DARK PEAK

ADAM J. WRIGHT

1

THE FOX

Relby, Derbyshire
December 21st, 1987

THE WINTER EVENING was gloomy as Mitch walked through the frozen moors with his sister. The dark clouds formed a low ceiling over the world and seemed close enough to touch. Mitch wondered if he could reach up with his gloved hands and sink his fingers into the grey substance, causing the clouds to burst and send snow falling down onto the landscape. He liked snow. Sarah did too. But Mitch knew the idea of reaching the clouds with his hands was a silly one so he kept them by his sides, one of them holding Sarah's hand in her cold, wet mitten.

He wouldn't normally hold his sister's hand but

she'd already slipped over twice on the ice and Mitch felt a duty to look after her. She was his little sister, after all. Maybe when she was nine, like him, she'd be able to walk across the moors without falling but until then, it was up to Mitch to keep her safe.

"Come on," she said impatiently, trying to run ahead and pull him along with her. "We'll miss it if we don't hurry."

He sighed the same way he'd seen Mum sigh when they were getting on her nerves, trying to show Sarah that he was more mature than she was. "I don't know why you're so excited," he told her. "I see foxes all the time."

"No, you don't, you liar."

He sighed again and tried to sound bored. "Sarah, the only reason I'm here is because you want to see the fox and you're not allowed to go onto the moors. So I have to come and make sure you're okay because I'm older."

"You're not allowed to go onto the moors either," Sarah reminded him as they trudged towards the distant woods where the fox had bolted. "I heard you telling Tilly that you are but you're not. You were just trying to sound big in front of her." A mischievous grin crossed her face. "You like her. Don't you?"

"Don't be silly," he said. Despite the cold snap in the air, his face felt suddenly hot. It was true, he did like Tilly. She was a tomboy, so she wasn't into dresses and dolls and all those girly things. Instead, she liked to do cool stuff like playing soldiers or exploring the stream that ran along the bottom of her dad's rapeseed field. Mitch liked her because she did all that cool stuff but he also liked her because she was pretty. He would never admit that to his sister, though.

Sarah pointed at his face. "You've gone red, that means you love her." Then she started singing, "Mitch loves Tilly, Mitch loves Tilly."

"Shut up," he said. "You'll frighten the fox away." He was also scared that Mum might hear Sarah and come outside to see what was going on. But when he looked back, it seemed as if a great stretch of moorland had suddenly appeared between them and the house. He hadn't realised they'd wandered so far. The walls that surrounded the garden where they'd been playing a short time ago looked small and far away. The black wooden gate Mitch and Sarah weren't supposed to open but had come through to get to the moors was almost invisible.

Suddenly, Mitch didn't want to see the fox anymore. He wanted to go home. It was getting late and Mum was bound to come out into the garden to see what they were up to eventually.

He wished they hadn't opened the gate and left the garden to play beyond the walls. If they'd stayed where they were supposed to, they wouldn't have seen the flash of red fur darting across the moors to the woods.

At first, Mitch had been just as excited about chasing the fox as Sarah, and scrambling down the incline from their house to the frozen expanse of the moors had been fun. But now they'd gone too far. It was getting dark and they were a long way from home.

He was about to tell Sarah that they should go back when she pulled her hand free of his and bolted towards the woods, leaving him holding her wet mitten while she sprinted across the frozen ground, squealing in excitement, "There it is! There's the fox!"

"Sarah, come back!" He tried to chase her but slipped on the ice, landing heavily on his side, his breath exploding out of him in a puff of mist. Scrabbling to his feet, he just had time to see Sarah disappear into the woods. "Sarah! Wait for me!" He ran for the trees, trying to ignore the pain in his side.

When he reached the woods, the evening gloom had deepened into a night-time darkness that was pure black beneath the trees. "Sarah, are you in here?" he whispered. He knew he should shout but something inside him wouldn't let him speak louder than a whisper, as if he should be quiet in here because something was lurking in the darkness and might come for him if it knew where he was.

He knew that was silly but he couldn't shake the feeling that something else was in these woods besides him, Sarah, and the stupid fox.

He told himself Sarah needed him and he managed to call her name. There was a touch of panic audible in his voice but he shouted loud enough that she should be able to hear him.

There was no reply.

He had to look for her, had to walk into the darkness beneath the trees.

You can do this, he told himself. *You've got to do this.*

He stepped forward and almost jumped out of his skin when a dead leaf crackled beneath his wellies. Trying to breathe normally again, his heart hammering in his chest, he entered the woods.

The trees around him began to rustle. He shrank back slightly. He was too old to believe in monsters, at least during the daytime, but right now standing alone in the dark woods with his heart hammering, he could believe anything. He'd seen programmes on telly about creatures that lived in remote places, creatures like Bigfoot and the Loch Ness Monster. There was even a name for the study of such creatures. Crypto-something.

These woods on the edge of the moors were remote. Had a crypto-something creature come out of the darkness and taken Sarah to its lair? Maybe she was alone in the dark right now, wondering why he hadn't come to save her.

That thought drove him forwards. He walked into the woods, searching the blackness beneath the trees for any sign of his sister. The rustling got louder and snowflakes began drifting down between the trees. Mitch breathed a sigh of relief. The sound wasn't a monster after all, just the snow rustling through the branches overhead.

"There are no monsters," he whispered to himself. "No monsters here at all."

The snowflakes were big and fat. They got in his eyes and stuck to his eyelashes, making it even harder to see. His cheeks and nose were numb with cold.

Sarah must be cold too and she's only got one mitten.

He called her name again but the snowfall seemed to muffle his voice. The flakes were falling so fast now that they formed a white wall all around Mitch. "Sarah," he shouted again but his voice barely croaked out of him.

It only took a few minutes for the ground to become a white, slippery blanket. He couldn't see the roots and branches hidden underneath the snow and every time he stepped forward, he had to be careful not to trip over them.

He suddenly felt that he was being watched and spun around to make sure no one was behind him. A dark shape detached itself from the dark shadows beneath a tree and ran towards him. He screamed and turned away from the shape, breaking into a run that he prayed was faster than that of the thing chasing him.

A buried root connected with his wellington and sent him sprawling in the snow. He landed hard, the air rushing out of him. He rolled onto his back so he could see how close the creature was.

The approaching shape became clear and Mitch saw red fur and a long, bushy, white-tipped tail. It was the fox that had lured them into the woods. Mitch scrambled to his feet and brushed snow off his jacket and trousers. The fox eyed him warily for a second before slinking into the undergrowth, its paw prints the only proof it had ever been there at all.

Mitch continued his search, trudging along carefully so he wouldn't fall over again.

The snowy woods looked like the land where the White Witch lived in *Narnia* and he wondered if this was all just a bad dream and he'd wake up soon, in his bed. Or maybe he'd come tumbling out of the wardrobe in his bedroom.

After wandering among the trees and calling out Sarah's name every two seconds, he realised he was lost. He had no idea which direction he'd come from. The heavy snowfall was filling in his tracks almost as fast as he was making them. No matter which way he turned, everything looked the same. More trees. More snow.

Then he heard Sarah scream. He'd heard her scream enough times in the past to recognise that sound anywhere.

He broke into a run, which was really a slow-motion bounding because of his efforts to avoid hidden roots and branches, and made his way to the area he was sure the scream had come from.

"Sarah? Are you okay?" He peered into the darkness, searching for her. She'd probably screamed because she'd slipped in the snow and fallen down, so he checked the ground to see if she was lying somewhere.

But all he could see on the ground was a set of boot prints, rapidly filling with falling snow. They weren't Sarah's; they were much too big.

He called out her name again and then, suddenly, the trees around him began to spin. Mitch didn't know if they were spinning or if he was spinning. His head felt cloudy. He couldn't think straight anymore, couldn't move, couldn't breathe. He was falling but he didn't know why. As his face landed in the freezing snow, the cold seeped into his entire body and the world around him faded away.

THE FIRST THING he heard when he woke up was voices. They sounded distant and muffled, as if they were on a television in a faraway room with the volume turned down. Mitch opened his eyes slowly but it was still dark in the woods and he couldn't see much. It had stopped snowing but he felt cold, colder than he'd ever felt in his life.

He suddenly remembered Sarah. Scrabbling to his feet, he called her name, shouting as loud as he could. But because he was shivering and his teeth were chattering, that wasn't very loud.

The voices in the woods got louder, closer. The beam of a torch cut through the darkness and shone on Mitch's face. He held his hands up against the glare.

"Over here," a man shouted. "I've found one of them."

The woods were filled with the sound of heavy boots running towards him. More torchlight appeared, bouncing up and down, illuminating the trees and throwing gnarled, twisted shadows all around Mitch.

He heard his mum's voice. "Mitch? Oh, my God, Mitch!" A moment later, her arms were around him and she held him tight. He expected her to feel warm but she didn't; she was cold, as if she'd been out here a long time.

After hugging him, she held him at arm's length to inspect his face. Tears ran down her cheeks. "Are you all right? You had me so worried."

Behind her, he could see two policemen in black jackets and a number of people from the village. Because their torches were still shining on his face, he couldn't see them clearly. He couldn't see if Sarah was with them.

"Did you find Sarah?" he asked Mum.

Her eyes widened. "What? Isn't she with you?" She looked at the area around them, her eyes searching.

"She ran away," he said.

She sagged against him heavily and they hugged again but this time it felt to Mitch that it was him who was comforting her, not the other way around.

She was sobbing, her tears wetting Mitch's neck.

The snow lay over the woods like a pristine, white shroud. All traces of Sarah had vanished.

2

ELLY

London
Present Day

WHEN HER PHONE BEGAN BUZZING, Elly Cooper tried to burrow deeper beneath the duvet and ignore it. Sleepily, she murmured, "Paul, please turn that off."

After a few seconds, during which the phone continued its incessant buzzing like an annoying insect, Elly realised that Paul wasn't next to her in bed. Then she remembered that she wasn't in her own bed at all, she was in a hotel in London. As she became fully awake, she also remembered that Paul wouldn't be in bed with her even if she had been at home. He was gone. From their bed. From their home. From her life.

Groaning, she reached out for the bedside table and grabbed the phone, peering through half-open eyes at the screen. It was Jen, her younger sister. Elly answered the call. "Jen, what the hell are you doing ringing me at this unearthly hour?"

Jen's voice held a note of concern. "What? Elly, it's half past ten. Don't tell me you're still in bed."

Shit. Elly's eyes flew open and she wrestled with the duvet so she could get out of bed. The sun was beating against the dark blue hotel curtains and she could hear the London traffic outside. *Half past ten, oh shit*. Her meeting with Glenister was at eleven and she had to take the tube all the way to Islington.

"Anyway, I called to see how you're doing now that Paul's gone," Jen continued. "If you're still in bed at half past ten, that answers my question. Do you want me to come over later? I have a free hour this afternoon before I have to pick William and Wendy up from school."

"No," Elly said, rummaging through her suitcase for a clean bra and pants. "I'm not at home, Jen. I'm in London."

"London? What are you doing there? Elly, you're not running away from your problem with Paul, are you? You need to be here and get it sorted, not run away to London."

Elly groaned in frustration. Even though Jen was

two years younger, she always acted as if she were the older sister, treating Elly like a child.

"I don't have a problem with Paul," Elly told her. "He has a problem with me, namely that I'm not the twenty-year-old blonde personal assistant he's been screwing for the past six months. And I'm not running away, I have a meeting with my agent, a meeting I'm going to be late for if I don't get a move on." She whipped off the underwear she'd been sleeping in and replaced it with the fresh set. No time for a shower. Glenister was just going to have to take her as he found her and deal with it.

"With your agent?" Jen sounded surprised.

"Yes, my agent," Elly said. "Paul may have left me but life does go on, you know." She padded into the bathroom, phone pressed between her ear and shoulder, and checked herself in the mirror, mussing her shoulder-length red hair with her fingers so that it looked like she was purposefully going for a tousled look.

The grey trousers and white blouse she was going to wear for her meeting hung on the back of the door in here. Elly had hoped that the steam from her morning shower would get rid of some of the creases the clothes had acquired while being shut in her case during the train journey from Birmingham yesterday. Too late for that now. She took the trousers and blouse into the main room and began to get dressed while Jen rambled on about Elly being in denial.

She put the phone on speaker and threw it on the bed. "I'm not in denial," she said as she slid the trousers up over her legs, "but I still have to make a living. Even more so now that I'm living on my own income alone."

"You sound so cold," Jen said. "You and Paul were together for five years. How can you be so nonchalant about it?"

Elly sighed and shrugged at the phone, even though she knew Jen couldn't see her. "What else can I be? Breaking down in tears isn't going to bring Paul back. And it isn't going to help me get on with my life."

There was a silence on the other end of the line for a moment and then Jen said, "Definitely in denial. And running away from your problems."

Elly groaned. "Jen, I haven't got time for this. The only place I need to be running right now is to Islington to meet my agent. I'll talk to you later." Before Jen could protest, she ended the call. She needed to clean her teeth and get her makeup on.

Ten minutes later, she was on Hammersmith Road outside the hotel. She flagged down a black cab and told the driver to take her to the Kensington Tube Station as quickly as possible.

"Where you going, love?" he asked her.

"I just told you, Kensington Tube Station."

"I mean after that. Where are you getting the tube to?"

"The Bellanger Restaurant in Islington."

"I'll have you there in fifteen minutes, love. The tube takes half an hour."

And costs about forty pounds less, Elly thought. But she knew she'd be late if she took the tube. Maybe this taxi driver was her saviour. Glenister had mentioned on the phone that he wanted to present her with a proposal for a new book. If she was late, he might give it to another writer. Elly knew how fickle the high-ups in the publishing business were and Glenister was no different. "Okay, get me there," she told the driver.

The vehicle's tyres screeched on the road as the cabbie pulled away from the kerb and joined the traffic heading towards Shepherd's Bush.

The day was bright and hot, the people walking along the pavement dressed in summer dresses and T-shirts. The cab windows were down, letting warm air smelling of dust and exhaust fumes into the vehicle. Elly closed her eyes and rested her head against the headrest, trying to compose herself for the meeting ahead.

Yesterday morning, she'd been at home in Birmingham. Glenister had called her at eleven and told her that he had something to propose to her regarding a new book and everything since then had been a frenetic race to get here: throwing a quickly-chosen assortment of clothes into her case, rushing for the train, and booking a last-minute room at the hotel from her phone during the train journey.

Jen had said she was running from her problems and Elly had denied it at the time but now that she thought about it, she'd been only too eager to get on the first train to London and escape the home she'd shared with Paul.

There was more to it than just running away though; she needed the book proposal Glenister was offering, whatever it was. Sales of her first true crime book, *Heart of a Killer*, had been great when the book had first been released six years ago, and had even propelled the book onto the *Sunday Times* bestseller list, but now they were waning.

Well, what did she expect, that the book would sell forever? There were only so many readers interested in Leonard Sims, the Eastbourne Ripper, and it seemed that everyone who wanted to read about his exploits had now done so. It was time for something new. She just hoped that Glenister's proposal was something interesting and that the agent didn't just want a book rehashing the cases of killers that had already been written about *ad infinitum* like Fred and Rosemary West or The Moors Murderers.

She'd rather write a book about something that interested her and hadn't been done to death already, but the truth was, she'd take any job if it meant a lucrative publishing contract. She still had a healthy bank account thanks to *Heart of a Killer* but that wasn't going to last forever. She needed to think about her future.

She'd always assumed that she and Paul would grow old together. Neither of them had spoken about it much, it had just been implied by the fact that they'd spent five years together and grown comfortable with each other.

Those five years had been good ones. For the past three, they'd been living together. All their friends had assumed that their relationship was strong, indestructible. Hell, even Elly had assumed as much. Until three nights ago when Paul had come home from work and told her that he was leaving her to be with his boss's PA. The indestructible bond between them had been destroyed totally.

Elly had thrown a glass vase full of plastic yellow flowers at Paul as he'd slinked out the front door. It had smashed against the door and Elly had fallen to her knees, crying among the glass shards and broken plastic. An hour later, she'd wiped her eyes and decided to get on with her life. Her tears weren't going to change anything.

Opening her eyes and looking out the open cab window at the buildings of Holland Park, she wondered if she was cold after all, like Jen had said. Breaking up with Paul should have affected her more. The fact that he'd been cheating on her should have made her feel incensed. But she felt nothing. After the initial flood of tears among the broken vase, there had been no further signs of grief. Just an emptiness inside whenever she thought of Paul.

Coming to London had helped, of course, by focusing her mind on the meeting with Glenister, not letting her dwell for too long on her ex-boyfriend.

The cab driver was true to his word and pulled up outside The Bellanger fourteen minutes after they'd set off from the hotel. It was exactly eleven o' clock.

Elly paid the fare and added a tip, reminding herself that if she'd taken the tube, she wouldn't have made it here on time. Rushing into the restaurant, she avoided looking into the mirrors set on the dark wood-panelled walls and instead searched for Glenister. She spotted him sitting in a booth near the rear of the establishment, past the bar where a number of people were sitting and drinking tea, coffee, and wine.

The Belanger's decor was art nouveau in style, with retro lamps on the tables and fittings and fixtures of brass and dark wood to match the walls. Elly walked past the bar to where Glenister was waiting.

She'd met Jack Glenister only on a few occasions, mostly when *Heart of a Killer* was accepted by a publisher six years ago. During the years the book had been in print, Elly's contact with Glenister had mostly been in the form of emails and phone calls.

The fact that he had called her here in person implied that he had something important to impart.

He looked up from the menu he was perusing as Elly approached the table and a warm smile lit his face. He'd hardly changed since the last time Elly had seen him all those years ago: same white hair parted carefully at the side and reaching down to his collar, same friendly grey eyes behind his gold-rimmed glasses, and same air of impeccability. He was dressed in a dark suit and midnight blue tie, and Elly self-consciously smoothed down her trousers with her hands. She knew she looked a mess and sitting with Glenister was going to make her untidiness even more obvious.

He stood and held out his arms, drawing her into a brief hug. "Elly, so good to see you again. Did you come on the early train?"

She realised he was excusing her appearance, believing it to be the by-product of getting up early this morning and spending hours on a train from Birmingham.

"No," she said, taking a seat opposite him at the table, "I arrived in London yesterday."

"Oh." His eyebrow rose slightly but he made no further comment. "Let's order and then I'll show you what I've got for you." He patted a brown leather briefcase that was sitting at his feet.

Elly looked at the briefcase. That innocuous piece of baggage could hold the key to her future. At the very least, it could hold the key to her survival for the next few months.

If Glenister was proposing a book, that meant he was also offering an advance from a publisher. Now that Elly and Paul had split up, the house they shared would have to be sold and Elly was going to have to find somewhere else to live. She was going to have to build a new life for herself and that would require money. Her world was falling apart but the contents of that briefcase could be her lifeline.

When the waiter came to the table, Glenister ordered a fillet of rainbow trout, Elly a salad with grilled chicken. She felt too nervous to eat anything more than that. As an afterthought, she added a glass of white wine to her order. If this meeting turned out to be a bust, at least she'd get a drink out of it, courtesy of her agent.

While they waited for the drinks to arrive, Glenister told her about one of his clients who had just signed a multi-million-pound deal with a major publisher for three crime novels. Elly was barely listening; her attention kept being drawn to the briefcase at Glenister's feet.

The drinks arrived after what seemed to Elly to be an age but was actually only a couple of minutes according to her watch. Glenister reached down and brought the briefcase up to the table. He popped open the clasps and lifted the lid, reaching in and pulling out a slim manila folder. He placed it on the table next to his glass of wine and returned the case to the floor. "Tell me," he said, leaning forward slightly, "what do you know about the Peak District in Derbyshire?"

Elly shrugged. She'd been there once as a child, spending a week in a caravan with her family. How old had she been? Eight? Nine? She remembered that Jen had been a pain in the arse the entire holiday, whining all the time. "Not much," she told Glenister. "There are a lot of hills there and it's popular with walkers. A scenic part of the country."

He nodded slowly. "I don't know anything about the place myself. I rarely leave London."

Elly found that easy to believe. She knew Glenister was London born and bred, raised in the East End. From humble beginnings, he'd moved ever upward in the publishing circles until he got to where he was today, living in luxury on the Chelsea Embankment. He still had a trace of his cockney accent but it was almost totally buried beneath his precise, controlled tones.

He opened the manila folder and took out a sheet of paper that had a page from a newspaper scanned onto it. He pushed it across the table towards Elly. "Ever hear of this?"

She looked down at the headline. SEVEN-YEAR-OLD GIRL GOES MISSING IN PEAK DISTRICT. The accompanying text was about a girl called Sarah Walker who had gone missing one night while walking in the woods with her brother.

Elly liked to think she was up to date with news stories like this but she'd never heard of Sarah Walker. Then she saw the date at the top of the newspaper page. "This happened thirty years ago."

"It did indeed," he agreed. He took another sheet of paper from the folder and handed it to her. "This was more recent."

Elly checked the date on the top of the scanned newspaper article first this time. January 2nd 2000. The headline read NEW YEARS EVE REVELLER MISSING. The article was about a 23-year-old journalist named Lindsey Grofield who had last been seen leaving a New Year's Eve party at a pub in Bakewell and had never made it home. She hadn't been seen nor heard from since.

"Are you saying there's a connection between these disappearances?" Elly asked.

Her agent shrugged and spread his hands. "I'm not saying anything of the sort. But some bright spark at Wollstonecraft Publishing who fancies himself a detective believes there might be." He reached into the folder again. "There's more. Have a look at this."

The article he gave her this time had a more sensational headline. BLACKDEN EDGE MURDERER STRIKES AGAIN! Beneath the headline, there was a black-and-white photo of a desolate piece of countryside that Elly assumed was

Blackden Edge. According to the article, the naked body of Josie Wagner, a 23-year-old nurse from Manchester, had been discovered at Blackden Edge, Derbyshire. Josie had been strangled to death and her body mutilated. The article was dated August 16th 1977.

The food arrived and while the waiter was putting the dishes down on the table, Elly did a quick mental calculation. Lindsey Grofield had gone missing twenty-three years after Josie Wagner's murder. It was a stretch to think there might be a connection between the two occurrences, or even a connection between Grofield and Walker's disappearances.

Grofield was twenty-three when she vanished, the Walker girl only seven. If there was one thing Elly had learned from interviewing Leonard Sims, it was that killers usually had a type. After all, that was how she'd been the only journalist Sims agreed to talk to. His victims had all been redheads and Elly had used that, making sure to include a photo of herself when she wrote to Sims at Broadmoor Hospital, requesting an interview.

"I'm not seeing a connection here," she told Glenister. "The timeline is too long and the young girl doesn't fit with the other two victims. If you take her out of the equation, you're talking about a strangling that took place in 1977 and a disappearance from a pub twenty-three years later. I think the wannabe detective at Wollstonecraft is making a huge leap of imagination to believe those two events are linked."

"Perhaps," Glenister said, "but the thing that piqued his interest is that 1977 headline. That's the front page of a local newspaper, the *Peak Observer* or *Gazette* or some such thing. It's vanished now, and in its heyday it probably had a circulation of no more than a hundred or so copies. The national tabloids reported on the story of the murdered nurse, of course, but none of them mentioned anything about a Blackden Edge Murderer. The only place that phrase appears is in the local rag."

"Okay, so you think there's a serial killer in Derbyshire that no one outside of that area knows about? The headline says "strikes again" so when did he strike before he murdered Josie Wagner?"

"Well, that's just it," Glenister said, "nobody knows. According to the fellow at Wollstonecraft, there are tales of this murderer passed down from parents to their children. 'Don't stay out after dark or the Blackden Edge Murderer will get you', that sort of thing."

Elly rolled her eyes. "Sounds like an urban legend, a cautionary tale they tell to their kids but do you think there's really a book's worth of material in it? What sort of book does Wollstonecraft want, an investigation of the legend or a true crime book?

Because if I'm to write the latter, there isn't much to go on."

Glenister gave her a thin smile and looked sheepish. "Well, they're not sure there's a book in this. If it turns out there really is a connection between that murder and those disappearances, then that's all well and good. The publishers will commission you to write a book on the subject."

Elly suddenly felt like her key to the future wasn't going to fit the lock of reality. "And if there isn't enough material for a book?"

Glenister shrugged. "Then they'll drop the idea and move on."

She jabbed her fingers at the newspaper articles. "You want me to investigate this without the promise of anything at the end of it? What about the proposal you were going to make?"

He gestured to the papers. "This is the proposal. It isn't a book proposal exactly but just think about it, Elly. What if you uncover a serial killer that no one has ever heard of? Think about the fame, the money. You'll be back in the charts before the book even comes off the press."

Elly sighed. "Jack, you and I both know there's not going to be a connection between any of these events. Just because someone at a publishing house thinks he's Sherlock Holmes doesn't make it so. He'll be still in a job working with other people's books while I go chasing after his delusional fantasy and end up with nothing to show for it."

"I'll be straight with you," Glenister said, taking a sip of his wine. "This is all I've got to offer you. Sales of *Heart of a Killer* have dropped off lately and no one knows who Elly Cooper is anymore. So, unless you want to go and interview the Eastbourne Ripper again and uncover something new for a sequel, this is it. What Wollstonecraft are proposing is to pay all your expenses for a two-week trip to Derbyshire. Snoop around a bit. When you return, we'll discuss what you have and they'll decide whether to follow up with a book proposal or not." He drained his wine and put the empty glass on the table.

They'd discussed a sequel to *Heart of a Killer* before. Elly always told Glenister that Sims had no more secrets to offer, that there was nothing more the Eastbourne Ripper could reveal about himself that would interest the public if it were published. But the truth was, she couldn't bring herself to talk to Sims again, to sit across a table from him. Not for any amount of money.

She had no desire to delve deeper into the mind of Leonard Sims. When telling her about the murders he'd carried out, he'd delighted in Elly's reactions. No matter how much she tried to hide her emotions from him, Sims always seemed to know what she was feeling and he played on that, describing every murder in intricate, gruesome detail.

He hinted at further crimes, ones which the police knew nothing about, but as soon as Elly had enough material for her book, she cut all contact with him. She couldn't bear to be close to that man again. It was like sitting across a table from a reptilian creature that was searching for its next decadent thrill and had decided that she would fit the bill just nicely.

Every time she had returned to her hotel room from Broadmoor, the first thing she did was stand under a very hot shower for a very long time because she felt as if the filthy essence of Leonard Sims were clinging to her skin.

So, a sequel to her bestselling book was out of the question and it looked like the best she could hope for from a publisher was a paid holiday in Derbyshire. She didn't think for one moment that a book was going to come out of the flimsy information she'd been given.

"I have a place for you to start," Glenister offered. "In fact, this is why it's caught the interest of the publishers. There was a fellow up in Derbyshire called Michael Walker, a well-to-do Lord of the manor type. He was the father of the girl who went missing in 1987. The police were interested in him at the time, brought him in for questioning on a few occasions, that sort of thing. Nothing ever came of it but that could be because he had connections with the powers that be. Maybe he got away with murder."

He took a bite of his trout. "Anyway, Michael Walker died a couple of weeks ago so perhaps some secrets will come out if you dig a little. People might be more willing to talk about Walker now that he's dead. And remember," he said with a wink, "you can't slander the dead so there won't be any fear of legal repercussions if your investigation leads to this fellow being the Blackden Edge Murderer."

Elly took a bite of her chicken salad. It was delicious but she wished she was eating it under different circumstances. Was Glenister hinting that he wanted her to set up Michael Walker as a murderer? She could imagine the sensation such a book would cause. Lord of the manor wealthy guy turns out to be a murderer and may even have killed his own daughter in 1987 and got away with it. Was that what Wollstonecraft Publishing wanted, a sensationalist book that was going to fly off the shelves, whether it was true or not?

"It sounds like you want me to put a spin on this," she told Glenister, "Accuse Michael Walker whether he was guilty or not."

"No, no, not at all," he said. "I'm merely pointing you in a direction that could turn out to be profitable for us all."

"And Michael Walker's family?" she asked. "How would they feel about this?"

"Well, his wife and son did a runner after Sarah went missing," Glenister said. "What do you think that was about? Maybe they knew something the police didn't. There were probably plenty of dark goings-on behind closed manor doors."

"You sound like a reverse snob," Elly told him. "This chap was rich and had connections therefore he must be a murderer?"

Glenister shrugged. "I don't know if that's the case but you must admit, it would make a good book."

Elly put her fork down, her appetite gone. "Do you want me to write the truth or a bunch of lies?"

"I want you to write what sells."

"Even if it points the finger at an innocent man?"

"I'm not asking you to point the finger at anyone, Elly," he said. "All I'm saying is that you have to look at this project with a view to writing something that has legs. If it means bending the truth here and there then so be it. All writers do it."

"I don't," she said. "*Heart of a Killer* was nothing but the truth." She gestured to the papers on the table. "I can't do this, Jack. I can't lay the blame for these events, which probably aren't even connected, at the door of a dead man who can't defend himself."

Glenister sighed resignedly. "I have to say, I wasn't expecting this. I thought you'd jump at the chance to do something new, be creative again. As soon as the publishers mentioned this assignment, you were the first person I thought of. You need this, Elly."

"I don't need to build my career on lies," she said, getting up. She felt a well of tears, borne of disappointment, rise in her eyes and she didn't want Glenister to see her cry. "I'll be back in a minute," she said, turning away from him and heading for the toilets.

The Belanger was filling up as the day wore on and now most of the tables were occupied with families or couples enjoying a good meal and each other's company on a lovely sunny day in London. Elly hurried her pace, feeling the first tears spill from her eyes. When she pushed through the door to the toilets, her cheeks were wet, her eyes stinging. Her breath hitched in her chest.

She stood at the sink and looked at herself in the mirror. God, she looked a mess. Taking a tissue from her handbag, she dabbed carefully at her eyes, trying not to ruin her makeup. She had no idea what she was going to do next where her career or her personal life were concerned. Everything familiar and comforting had somehow slipped out of her grasp.

Her phone buzzed in her handbag, telling her she had a text. She took it out and felt her heart sink even further when she saw Paul's name on the screen. His text was simple: *Coming round to the house Saturday morning to pick some stuff up.*

She remembered when his texts to her had been

filled with emojis of hearts and smiley faces. He used to always end his messages with a large X. Now, after five years together, it had come to this; a plain statement of fact that was devoid of any emotion at all.

Today was Thursday, which meant she'd have to face Paul the day after tomorrow. She wasn't sure she could do it. She didn't want to be sitting at home waiting for him on Saturday morning, as if she had nothing better to do than watch him collect his things and take them out of the door to his new life.

Well, maybe she wouldn't be there when he turned up on Saturday morning. He had a key, so he could let himself in. Elly would make sure she was somewhere else.

The idea of two weeks in Derbyshire suddenly didn't sound so bad after all. At least she'd be able to get away from the Paul situation, and maybe the break would be good for her mentally. Her problems might seem less significant if she were standing in the middle of a desolate moor or on top of a craggy hill.

She'd have to do what Glenister and the publishers wanted, of course, but that was the price she was going to have to pay to put some distance between herself and her problems. Besides, maybe the late Michael Walker *was* connected to the murder of the nurse and the disappearances of the other girls, including his daughter. She couldn't dismiss it out of hand before at least investigating the possibility.

She began calculating the logistics. If she caught a train back home to Birmingham later today, she could pack a few things, get a good night's sleep and drive to Derbyshire tomorrow. If she set off after lunch, she'd be there by late afternoon if the traffic was light.

Deciding that plan was her best option right now, she returned to the table where Glenister was drinking a second glass of wine.

"I'll do it," Elly said, sitting down. "I'll go to Derbyshire and look into the disappearances of these girls. If I find that there's a link between the disappearances and murder and a link to Michael Walker, I'll report back accordingly."

"That's all anyone is asking," Glenister said.

"I have one condition," she said.

His face darkened slightly. "What's that?"

"I want to start tomorrow. The publishers are going to sort out my accommodation."

He nodded. "I'm sure they can arrange that."

"Then I'm in."

"Excellent. I'm sure you won't regret this, Elly. Who knows where this could lead? Shall we drink to it?" He held up his half full wine glass.

"I can't," Elly said. "My glass is empty and I've got a train to catch."

3

THE CALL

It began to rain just as Mitch was finishing the Rileys' hedge. As the first fat drops of water spattered down on him, he switched off the hedge trimmer and slid his ear defenders down so they hung around his neck. The smell of petrol from the trimmer's engine hung in the air, tainting the fragrance of freshly-cut grass from the lawn Mitch had cut before attacking the hedge.

Luckily, he'd already raked the grass cuttings up, or he'd be dealing with a damp mess right about now because the rain was pelting down harder and faster every second.

He ran across the lawn with rain in his eyes and hedge trimmer in hand. He reached the front gate and sprinted onto the street where his orange Jeep Renegade was parked. After throwing the trimmer into his covered trailer, where it lay alongside the lawn mower and other tools that were already in there, Mitch clambered into the driver's seat.

Maybe he could go back and collect the hedge clippings when the downpour had passed over. He was already drenched, his T-shirt and jeans clinging to him and cold rainwater rolling down his face from his soaked hair.

He dug into his jeans pocket and grabbed his phone. He might as well tell his afternoon clients that he wasn't going to be coming to tend their gardens. Even if the rain stopped now, their lawns would be too wet to mow.

There was a missed call from an unknown number on the phone. Probably someone calling to ask about his rates. He was about to bring up the contact list to get the numbers of today's clients when the phone rang. This time, the caller wasn't unknown; it was his ex-wife, Jess.

He answered immediately, hoping she wasn't calling with some reason why Leigh, their twelve-year-old daughter, couldn't stay with him for the weekend. "Hey, Jess."

"Mitch," she said, sounding worried. "Is everything all right?"

"Yeah, I'm fine despite the heavens opening up on me. Is Leigh okay?"

"She's still at school. Looking forward to spending the weekend with you."

"Well, that's good. So you're not ringing to cancel?"

"No, not at all," she said. "Don't forget you can pick her up in the morning tomorrow. The school is having an inset day."

"Yeah, I remember."

"The reason I'm ringing is because I was just wondering if you've had a call from someone named John Mercer?"

"I got a missed call. Why?" He watched the rain on the windscreen. The water moved in snake-like rivulets that raced down the glass.

"He rang here earlier," Jess said. "He wanted to get in touch with you. I gave him your number."

"Potential client?" he asked. "I'm not sure why he'd ring your house. Sorry about that." If someone had rung Jess's house to get in touch with him, they must have been looking at a very old ad for his gardening service. He hadn't lived at the house in Monarch Gardens for over four years.

"No, he's not a client. He said he was a solicitor. Hang on, I wrote it down." There was a pause, and then she said, "Mercer and Robinson Solicitors, Matlock, Derbyshire."

The wet clothes clinging to Mitch's body suddenly felt very cold against his skin. He shivered. "Did he say what he wanted?"

"No, he just said he wanted to contact you. I gave him your mobile number. I thought that since he was calling from Derbyshire, it might be about..." Her voice trailed off. She knew there was no need to complete the sentence.

"Sarah," he said.

"Yes."

"I can't think of any other reason why someone from Derbyshire would be ringing me."

"I don't think it's bad news," she said. "If it was something bad, surely the police would be trying to contact you, not a solicitor."

She was right about that. If the Derbyshire police had found Sarah's remains, they'd be ringing him themselves, not getting a solicitor to do it. So who the hell was John Mercer?

"I'll call him," he told her. "Otherwise, I'm just going to be wondering what he wants."

"Okay, see you later," she said casually.

"Yeah, see ya," he said before ending the call. The way he and Jess spoke to each other now, it was as if they were nothing more than acquaintances. Yet she had been the woman who had made him want to settle down when he'd been living a nomadic existence.

After Sarah's disappearance, his mum moved herself and Mitch around the country constantly, as if she were running away from something, and that meant his education suffered. Most of the time, she had kept him out of school altogether.

So, while she went to work doing whatever job

she'd found in whatever town they were currently living in, he went from house to house in the neighbourhood and asked the neighbours if they'd like their lawns mowed, hedges trimmed, or leaves raked. He used their own tools at first but as he gradually earned more money, he had bought his own gear.

What started as a way to earn a little pocket money and keep him occupied while his mum was at work became a lucrative business. He discovered he was good with his hands and he expanded his services to include repairing fences, fixing broken gutters, and rebuilding garden walls. He also had an eye for design and sometimes suggested to his clients how he could better reshape their borders and lawns.

At the age of eighteen, he studied at night school for the English and Maths qualifications he'd missed out on and also began a qualification in horticulture.

His mum never got to see him get those qualifications because she died of lung cancer before he finished his course. The cancer came out of nowhere and took her quickly, leaving Mitch alone in the world. Even after his mum was gone, he continued the nomadic lifestyle she'd drilled into him.

It was only when he had met Jess that he thought about settling down. They met in a cafe in Banbury in 2002. It was late spring and he'd been fixing fences and gutters all day after a freak gale the night before had wreaked havoc on many of the local properties. Sipping a coffee and eating eggs and toast, he noticed that the girl at the next table was reading a paperback copy of Val McDermid's *The Wire in the Blood*, the second book in a series about a clinical psychologist named Tony Hill who helped the police solve crimes, usually murder.

He'd read the book himself and enjoyed it, so he asked the girl how she was finding it. That led to a conversation about a TV show based on the books that was supposed to be coming out later that year and then a lengthy discussion about murder mysteries. They ended up exchanging numbers. The rest was history. But it was a history that was cut short in 2013 when he discovered Jess was having an affair with Andrew Tomkins, her boss at the architectural firm where she worked.

He wasn't sure why he was still dwelling on that after four years had passed.

He scrolled to the missed call on the phone and pressed it with his thumb. While it dialled, he put the phone's speaker on. The sound of a phone ringing on the other end of the line filled the Jeep, clashing with the rhythmic drumming of the rain on the roof.

There was a click and then a woman answered. "Mercer and Robinson. Jane speaking. How may I help you?"

"Hi," Mitch said. "Could I speak to John Mercer, please?"

"Just a moment and I'll see if he's available. Who's calling, please?"

"My name's Mitch Walker. Mr. Mercer has been trying to contact me."

Another click followed by silence. The falling rain ticked off the seconds and he counted them. After thirty-two, a man's gruff voice came out of the speaker, "Hello, Mr. Walker, I'm John Mercer. Thank you for returning my call."

"I need to know why you were calling me," Mitch told him. "I don't usually get phone calls from solicitors." The words came out more aggressively than he'd intended. He was mentally preparing himself for the worst.

His earlier assertion that this couldn't be bad news was crumbling away. If someone—anyone—was ringing him from the area where Sarah went missing thirty years ago, they had to be ringing about her. The police must have found her body in the woods, on the moors, or buried in a riverbed and this man was calling to tell Mitch the facts. *So sorry, Mr. Walker, but your sister's dead body has been discovered in an abandoned cave. Have a nice weekend.*

"I'm afraid I'm calling with some sad news," Mercer said.

Mitch felt a pain in his hand and looked down. He was gripping the steering wheel so tightly that his fingers were white.

"It's about your father," Mercer said.

"My father?" Confusion hit him like a freight train. "What do you mean? I haven't seen him since I was nine years old. Why are you contacting me about him now?"

The confusion was crowded out by relief as Mitch realised this wasn't about Sarah at all. He took a deep breath and let it out slowly, relaxing his grip on the steering wheel.

There was a pause while Mercer considered his words, then he said, "I'm afraid he's passed away." He spoke the words softly, as if they might have had some impact on Mitch and he was trying to lessen the blow. But Mitch felt nothing at all. Any emotions he had towards his father had disappeared years ago.

He'd been gone from Mitch's life a long time. The news that he was dead meant no more to him than hearing about the death of a stranger.

When he said nothing, Mercer continued. "Your father came to my office five years ago and asked me to prepare his last will and testament. He named you as his sole beneficiary, Mr. Walker."

"What? Why would he do that?" He tried to imagine his father walking into a solicitor's office and speaking his name after not seeing him for over thirty years. How did he even know Mitch was still alive?

"You are his son, Mr. Walker," Mercer said. "Surely you can see why he would leave everything to you."

"No, I can't. I can't see why he left anything to me at all. I haven't seen him since I was nine."

"From what I understand, that wasn't your father's choice."

He was right about that. After Sarah disappeared, Mitch's mum took him away from Derbyshire and kept the two of them constantly on the move.

"He left you quite a sizeable estate, Mr. Walker," Mercer continued, "including Edge House."

Edge House. The name conjured images of long hallways and large rooms with arched windows. And there had been a walled garden with a black wooden gate in the rear wall that led to a steep incline and the moors beyond.

Mitch had no desire to return to that house. Its walls housed too many bad memories. As well as those of Sarah's disappearance, there were others that floated out of reach when he tried to remember them. Yet they haunted his dreams in the dead of the night when he wanted nothing more than to forget them.

If he only had himself to consider, he'd tell Mercer that he wasn't interested in his father's estate. As far as he was concerned, he wanted nothing more to do with Derbyshire. But there was Leigh to think about too. Edge House probably had a lot of value, although he had no idea what condition the place was in now. And whether Mitch liked it or not, the house was part of her history.

He'd promised Leigh that he'd take her hiking on the weekend. She'd been reading books about the S.A.S. and survival and had been watching Bear Grylls on TV. Wanting to encourage her interest in outdoor pursuits, Mitch had told her they could go to the Avon Valley and walk along the river with packed lunches in rucksacks. It wasn't exactly a remote wilderness but it would be a good way to see if she really wanted to explore the great outdoors in person or just watch it on TV.

The Peak District, where Edge House was located, was all rugged landscape. What better place for his daughter to experience the outdoors? They could stay at the house and then he'd arrange for Mercer to oversee its sale and they'd never see it again. Mitch's final memories of Edge House would be happy ones.

"All right," he said to Mercer, "what do I have to do to get the keys?"

"There are some documents to sign and then the estate will be passed over to you in its entirety."

"I'll be at your office tomorrow afternoon," Mitch said. He ended the call. The rain continued to bounce off the Jeep's roof.

He hoped visiting Derbyshire with Leigh would change his perspective on the place. Because right now, it was a place of ghosts and nightmares.

The place where his sister had vanished into thin air.

4

THE KEY

"Are we there yet?" Leigh asked.

"Not far now." Mitch kept his eyes on the road, struggling to see through the rain-drizzled windscreen between each swish of the wipers. They'd been driving for almost two hours and had spent almost thirty minutes of that time stuck in traffic, crawling along the monotonous motorway past roadworks while the rain beat down on the roof of the Jeep.

Eventually, they'd left the motorway—but not the rain—behind and now they were driving along a winding road bordered by high trees and hills on the left and a view of rolling, rain-swept farmland on the right.

According to the Jeep's GPS, they were less than ten minutes from their destination. Mitch had thought that returning to this area of the country would bring back childhood memories but, despite the fact that he'd spent the first nine years of his life here, he was drawing a blank so far. He remembered bits and pieces of his years in Derbyshire but the memories always seemed fleeting. The sight of the countryside, which must have been familiar to him at one time, didn't solidify any of the nebulous images that floated around in his head when he tried to remember his childhood.

He remembered Edge House as a big, rambling place with shadowed corners and dark hallways but he realised he might be remembering it that way because of what happened later. The shadowed corners could be gaps in his memory or things his mind had later blocked out. He was sure the childhood years he'd spent at the house hadn't been good ones, even before Sarah disappeared. He just couldn't remember exactly why that was.

Leigh sighed dramatically. "Is the rain ever going to stop? You said we could go hiking."

"We can still hike in the rain," he said. "We can walk up one of the big hills they have around here and eat sandwiches when we get to the top. We'll be able to see for miles."

"Sandwiches?" Leigh wrinkled her nose slightly.

"You like sandwiches."

"Not outdoors. They don't taste right outdoors."

"Okay, so we can have a meal at one of the pubs. I bet they'll have fish and chips."

She nodded. "Okay."

"We're going to have a fun weekend," he assured her.

She was silent for a few moments, watching the trees roll past her window. Then she said, "Mum said you're going to sell a house while we're here. Is that going to take long?"

Mitch shook his head. "No, I don't think so. I'm not going to sell it myself, I'm going to leave someone else in charge of that. So it won't interrupt our weekend."

"Mum said the house used to be your house when you were a boy."

"That's right. I lived there a long time ago but I can't remember much about it. So we get to explore it while we're staying there. It's a big house and it's got a big garden."

Leigh wrinkled her nose again. "Sounds creepy."

"I'm sure it'll be fine." They passed a sign that said *Matlock* and drove past a pub, then beneath a bridge. Beyond the bridge, the road was lined with various shops and businesses. The GPS said they'd reached their destination and Mitch looked around for Mercer and Robinson Solicitors.

A couple of people were huddled beneath an umbrella outside a furniture shop but, other than that, there were no other pedestrians. The road ahead continued farther north past a train station and a large Sainsbury's supermarket and that seemed to be where all the traffic was heading. Mitch spotted a sign that said Mercer and Robinson Solicitors and turned onto a side road to find somewhere to park. He slid the Jeep in between a couple of parked cars and killed the engine. The rain drummed on the roof like impatient fingers tapping out an unknown rhythm.

Mitch grabbed their waterproof jackets from the back seat and they put them on. It was awkward in the confined space of the vehicle but after a couple of minutes, they were ready to face the rain.

"Let's go," Mitch said, throwing his door open and stepping out into the downpour.

Leigh followed, pulling the hood of her light blue jacket up over her head. "Dad, you need to put your hood up too."

"It isn't far," Mitch said, "I'll be okay." He led her back to the main road and to the door beneath the Mercer and Robinson sign. The black lettering on the glass door confirmed this was the right place. Mitch opened the door for Leigh and then followed her inside, out of the rain.

A flight of steps covered in light green carpeting led up to the next floor. At the top, the landing had been converted into a small waiting room with the addition of a half dozen plastic chairs and a low wooden coffee table littered with various magazines. There were two closed doors with black lettering painted on their frosted glass panels, one bearing the name William Robinson, the other John Mercer. An open hatch showed a receptionist's office. A grey-haired woman in her fifties was typing on a computer. When she saw Mitch, she looked up. "Mr. Walker? Mr. Mercer will be with you shortly if you'd like to take a seat."

Mitch nodded and sat down in one of the plastic chairs. Leigh scoured the beauty magazines on the table, picked one, and took a seat next to him. She pulled down her hood and leafed through the glossy pages.

The waiting area had a damp smell, as if people had come in from the wet street over the course of the day and left behind droplets of rainwater and splashes of mud from the dirty puddles outside.

After a couple of minutes had passed, the receptionist appeared at the hatch and said, "If you'd like to go in, Mr. Mercer will see you now." She indicated the door bearing Mercer's name.

"Come on," Mitch said to Leigh. He didn't want to leave her out here on her own while he was in the office with Mercer. A feeling of unease crawled inside him. He'd felt it since they'd arrived in Matlock and had dismissed it as his mind playing tricks on him. He was returning to the place where Sarah had gone missing, so there was bound to be some emotion involved. But even so, he took Leigh into Mercer's office with him.

Mercer was tall, white-haired and balding, with

small gold-rimmed glasses perched on his nose. He wore a crumpled dark blue pinstripe suit. His desk, devoid of anything other than a gold pen and a closed hardbound notebook, took up half the space in the small office. Mercer was standing beside it when Mitch and Leigh walked in.

"Mr. Walker," he said, coming forward and extending his hand, "it's good to see you. It's a shame that our meeting is under such sad circumstances."

"I told you," Mitch said, "I didn't know my father." He shook the proffered hand, noting Mercer's weak grip.

"And who do we have here?" Mercer asked, bending over to look closer at Leigh.

"This is Leigh, my daughter." Mitch reflexively put his hands on her shoulders and drew her slightly closer.

"Hi, Leigh. Has your daddy told you about the house you own now? It's a lovely house with a big garden. I'm sure you'll enjoy playing there."

Leigh shrugged but said nothing. Mercer retreated behind the desk and sat down, inviting them to do the same by waving his hand at two seats on the client side of the desk.

"Now then," Mercer said when they were all seated, "do you have any questions, Mr. Walker?"

"Just one. Will you be able to handle the sale of the house after I return home to Leamington Spa on Sunday?"

Mercer looked shocked. "You want to sell Edge House? But you haven't even seen it yet."

"That place holds nothing for me other than bad memories. Leigh and I are going to stay there this weekend and do some hiking but after that, I want the place gone from my life."

"Well, yes, if you're sure that's what you want." Mercer removed his glasses and wiped them with a handkerchief. "We'd have no trouble selling the property, no trouble at all."

"Good," Mitch said.

"Now if I can just see some ID, we can get the papers signed and I'll give you the keys." Mercer opened a drawer in the desk and produced a sheaf of papers. "As well as Edge House, your late father's estate includes his vehicle and a sum of money. So I'll need your bank details to get the amount transferred into your account."

"Of course," Mitch said, reaching into his jeans pocket for his wallet. "Exactly how much are we talking about?"

Mercer put the glasses back on his nose and peered through them as he leafed through the papers. "After paying his creditors, taxes, and solicitors' fees, the amount of cash your father left to you comes to two hundred and thirty-three thousand pounds."

Mitch stopped himself from saying anything because he wasn't sure he could trust his mouth to work properly. Leigh said, "Wow," for both of them.

Mercer smiled and nodded. "Michael Walker was a wealthy man. As well as the cash, there is a safe deposit box held at one of the banks in town. Its contents are unknown. This is the bank's address and phone number." He passed Mitch a business card. "Safe deposit boxes are being phased out and your father was only allowed to keep one because of who he was."

"Okay," Mitch said. He wondered how much the contents of the safe deposit box would add to the £233,000 he'd already inherited. Whatever was in that box had to be worth a lot of money for his father to lock it away in the first place.

"Exactly how much is the house worth?" he asked Mercer.

The solicitor raised his eyebrows. "Well, it's difficult to come up with a figure off the top of my head. The property will need to be valued, of course."

"Yes, but you must have some idea."

Mercer contemplated for a moment. "Well, considering the location and size of the house and the surrounding land, I suppose the property is worth something in the region of two and a half to three million pounds."

Leigh gasped. "Dad, we're rich. Like, really rich."

"Yeah, I guess we are." Mitch had always wanted to be able to provide for his daughter's future and had squirrelled money away whenever he could for that purpose. But his gardening business was seasonal and his savings dwindled during the years when the cold bite of winter arrived early or lingered longer than usual. But now, that didn't matter. He'd been given a means to provide for Leigh, even if it had come from an unexpected source.

He reached for the gold pen on Mercer's desk and said, "Where do I sign?"

TEN MINUTES LATER, Mitch and Leigh were on the street again, only now, Mitch had a simple metal keyring in his hand and on that ring were two keys: the key to the front door of Edge House and the key to his father's safe deposit box, which was inscribed with the number 208. The keys to the other doors in the house, and his father's Land Rover, were apparently inside the house, hanging on a hook near the back door.

It was still raining so Mitch walked quickly along the pavement, Leigh following close behind. "Let's get some supplies from the supermarket before we go to the house," Mitch suggested as they reached the Jeep. "You want pizza tonight?"

Leigh nodded. "Will they have ham and pineapple?"

"I should think so, although I have no idea why you'd want that when there's such a thing as pepperoni." He unlocked the vehicle and climbed in.

Leigh got in and shot him a mock exasperated look. "Really, Dad? You're going to diss ham and pineapple?"

"Can that even be called a pizza?' he asked, starting the Jeep.

"You know it can! It is. It's a recognised type of pizza," she said.

As soon as the engine kicked into life, a beep sounded from the dashboard. Mitch looked down and groaned when he saw the vehicle info display. Apparently, the rear tire nearest the kerb had zero air pressure.

He opened his door and leaned out to take a look at it. The tyre was totally flat. The Jeep's computerised monitoring system hadn't warned him of reduced pressure, so he was sure there hadn't been a slow leak. And if the tyre had blown, surely he'd have heard it.

When he got out and crouched down next to the tyre, he saw why he'd had no clue about the puncture. It had been just fine when he'd parked here earlier. But since then, someone had come along and slashed through the side of the tyre with a knife. There was a two-inch-long straight-edged tear in the rubber.

"Dad?" Leigh shouted. "Is everything okay?"

"Yeah," he said, leaning in through his door. "I'm just going to have to put the spare tyre on the Jeep before we go anywhere."

"Oh. Did we drive over a nail or something?"

He nodded. "We must have." No need to upset her.

Returning to the rear of the Jeep, he opened the boot and took out the spare and the jack. Squinting against the rain, he peered along the street in both directions. Nothing but rain hissing down onto empty pavements.

Yet Mitch felt as if he was being watched.

The rain pounds the street outside the cafe. It bounces off the pavement where Mitch Walker crouches next to the rear wheel of his Jeep and loosens the wheel nuts with a tyre iron. It's too warm in the cafe. There's condensation on the windows. I have a steaming cup of tea on the table in front of me.

Because of the weather, the cafe is busy. Most of the customers are only here to escape the rain. But being inside the cafe is almost worse than standing outside in the downpour. The air in here is heavy with the smell of grease. The fluorescent light tubes set into the ceiling are too bright. Someone has turned the heat up but instead of being pleasant, it's stifling.

There's a radiator right next to my booth, belting out enough heat to melt the polar ice caps. I'm hot but I'm not going to move. There aren't any other unoccupied window seats from which to watch Mitch deal with my handiwork.

The Swiss Army knife I used to slash the tyre is in the pocket of my raincoat, folded on the bench next to me. It's a good knife. Reliable. I'm still not sure why I used it to slash the Jeep's tyre but my not knowing doesn't bother me. Sometimes we have to act without thinking. Sometimes the best things in life come from acting emotionally, with no fear of consequences.

Watching Mitch labour in the rain isn't exactly one of the best things in life but it's satisfying enough for now. How dare he show up here after all this time? Perhaps he thinks he's going to carry on where his father left off. That won't do. That won't do at all. So my welcome-home present in the shape of a rip through the rubber of his tyre is just a warning.

"Can I get you anything else?"

The voice startles me and I look up to see the blonde waitress who served me the tea. There's a smile on her face, expectation in her eyes.

"I'm fine, thanks," I tell her.

She looks past me to the street where Mitch is sliding the jack under the Jeep. The little girl—I don't know her name yet—is sheltering from the rain in the doorway of a closed antique shop.

"Oh, that poor man," the waitress says with genuine concern. "What a dreadful day to get a flat."

I nod noncommittally and sip my tea.

She leaves me alone and goes to serve the family at the next table. I watch her as I drink more tea. She's tall and moves with confidence, nodding slightly like a flower in a breeze as she writes on her order pad. *What flower does she remind me of? Something bright and tall. A cornflower. Yes, that's it.*

I close my eyes and conjure the image of a field to my mind. It's a field I know well. Isolated and away from the beaten path. I imagine a patch of bright blue cornflowers in the corner of the field, swaying slightly in the breeze. How nice it would be to visit those flowers and run my hand over their nodding heads. I would nod back at them, just a slight movement of my head. A secret nod. Just enough to tell them I know their secret. I know what lies beneath, buried in the soft earth where their roots burrow and quest.

Cornflower—that's what I've decided to call her now—goes to the kitchen to place the family's order. I turn my attention back to the show outside where Mitch is struggling to get the tyre off the Jeep. He glances up and down the street every now and then, as if he knows he's being watched but doesn't know where from.

He's grown up a lot since the last time I saw him. His face is more mature, obviously, but it looks like some of that maturity was hard won. His eyes are wells full of emotion. His body, which looks trim and fit, seems to be weighed down by something that is beyond the physical. He's been hurt in the past. I recognise it all too well, just as I can see it in the eyes of the still-smiling Cornflower as she reappears from the cafe kitchen. Just as I can see it in my own face when I look in the mirror.

I don't want to think about that now. I just want to watch Mitch struggle in the rain. If he thinks he's going to return here after thirty years and it's all going to be plain sailing, needs to think again.

I'll make sure he leaves again soon.

One way or another.

5

EDGE HOUSE

After hurriedly changing the tyre in the rain, Mitch threw the flat into the boot along with the jack and drove to the supermarket, where they picked up some essential supplies, including a pepperoni pizza for himself and a ham and pineapple for Leigh.

He knew he should go to the nearest garage and buy a new tyre, because now he'd be driving without a spare and if he got another flat, they'd be stuck. But something inside him, some deep-seated instinct nestled in the back of his brain, made him fear staying too long in Matlock. The fear was irrational, he knew, but it was strong enough to make him constantly glance at the rear-view mirror after they left the supermarket, checking to see if someone was following them out of town toward the Peak District.

It was only after they'd left the main road behind and been driving for twenty minutes along narrow roads that wound around rolling hills and through tiny villages that Mitch was sure there was no one behind them, no dark car driven by a person unknown following them to Edge House.

The rain lightened to a drizzle but black clouds rolled over the peaks of the high hills in the distance, threatening another downpour. The hills closer to the road were gentler slopes, cultivated into farmland. Dry stone walls divided viridian pastures and bright yellow rapeseed fields. Mitch knew that under different circumstances, he would have appreciated the view but right now, he only felt a knot of anxiety, knowing that each second of passing time brought them closer to the house.

"You okay, Dad?" Leigh had been playing on her iPad for most of the journey but the sight of the high, distant hills had made her sit up and take notice of her surroundings. She'd probably seen something in Mitch's face that worried her because there was a look of concern in her eyes.

"I'm fine," he assured her.

"You don't look fine. You look like you're scared of something."

He forced a grin onto his face. "It just feels weird returning here after all these years. Imagine if you were as old as me and you went back to a place you can barely remember." He was downplaying his real feelings, he knew, but how could he explain to Leigh that he was actually scared to see Edge House again? That he felt the sight of the place would trigger some long-forgotten memory, something that should remain hidden in the shadows of the past where it couldn't hurt him?

"I think I'd like it," she said. "It'd be fun."

"Well, that's because you're adventurous," he told her.

Leigh nodded in agreement and then said, "I think you're sad because being here reminds you of your sister."

Where had that come from? He and Jess had only mentioned Sarah a couple of times in front of Leigh. She hadn't seemed too interested in the subject at the time but she'd obviously filed the information away somewhere in her head and was now putting two and two together.

"Well that's probably part of it too," he said. "When my sister disappeared, it tore my family apart. My mum and I moved away and I never saw my dad again."

"That's sad," she said, turning to look out of her window at the distant landscape.

Mitch wondered if she was thinking about the rift in her own family. A mum with a new boyfriend, and a dad she only saw on weekends. He tried to be there for her as much as possible, on the phone and on video calls as well as seeing her as often as he could, but he knew Leigh had been affected by the split between him and Jess, probably deeper than either of them realised.

"Hey, you know you can see me whenever you like, right?" he asked her lightly.

"Yes, I know." She didn't turn to look at him, keeping her attention on the view beyond her window or the rain streaking down the glass, Mitch wasn't sure which.

It had been more than a year now since he and Jess had split up and he knew that time would never heal the wounds that had been dealt to both him and Leigh by the breakup. He remembered the moment he'd found out about Jess's affair as if it had happened yesterday. It had been a hot summer evening and he'd been out on the drive in front of the open garage, taking the lawnmower apart and cleaning the blades and internal workings. As he was wiping dead grass off the lawnmower blades, a phone began to ring. At first, he didn't recognise it as Jess's phone because it wasn't her ringtone. Usually, her phone blared out a Scissor Sisters song when someone was calling it. But the song Mitch heard now was "Stay" by Rhianna.

He stood up from where he'd been crouched over the mower and turned his attention to the garage where Jess's silver-coloured BMW was parked. The song was definitely coming from inside the car.

Jess was inside the house, taking a shower after her day at work. The architects firm where she worked often called her outside of office hours to talk about some project or other and sometimes Jess had to go back to the office to sort out a problem, so Mitch went to the car, opened it, reached in and grabbed the phone from where Jess had forgotten it in the cup holder between the seats. If it was important, he would go up to the bathroom and tell her she needed to call the office.

Rhianna was still singing. The name displayed on the screen was Andrew. Jess had mentioned Andrew in passing on a few occasions. Andrew Tomkins. He was some high-up at the firm. Not Jess's boss as far as Mitch knew but definitely one of the managers and probably someone whose call Jess wouldn't want to miss. Deciding to take a message for her, he slid his thumb across the screen to answer the call.

The voice on the other end of the line was smooth, overly-friendly. "Hey, babe, where are you?"

Mitch tightened his grip on the phone as if by doing so he could strangle off the words coming from it. Babe? Mitch sometimes addressed Jess as babe but only as a joke because she'd once told him how much she hated it.

"You there, Jess?" the voice asked.

Mitch cleared his throat, suddenly realising that he'd been holding his breath. "Who is this?"

"Shit." The man hung up.

Andrew Tomkins had sounded like a man who'd

been caught doing something he shouldn't when he'd spoken his final word and ended the call but it wasn't Tomkins' words, not even the "babe," that made Mitch's heart drop into his stomach. When he'd first spoken, when he'd thought he was speaking to Jess, Tomkins had spoken in that tone reserved for lovers and confidants.

With the phone still gripped tightly in his shaking hand, Mitch went into the house to find Jess. He had no idea what he was going to say to her. He found her in the bedroom, wrapped in a towel, her hair still wet from the shower.

She turned to face him, smiling. Mitch tried to remember how long she'd been taking a shower after coming home from work. She never used to do that; it was a recent habit. Was she coming home and washing Andrew Tomkins away before she spent time with him and Leigh?

"Andrew Tomkins called," Mitch said, holding the phone out to her.

His voice was flat, not accusatory in the least, but Jess must have seen something in his face because after she took the phone, her eyes fell to the floor and she took a deep breath before asking, "What did he tell you?"

The hollow feeling Mitch had felt in his gut while ascending the stairs to the bedroom was slowly turning into anger. "He didn't tell me anything. He wanted to speak to you...babe."

She flinched at the word. Then she sat on the bed, threw the phone on the pillow, put her face in her hands, and began to weep.

Mitch stood there dumbly, watching her. He wanted to ask her why, needed to know what it was about her life with him and Leigh that wasn't good enough for her. But he didn't ask those things. Instead, he simply turned around and left the room.

Later, Jess found him sitting on the sofa in front of the TV. But the TV was turned off. Mitch was staring at the blank screen. She told him then that she wanted a divorce. She wasn't happy anymore. She wanted more from life than she was getting from their marriage. He didn't need to worry about seeing Leigh; she'd let him see his daughter whenever he wanted.

Mitch sat there staring at the blank screen, listening to her words but not really focusing on them, as if they were irritating flies buzzing at the periphery of his awareness. He was thinking about Leigh, who was at her friend's house down the street for a sleepover. Who was going to break the news to her? Would she understand what was happening or would she blame Jess, or him, or both of them? How was this going to affect her life, not only now but when she was older and in a relationship herself?

"Dad, isn't this where you used to live?" Leigh asked from the passenger seat, bringing Mitch's thoughts to the present again. She was pointing at a white sign ahead that said *Relby*.

"This is the village," he said.

"Awesome," she said, sitting up in her seat, "I can't wait to see the house."

Mitch didn't share her enthusiasm. He was looking forward to spending the weekend with Leigh and hiking on the hills and moors with her but as far as the house was concerned, he could live the rest of his life without ever seeing it again and he wouldn't miss it. They were only staying there this weekend because it was free accommodation.

He pressed his foot on the brake as the Jeep trundled over a stone bridge. The bridge spanned a wide, dark river that seemed to mark the village boundary. Beyond the bridge, the main road was lined with two-storey stone houses, a Post Office, a couple of shops, and a large church watching over the village from a slight slope. A large white building served as the local pub. A wooden sign high on its wall showed a painting of a mermaid brushing her long golden hair as she sat on a rock at sea. Beneath the painting, the pub's name, *The Mermaid*, was painted in black on the white wall.

"Maybe we can eat there," Leigh said. "There's a sign outside that says they serve food."

"We'll see," Mitch said. When he'd suggested to Leigh earlier that they might eat at a pub, he'd meant the pubs in the surrounding area, not the local in

Relby. There would probably be patrons in there who knew his father and remembered Sarah. This was a small village and things like a young girl's disappearance weren't soon forgotten, sometimes even after thirty years had passed. Mitch didn't want to be recognised by a villager and have to listen to them tell him what a tragedy Sarah's disappearance was. He knew better than anyone the full impact of that tragedy.

The drizzle of rain became a torrential downpour, drumming on the Jeep's roof and misting the windscreen. Mitch turned the wipers on.

"So where's your house?" Leigh asked, looking at the houses on both sides of the road.

"It isn't in the village," he said, checking the GPS because he wasn't exactly sure himself where Edge House was in relation to Relby. The digital map on the dashboard seemed to suggest the house was a couple of miles north of here.

They left the village behind and drove for another mile before the GPS announced a left turn ahead. Mitch scanned the road but couldn't see the turn, despite the voice's assertion that it was only two hundred yards in front of them. Mitch applied the brakes, checking the map on the dash and the left-hand side of the road. There was nothing there but impenetrable woods.

Then the GPS said, "Turn left," and Mitch saw a narrow track barely as wide as the Jeep leading into the woods. The entrance to the track was flanked by two grey stone pillars that were topped by statues of sleeping lions. Carved on the left-hand pillar, beneath the lion, was the word EDGE. The right-hand pillar bore the word HOUSE. A small white sign tied to the trunk of a fir tree read PRIVATE ROAD.

"This is it, Dad," Leigh said excitedly.

"Yeah, this is it." Mitch took a breath and turned left, guiding the Jeep between the pillars and sleeping guardians. The trees on either side of the track formed a canopy that blocked out the light, keeping the track in deep shade.

A half-formed memory returned to Mitch, a memory of running along this track at night. He was sure he'd been wearing pyjamas at the time, the soles of his bare feet scratched and cut by twigs and stones. He'd been running towards the road, away from the house. And when he'd looked back over his shoulder, he'd seen a single light burning in one of the windows and he'd feared whoever was in that lit room.

He tried to remember more details but the memory was hazy, like a dream that flees as soon as the dreamer awakens.

Ahead, the track snaked left and then right again and the trees gave way to a large semi-circular lawn and the house that lay beyond.

Mitch felt the knot in his gut tighten slightly.

There were no trees behind the house. Beyond the walls that contained the garden, the land fell away sharply. This feature of the terrain was obviously what gave the house its name. It also meant that to anyone approaching the house, the imposing structure was framed against the sky. Mitch guessed that such an effect would make the house appear pleasant on sunny summer days but at the moment, the dark storm clouds rolling over the distant moorland lent the house an ominous air.

Edge House had been designed in Victorian times by an architect in love with the Gothic Revival style. It stood three-storeys high with arched and leaded windows that reflected the dark clouds on their rain-streaked panes. The house's gables faced the lawn and were high-peaked, making the dark slate roof slope steeply. At the rear of the house, the conical roof of a tower could be seen. Mitch couldn't remember a tower from his childhood and wondered if it had been added after he and his mother had left in 1987.

Among the arched windows, Mitch recognised the one that had featured in his dream-memory, a large window on the top floor with stone tracery patterned to resemble interlocking vines. He tried to remember who had been in that room, whom he had feared when he was fleeing along the track towards the road, but nothing came to him. The memory remained dark. Had the room's occupant been his father? And why had Mitch been running away towards the road?

Unable to find an answer to that question, he drove up to the house, tyres crunching on the gravel that surrounded the lawn, and killed the engine.

He looked over at Leigh, who'd been strangely quiet since seeing the house. She was staring wide-eyed at the building, seemingly stunned into silence.

"Well, what do you think?" Mitch asked.

"It's awesome," she said, then added, "but also a bit creepy."

"Creepy, huh?"

"Yeah, it's like something out of *Dracula*."

Mitch laughed and said, "I'm sure it won't be as creepy inside. Come on, let's have a look." He got out of the Jeep and ran over to the front door to avoid getting too wet. Leigh joined him.

The arched front door was made of heavy wood with a black iron handle and ornate lock. A brass lion's head knocker stared at them, snarling. Mitch fished the key out of his jeans pocket and pushed it into the lock. There was a loud click when he turned it. Steeling himself, he pushed the door open. Beyond the archway a gloomy foyer awaited.

"You first," Leigh said, her voice barely a whisper.

Mitch steeled himself again and stepped over the threshold and into the gloom. He found a light switch on the wall and clicked it on. Overhead, an ornate iron chandelier whose arms were fashioned to look like tendrils of ivy flickered to life. The walls of the foyer were dark and wood-panelled, with paintings of hunting scenes here and there. A wide flight of stairs led up to the next floor, the wooden banister highly-polished from the touch of many hands over the years. A Persian rug, predominantly coloured red and gold, lay at the foot of the stairs on the dark wooden floorboards. Mitch wondered why the rug was positioned there and not in the centre of the room where it seemed to belong. He realised he had no idea about his father's taste in interior decoration other than the fact that the man had obviously liked hunting scenes and thought an ornate carving belonged on everything.

There were closed, heavy wooden doors on either side of the foyer as well an open door straight ahead. Through the opening, Mitch could see a short passageway that led to the kitchen at the back of the house.

At the top of the stairs, a huge window framed the dark sky and cast a dull light onto the landing above.

Mitch felt Leigh's arm snake around his. She pressed herself close to him.

"There's nothing to be afraid of," he said. "It's just a big old creepy house." He realised he was whispering.

"I told you it was creepy," she said.

"If you don't want to stay here, we can find a B and B or a—"

"No, it's okay," she said. "It's like being in a ghost story. I can't wait to tell Jasmine and Laura at school. They'll be so jealous when I tell them I stayed in a haunted house."

"It isn't haunted," Mitch said. But then he wondered if that was true. He didn't believe the house was infested with ghosts or spirits or anything like that, but memories could come back to haunt people, couldn't they? Wasn't it possible that being in a place where a bad thing had happened could make an unremembered past claw its way to the surface from the deep grave of lost memory? *Where a bad thing had happened?* Where had that come from? Sarah's disappearance was bad, of course, but it hadn't happened in the house. He supposed he was connecting the house to the disappearance because this was where he'd been living at the time.

"Well, I'll still tell them it was. They won't know any different." Leigh released her grip on Mitch's arm and indicated the closed doors. "Which way are we going to go exploring first?"

"Let's try the kitchen," he suggested. It looked bright and airy back there, a welcome relief to the dark walls and floor of the foyer. At the end of the short passageway, he and Leigh found themselves in a kitchen that was long and wide, with modern strip lights that seemed to defy the Gothic design of the rest of the house. The walls were painted in a light grey colour, the cupboards slightly lighter. One wall was almost entirely made up of a row of large arched windows that overlooked the walled garden behind the house. The windows let in copious amounts of light despite the bad weather, lending the kitchen an air of breeziness.

Mitch went to the windows and looked out at the garden. It was overgrown and wild, the moss-covered walls festooned with ivy and other creepers. Weeds ran rampant in the flowerbeds, choking to death the few remaining flowers as they had already done to their brothers and sisters.

"Dad," Leigh said, "I think we've been burgled." She was pointing at the back door, which was slightly ajar, letting in a light drizzle of rain that spattered onto the chessboard-patterned black and white floor tiles.

Without touching anything, Mitch checked the door. The wood around the lock was splintered, as if the door had been forced open. Using his elbow, he opened the door and checked its exterior. There was a shallow indentation where something had been used as a battering ram to gain entry.

Taking Leigh's hand, he led her back through the house to the front door and out to the Jeep. He had no idea when the house had been broken into and for all he knew, someone could still be inside. Once they were inside the Jeep, he called the police. After being put through to a desk sergeant at Buxton police station and explaining that he was the owner of Edge House and he'd found the place broken into, he was told to wait for an officer to arrive and not to go back into the house.

That last part was easy. Mitch had no desire to go back into the house and would be glad when Sunday arrived and he left it for the final time.

6

BATTLE

THE POLICE ARRIVED HALF an hour later but not in a patrol car. Instead, the vehicle that came rolling up the drive and crunching over the gravel was a green Range Rover. A man in a light brown trench coat and tweed hat got out of the driver's side and came running over to the Jeep, his body stooped, one hand pressing his hat to his head is if he were exiting a helicopter. When he got to Mitch's window, he made a winding signal with his free hand. Mitch was already opening the window. It buzzed down, letting in the rain.

"I'm DCI Stewart Battle," the man said, fishing his warrant card from the pocket of his coat and showing it to Mitch. "Are you the gentleman who reported the break-in?"

"That's right." Mitch guessed the policeman to

be in his late fifties. He had a weather-worn face and a bushy salt-and-pepper moustache.

"Just wait here, sir," Battle said. "DS Morgan and I will check the property and make sure it's safe." He turned to a dark-haired young woman who was getting out of the Range Rover and gestured for her to follow him into the house. She did so.

When they'd both disappeared inside, Leigh asked, "Are they the police?"

Mitch nodded. "I was expecting a uniformed officer but those two are detectives. A Detective Chief Inspector and Detective Sergeant." It seemed like a waste of resources to send two detectives to check out a break-in. Maybe that was what happened when you were lord of the manor; the police pulled out all the stops.

Battle appeared at the front door ten minutes later and waved that all was clear.

When Mitch and Leigh joined the two detectives in the foyer, Battle gave them a short-lived smile. "All clear, sir. I'll get a forensic officer out here to take fingerprints. There might be something useable on the door or perhaps upstairs where it looks like they spent the most time. Now, if you can tell us what's been stolen, we can see about catching whoever did this." He took out a small black notebook and flipped it open.

"I have no idea what's missing," Mitch said. "We've only just arrived here."

Battle nodded slowly. "I see. Well, we can ask Mrs. Jenkins about that, I suppose."

"Mrs. Jenkins?" Mitch asked.

"The housekeeper," Battle said. "You are Mitchell Walker, correct? Son of Michael Walker?"

Mitch nodded. "I am."

"Your father employed a housekeeper. Mrs. Lily Jenkins. She'll be able to tell us if anything has gone missing. In the meantime, what I find interesting about this break-in is what the thieves didn't take."

"I don't understand what you mean," Mitch told him.

"Well, the television is still in the living room. The keys to your father's Land Rover are hanging up by the back door but the vehicle is still in the garage. There's even some cash lying around. What thief would leave cash behind?"

"They must have taken something," Mitch said. "Otherwise, why did they go to the trouble of breaking in?"

Battle's grey eyes looked at Leigh, then back at Mitch. "Mr. Walker, would you mind if DS Morgan took your daughter into the living room to watch television for a while?"

"No, that's fine." Mitch turned to Leigh. "Is that okay with you?"

Leigh nodded.

The Detective Sergeant smiled at her and said,

"My name's Lorna. Shall we go and see if we can find anything good on the TV?"

Leigh nodded again and followed her through the door that led to the living room. Mitch heard her telling the DS, "I've got a friend called Laura. Her name sounds like yours but I think Lorna is nicer."

Battle turned to Mitch. "If you could come with me upstairs, sir, there are some clues regarding the thieves' motive for breaking in." He went to the staircase and Mitch followed. They ascended to the next floor and Battle led Mitch along a long hallway to an open door. "We've checked the other rooms," he said. "Most of them are empty. The thieves went through your father's bedroom but there wasn't much in there apart from a bedside table, a wardrobe, and a bed. It seems the room they were most interested in was this one, your father's office."

The room contained a large polished mahogany desk, and an executive-type leather chair sat by the window. Bookshelves ran along one side of the office but the books had been scattered onto the floor, revealing a safe built into the wall. The safe door had been attacked with a drill and bore three small circular holes.

"Total amateurs," Battle said. "It isn't exactly a top-notch safe but they still couldn't get in, even with a drill and all the time in the world. Of course, by the time they drilled the third hole, they must have realised they were wasting their time anyway." He pointed at the safe door. "Have a look in there."

Mitch went over to the safe and put his eye to one of the holes. The light coming in through the other two holes was enough to make out what was inside. Nothing. The safe was empty.

"The usual method of drilling a safe is to make one hole and use a precision instrument to open the door," Battle said. "Whoever did this had no idea what they were doing. Perhaps they drilled the other two holes just to see what was inside." He chuckled. "I'd like to have seen their faces when they discovered it was empty."

"What do you think they were looking for?" Mitch asked.

"I don't know but it was something specific, something that they thought would be in this safe. And it must have been of more value to them than the things they ignored like the television, the Land Rover, and the cash. Not to mention the paintings on the walls that I'm sure would fetch a pretty penny." He sighed. "This makes me wonder if we should reopen the investigation into your father's death. At the time, we couldn't find any evidence of foul play, but this"—he indicated the safe—"makes me think we might have missed something."

Mitch realised he had no idea how his father had died. At first, when John Mercer had rung him, he hadn't wanted to know, but now the detective's words were piquing his interest. "There was an investigation into my father's death? Was that because he died in suspicious circumstances?"

"We didn't think so at the time," Battle said. He narrowed his eyes slightly. "You do know how he died, don't you?"

Mitch shook his head.

Without answering, Battle left the room and walked back along the hallway and down the stairs. Mitch followed.

When they were both standing in the foyer, Battle pointed up at the landing they had just descended from. "Your father fell down the stairs from the landing. We're not sure if he wandered out from his bedroom during the night and tripped or if he was going up to bed and lost his footing. The housekeeper found him the following morning." He pointed at the Persian rug. "If I were you, I wouldn't move that rug, at least not while your daughter is around. The clean-up crew did the best they could but these old wooden floors tend to soak up liquid and there was a bit of blood."

"Understood," Mitch said.

Battle hesitated for a moment as if he were deciding whether to say something or not. At last, he said, "While we're on the subject of hidden things, Mr. Walker, if you come across anything unusual, will you let me know?" He took a business card from his pocket and handed it to Mitch.

Mitch frowned, confused. "What do you mean by unusual?"

Battle shrugged. "I'm not exactly sure, to be honest. Look, I'll be straight with you. Over the years, there have been a number of disappearances in this area. A couple of times, your father's name came up as a person of interest. I'm not saying he had anything to do with the crimes we were investigating but, because of who he was and who he knew on the force, some leads weren't looked into as deeply as they might have been otherwise. Those crimes were never solved."

"Disappearances?" Mitch said, "You mean like Sarah's disappearance? You think my father was involved somehow?"

Battle held up his hands. "I'm talking about a number of crimes, some of which occurred before you or your sister were born." He sighed. "I was only a young copper at the time and when I was told to leave something alone, I did so without question. But those kind of cases, the ones that go unsolved, tend to stick with you. You think about what might have been missed."

Mitch didn't know what to think. Battle might be clutching at straws, trying to rectify some mistake from his past, or attempting to solve a case that got away, but without more information, Mitch couldn't help the detective. And even though he'd hardly known his father, he wasn't ready to accept that the man might have been a killer or a kidnapper or whatever it was that Battle was insinuating.

"I can see you're conflicted," Battle said. "Forget I said anything. I'll just get my DS and head back to the station."

"Fine," Mitch said, sensing that some sort of barrier had descended between him and the detective.

"DS Morgan, we're leaving," Battle shouted toward the living room door.

Lorna Morgan appeared with Leigh close behind her. "I hope you enjoy your weekend," she said to Leigh before following her boss to the front door.

Before he stepped over the threshold and into the rain, Battle turned to Mitch. "We'll probably never know what the thieves expected to find in that safe, Mr. Walker, but if you do find out, please call me. I don't like unsolved mysteries." He strode across the gravel and climbed into the Range Rover, DS Morgan in tow.

Mitch watched them drive away and then turned to Leigh. She gave him a thin smile but he could see a worried look in her eyes.

What the hell had he been thinking by bringing her here for the weekend? He should have taken her hiking somewhere closer to home, not brought her here, where the house had been violated and the blood stained the floor.

"I've got an idea," he said. "Let's find a nice hotel."

She brightened immediately and the fact that she would have stayed here without complaint even though she obviously hated the idea broke Mitch's heart. "Are you sure?" she asked.

He nodded. "Very sure."

"Okay." She was out the front door before Mitch had a chance to take the keys out of his pocket.

As he was locking the door, he noticed the safe deposit box key on the ring. Battle had said they'd probably never know what the thieves had been looking for in the safe but maybe this key held the answer. Maybe Michael Walker had moved whatever items were in the safe to the box at the bank. If they were so valuable that someone was willing to break into the house to get them, it made sense.

He got in the Jeep, where Leigh was waiting, playing a game on her iPad, not looking at the house. Feeling another pang of guilt that he'd brought her here, Mitch started the engine and followed the gravel path around the lawn to the track that led through the trees back to the main road.

When they were on the track, he glanced at the house in the rear-view mirror. It sat silently in the storm, its unlit windows watching him leave like dark eyes.

7

STORM

WHEN ELLY ARRIVED at her Peak District accommodation, the sight of it was almost enough to douse the flames of frustration that had been burning inside her since leaving Birmingham. She'd left her house almost three hours ago, after eating a light lunch that consisted of a microwaved lasagne and a couple of pre-packaged green leaves that could hardly be called a salad.

After wolfing down half of it and chucking the rest in the bin, she'd tossed her suitcase into the boot of her old Mini and set off north on the M6 Motorway. She'd found herself stuck in dawdling traffic almost immediately because there were miles of roadworks. Too late, she realised that the SatNav was guiding her onto the M6 Toll Road and she'd had to pay five pounds to continue her journey.

After exiting the toll road, she'd been stuck in

queuing traffic again thanks to more roadworks. And the whole time, her car was being pounded by the bloody incessant rain. The spray made it difficult to see the road ahead and she'd spent most of the time wiping the inside of the windscreen with tissues because the Mini had a condensation problem.

When she'd finally left all that behind and hit the winding country roads, the SatNav had fallen off the windscreen and onto the passenger seat because of the condensation. Elly had stuck it back onto the glass but almost crashed into a hedge in the process.

Her entire journey had been fraught with frustration but as she arrived at the place she'd be staying for the next two weeks, she told herself it had all been worth it.

She'd expected Wollstonecraft Publishing to find a hotel for her to stay in, but instead, they'd rented a holiday cottage. It even had a name: Windrider Cottage. Situated on a hill overlooking the moors and totally isolated, it was exactly what Elly needed right now, somewhere to escape from the rest of the world for a while. There was a pub a few miles back down the road so she'd have somewhere to go if she felt like human interaction, but apart from that, she was going to be alone with her thoughts for the next fortnight.

The cottage was quaint, built of white-painted stone with a neat little garden at the front behind a low iron fence. Elly parked the Mini on a paved area next to the gate and rushed through to the cottage's front door, trying to reach the porch before the rain could soak her. There was a metal key safe on the wall and she punched in the combination she'd been given in an email from the cottage's owner. After opening the safe and grabbing the shiny silver key inside, she unlocked the door and stepped into her new-found refuge from the outside world.

The first thing she noticed was that the place smelled fresh. That was always a plus. A door on the left opened into the living room, which had a stone fireplace, TV, and a plush-looking sofa and easy chair. On the opposite side of the entrance hallway, there was a dining room equipped with a table and four seats as well as a bookcase filled with paperback novels and board games. A set of narrow steps led up to the bedrooms.

Elly walked past these rooms to the rear of the cottage where the kitchen was situated. It was a modest size but more than big enough for her, and the view from the large window over the sink took her breath away.

There was a small, unremarkable, lawn but the cottage didn't need anything fancy back there because beyond the lawn, the hill sloped away and offered a stunning view of the moors and peaks. Elly was a city girl through and through, having lived in places like Manchester, London, and Birmingham all her life, but at that moment, she wanted to go outside despite the rain and view the scenery without a barrier of rain-smeared glass separating her from the landscape. She wanted to be a part of it.

To hell with it, she thought and went to the back door. The key was hanging on a hook on the wall. Elly took it and opened the door, stepping out into the pouring rain. She walked across the lawn, sliding on the wet grass because her trainers had no tread on their soles, until she reached the slope of the hill. She stood there, drinking in the view.

If anyone had asked her what a moor would look like from the top of a hill, she'd have said it would look dull, coloured brown and dark green with nothing to break up the visual monotony. But the moor that stretched out before her now was anything but dull. As well a mixture of emerald green and coffee brown grass, there were mauve-coloured patches of fern and dark shadows beneath lone trees that seemed to be standing in a roiling sea as the wind blew the tops of the long grasses this way and that. Pools of real water scintillated beneath the thick storm clouds, reflecting various shades of the grey and blue sky.

Clouds and mist obscured the peaks of the hills, shrouding them in mystery. Elly wanted to climb up into the haze and hide within it as if it were a protective cloak.

She'd never felt a part of anything as strongly as she felt a part of the wild landscape before her. The rain lashed against her face, stinging her, but she welcomed it, imagining that it was washing away her features in the same way that it had eroded and shaped the tall hills.

Her phone rang, bringing her out of the spell the landscape had cast on her. Elly cursed, feeling suddenly cold as she realised the rain had soaked through her T-shirt and jeans. Heading back inside, she pulled the phone out of her pocket and saw the word MUM on the screen. She hadn't told her mum about the trip to Derbyshire but had no doubt that Jen had told her everything.

She almost regretted calling her sister last night and telling her of her plans to visit the Peak District because now her mum would be calling to find out more details. There was nothing she liked more than talking to Elly about her life so she could tut in disappointment or simply say, "Well if that's what you think is best, dear," in a way that said it wasn't what *she* thought was best. Not at all.

Jen was spared their mother's disappointment, of course. She could do no wrong because she had a husband and two kids and as far as their mum was concerned, that was what a woman should aspire to. Elly didn't begrudge her sister because she'd rather live life her own way, even if it meant she had to put up with disapproving comments every now and again.

She answered the phone. "Hi, Mum."

"Elly, can you hear me? Jen tells me the

publishers are sending you to Derbyshire on some fool's errand. What's it all about, dear? Perhaps you shouldn't go."

"It's too late for that," Elly said, "I'm already there."

"Oh dear." Her mother sounded as if she'd just learned of the death of her closest friend.

It's fine, Mum." Elly brushed her wet hair away from her face and walked through the cottage to the front door. She went out to the car and, with the phone pressed between her ear and shoulder, retrieved her suitcase from the boot. "And what do you mean by fool's errand?" she said as she re-entered the cottage and placed the suitcase on the dining room table.

"That's what Jen said."

Elly was sure that wasn't what Jen had actually said at all but was, in fact, what her mother thought.

"She said they've sent you there to look for a serial killer who doesn't exist," her mum continued. "It all sounds very odd to me."

"It isn't odd, Mum, it's a job." Elly opened the case and took out the folder Glenister had given her as well as a large-scale map of the area with Edge House, the house where Michael Walker had lived, circled in black pen.

"Elly, are you sure you're doing the right thing? Now that Paul's left you, you shouldn't be gallivanting around the country. You need to stay close to home, find someone else, someone who might put a ring on your finger."

Now that Paul has left you. Wow, her mum really wasn't pulling her punches today. Never mind being tactful and saying something like, "Now that you and Paul have split up." Nope, Mum just jumped in there with both feet. She probably thought Paul was a hero for putting up with Elly for so long.

"I need to work, Mum. Now that Paul has gone, I only have my own income to live on." She got her camera out of the case and placed it on the table next to the map. Digging under a pile of jumpers, she found her notebooks and pens and dumped them on the table too.

"Well, that's exactly what I mean," her mum said. "You find the right man and he'll look after you for the rest of your life. You won't need to go chasing imaginary serial killers. Somewhere out there, there's a right man for every woman. There's even one for you."

"He's probably as imaginary as the serial killer," Elly said.

There was an exasperated sigh on the other end of the line. "Your father and I are worried about you. What if this serial killer isn't imaginary? What if he goes after you because you're looking for him? It happens, you know. I've seen *Luther* and *Midsomer Murders,* I know how these things work."

Now it was Elly's turn to sigh. "This isn't a television show and the man I'm investigating is dead, so I think I'm quite safe."

"Dead? Why are you investigating a dead man?"

"It's a long story. I've got to go, Mum. I got soaked by the rain and I need to take a bath. I'll call you sometime in the week. Give my love to Dad."

"Well, just make sure you do call. And remember, men don't like women who are too adventurous. Perhaps when you get back home you'll settle down a bit."

Elly ended the call and put the phone on the table. The calm she'd felt outside in the rain was shattered. Now, she felt as if her nerves might snap. Taking a deep breath, she told herself that her mum meant well. There was no point stewing over it. And she really did need to take a bath. Her clothes were sticking to her skin, making her feel cold and clammy.

She closed the suitcase and took it upstairs, where she chose a bedroom for herself. It was smaller than the master bedroom but where the master was at the front of the cottage and looked out over the road, the one Elly chose was at the rear and overlooked the moors and the hills. She put the case on the bed and took out her pyjamas, which consisted of plain white cotton bottoms and a top that had a red heart on the left breast.

She took them into the bathroom where a large corner tub waited. "Just what the doctor ordered,"

Elly murmured to herself as she turned on the hot tap. There was a bottle of lemonade-scented bubble bath on the windowsill so she added some to the water and undressed while the bubbles frothed up, filling the bathroom with a sweet citrus scent.

When the tub was full, Elly got in and sank into the hot water, closing her eyes and letting her mind drift.

Ten years ago, she'd taken meditation classes at the local community centre, thinking they would help her control her emotions. She knew she had a tendency to fly off the handle at times and it was something she wanted to work on. The classes had done nothing for her and she'd spent the hour during which she was supposed to be "watching her breath" thinking about problems at work, worrying about problems in her personal life, opening her eyes and checking the clock on the wall, wondering if the other students in the class were really just pretending to be peaceful of if their minds were whirling too, and contemplating whether she should stop at the chip shop on the way home or order pizza.

The calm that she'd longed to experience (and that was something that the teacher would have frowned at because they weren't supposed to long for anything during that hour and were supposed to "leave desire at the door") had eluded her. But at this moment, lying in a bath in a cottage in the middle of nowhere with a storm raging outside and rain cascading against the windows, she felt calmer than she'd ever felt in her life.

Maybe reaching rock bottom made her appreciate the beauty in simple things. Declining book sales, Paul's departure, and an uncertain future had pushed her life into a downward spiral and it was only now that she understood the allure of a stormy landscape that she wouldn't normally have noticed and appreciated being isolated from the rest of the world in a way that was not lonely and sad but energising and peaceful.

Despite everything, she felt suddenly optimistic about the task ahead of her. If Michael Walker was a murderer, then she would prove it. If it turned out he wasn't, she would investigate further until she found the truth.

What if Michael Walker was innocent and the real killer was still out there somewhere? She might be on the brink of something huge here. She could actually bring a murderer to justice.

Her phone rang downstairs, bringing Elly out of her reverie. She waited for the ringing to stop, for the call to go to voicemail, so she could relax again.

But the moment was gone. And the calmness she'd experienced was gone too, replaced by a burning enthusiasm to pore over the articles in the folder Glenister had given her. She reached for the plug in the tub and pulled it. While the water was draining away, she got out and dried herself quickly before slipping into the pyjamas.

She padded downstairs and opened the folder.

A loud pounding shook the front door and Elly nearly jumped out of her skin. She shrank back, her heart in her mouth. Then the windows rattled in their frames and she realised the cottage was being rocked by a clap of thunder.

She looked out at the rain-swept road in front of Windrider Cottage. Her Mini looked small and insignificant parked out there.

The thought she'd had in the bath returned. What if the amateur sleuth at Wollstonecraft Publishing was wrong and Michael Walker was innocent? That meant there was a killer on the loose in this area. He could be anywhere, maybe even out in this storm, looking for his next victim.

Shivering, she returned to the table and spread the newspaper articles out. The names of the lost girls stared up at her. Josie Wagner. Sarah Walker. Lindsey Grofield.

Elly touched each name in turn. Three girls separated by time but possibly connected by fate.

"I promise I'll find out what happened to you," she whispered.

8

THE VAULT

On Saturday morning, after eating a fried breakfast at the Premier Inn they'd spent the night in, Mitch and Leigh walked across the car park to the Jeep. They were dressed in hiking gear and Mitch had a rucksack slung over his shoulder. The storm had blown itself out during the night and now the sky was bright blue with a few white clouds dotted here and there. Mitch had packed their waterproof jackets into the rucksack but he was hoping they wouldn't need them.

"Listen," he said as he opened the boot and slung the rucksack and his walking boots inside, "before we go walking, we need to go to Matlock again and pop into the bank. I need to close the account for the safe deposit box."

He felt a little guilty that this weekend, which was supposed to be about spending time with Leigh, was becoming more about wrapping up his father's business.

"You know what?" he said, getting into the Jeep. "Forget I just said that. Let's go hiking. I'll deal with the bank next week." He could come back on his own on Monday and sort the account out, after Leigh had gone home.

"Oh, okay," Leigh said, looking disappointed.

"What's the matter? I thought you wanted to go hiking?"

"I do but I want to know what's in the box too. Maybe it's full of diamonds or something."

"Maybe it is," he said. He couldn't discount the possibility. "Shall we go and have a look then?"

Leigh nodded. "We can go walking after. Maybe we'll have a rucksack full of diamonds."

"That sounds like it'd be heavy," Mitch said.

"I'd carry it," she offered.

He laughed. "Yeah, I bet you would. Okay, let's go and see what's in the box. I need to get a new tyre anyway if we're going to be driving into the wilder parts of the Peak District."

They arrived in Matlock half an hour later and Mitch managed to find a garage that specialised in tyres and exhausts. He left the Jeep there so the mechanics could fit a new tyre to replace the one that had been slashed and put the spare back in the boot where it belonged.

Taking the rucksack, in case the safe deposit box

really did contain something that was heavy, he and Leigh walked into town. They found the main street easily and entered the bank. It was busy with customers, which Mitch expected was the usual for a Saturday morning. When he explained to a teller who he was, she went to fetch the manager.

Less than a minute later, a blonde woman in a dark blue jacket and skirt appeared from a back room and walked over to Mitch. "Hi, Mitch" she said, smiling. "It's great to see you again. How are you?" She spotted Leigh and crouched down to face her. "And who is this young lady?"

"I'm Leigh."

"That's a nice name. I'm Tilly. I'm your dad's cousin."

"Are you?" Leigh asked, wide-eyed and surprised.

"Yes," Mitch said, recognising Tilly as she stood up again. "Yes, she is." He hadn't seen her since they were both nine years old but her features hadn't changed all that much. The years had been kind to her. He remembered Sarah once joking that he was in love with Tilly but the truth was, he had respected her because she was tough and adventurous. He wondered if she still had that streak of daring within her or if it was something the years had changed.

"Come through to my office," Tilly said. "We can catch up while we deal with your dad's account." She led them through a door that revealed a number of glass-walled offices where advisors spoke to customers. Tilly walked past these offices to a door at the end of the corridor that bore her name: Tilly Walker. Mitch wondered why she'd never married. Or maybe was divorced and using her maiden name.

"So how are things?" Tilly asked as she ushered them into the office. "What have you been up to?"

"I've been running a landscape gardening business," Mitch said. "It looks like you've done all right for yourself. Bank manager. Impressive."

She grinned. "Remember when we were young, though? I always said I wanted to be an explorer and travel to uncharted lands. Things didn't exactly turn out that way."

Mitch had a sudden flash of life before Sarah's disappearance. He and Tilly had spent a lot of time together, along with their younger siblings Jack and Sarah, exploring the woods and fields around Edge House and the house where Tilly and Jack lived. That house's name eluded him for a moment then sprang into his mind. Blackmoor House.

"How is Jack?" he asked.

Tilly's face darkened. "I wouldn't know. I haven't exactly been in touch with my family for a while. I saw them at your dad's funeral, of course, but we didn't speak."

"Sorry, I didn't mean to pry." The truth was, he *hadn't* meant to pry. He remembered Jack as a little shit and had only asked about him out of politeness.

"No, no, it's fine," Tilly said, her face brightening again. "Look, we should get together sometime and have a good chat. We've got a lot of catching up to do." She took a business card from a clear plastic holder on the desk and scribbled something on it in pen. She handed it to Mitch. "That's my personal number. Give me a ring and we'll get together sometime."

"Sure." Mitch tucked the card into his wallet. He didn't mention that after this weekend, he didn't plan to ever be in this area again.

"These are the documents you need to sign and then I can release the contents of your dad's safe deposit box to you," Tilly said, sliding papers across the desk to Mitch. "His is the last box we've got at this branch. We only let him keep it because he was one of our best customers." Sadness showed in her eyes and she cleared her throat, clearly holding back tears.

"I'm sorry," Mitch said, "it must have been a shock when he died." It seemed strange that his cousin was more affected by his father's death than he was but she'd known Michael for the past thirty years while Mitch had been gradually forgetting all about him.

"I saw him just two days before," she said. "He came in to put something in the box, actually. He sat right where you're sitting now, holding a manila envelope he was going to take to the box, and he chatted about the weather as if it was any other day, you know? He had no idea that in two days' time, he would be gone forever." She opened the desk drawer and took out a box of tissues. Dabbing her eyes, she said, "I'm sorry, Mitch."

"No need to apologise," he said as he signed the papers. He looked over at Leigh, who was staring at Tilly with a look of sadness in her own eyes. Mitch touched her arm, drawing her attention. "Hey, it's okay," he said.

Leigh smiled thinly, making Mitch again wish he'd left all of this business regarding his father until next week, when Leigh could be left out of it. He'd planned to visit Mercer and Robinson to drop off the keys after picking up the Jeep but now he decided to come back on Monday to do that. Even though it meant driving back to Leamington Spa tomorrow and then back to Matlock the day after, he'd gladly do that to spare Leigh getting involved in any more of this mess.

The sooner Edge House was sold and he could put all this behind him, the better.

"Right," Tilly said, getting up and smoothing her skirt with her hands. "I'll take you to the box."

They followed her out of the office and through a door protected with a digital combination, then down a flight of stairs to another door, this one made of steel and also locked with a combination lock as well as a key. Tilly opened the door and turned on the lights in the room beyond. The room was small, with a table at its centre and numbered, locked steel doors lining the walls. Each door had two locks. The overhead light was too bright for such a small room and cast everything in a stark whiteness. The fluorescent tube buzzed and flickered.

"We have one key and the customer has the other," Tilly explained, lifting a set of keys and selecting one. She went to box 208 and inserted the key into one of the locks, unlocking it before saying, "I'll leave you to it," and leaving the room. She closed the door behind her.

"Open it, Dad," Leigh prompted.

Mitch unlocked the steel door and removed the metal box inside, placing it on the table in the middle of the room. He opened the lid and looked inside.

"Is that it?' Leigh asked, disappointed.

Inside the box was a single, fat, manila envelope. Mitch reached in and took it out. At first, he thought the envelope contained cash, a stack of notes maybe, but the longer he held it, the more it felt as if there was a book inside.

"Maybe we were a bit optimistic when we said it might be a box full of diamonds," he told Leigh.

She shrugged. "Maybe it's a treasure map."

"I don't think so," Mitch said, opening the envelope and looking inside. "It looks like some sort of journal." He slid the book out onto the table. It was thick, bound in black leather, and wrapped with a long, black leather cord.

He unwrapped the cord and flicked through the pages. They were filled with handwriting in black pen and pencil sketches of places and people. "Looks like some sort of journal," he said.

"What does it say?"

He held it up so she could see the thickness of it. "I don't know. There must be hundreds of pages here. It'd take a long time to read it."

She held out her hand. "Let me have a look at it."

"No, we're going hiking. We don't need to concern ourselves with this, okay? We're supposed to be trudging over those hills, not reading old diaries in bank vaults. Come on." He slipped the journal into the rucksack beneath his waterproof jacket and knocked on the door.

Tilly opened it. "Everything okay?"

"Everything's fine," Mitch told her. "Leigh and I are going hiking now."

"Great," she said, leading them back up the stairs. "Have a nice time. And be sure to give me a ring so we can catch up."

"Of course," Mitch said. Tilly seemed to genuinely want to hear from him so he decided that he'd call her when he came back on Monday. He couldn't see any harm in having a drink with her and reminiscing about their childhoods. Maybe such a conversation would shake loose some of the memories that seemed to be stuck in an uncharted part of his brain where his recall was forbidden to travel.

When he and Leigh got outside, she turned to him and said, "Dad, is Tilly really your cousin?"

"Yes, she is."

"Does that mean she's my aunt?"

"No, not exactly."

"Oh," Leigh said as they walked back along the main street towards the garage. "Well, anyway, I like her. She's nice."

"I'm sure she is."

They arrived at the garage. The Jeep was sitting in one of the parking bays, sporting a brand-new tyre.

"Okay," Mitch said, "let's go inside and pay and then we can get onto those hills." He made a mental note to himself to keep the focus of the rest of the weekend on Leigh. There was no need to waste any more time talking about ancient history.

He'd return on Monday and put the sale of Edge House into the hands of John Mercer. He'd catch up with Tilly, as he'd told her he would, but then he was done. The only real link he had with this place was Sarah and he had to accept the fact that he'd never know her fate.

The past was dead and gone. It was time to finally bury it.

I DRIVE SLOWLY past Manchester Piccadilly train station, peering through the windscreen at the people coming out through the doors and onto the night-darkened street.

Some of them are commuters, arriving home late with briefcases clutched beneath their arms. Others are travellers who have caught the train here from the airport. They drag loaded suitcases behind them and search for taxis as soon as they come out of the station.

These are not the people I am looking for tonight. The ones I want are those who no longer belong to the world. They are running away from something back home, coming to the city to hide from their past. They are the lost.

They are easy to spot and I see one wander out onto the street. Unlike the people climbing into taxis or walking to the car park to collect their vehicles and drive home, she ambles aimlessly on the pavement. She has nowhere to go, nowhere to be. No one is expecting her arrival and no one will miss her when she vanishes.

I don't drive over to her immediately. There is no need to hurry. She isn't going far on foot and even if I do lose her, there are plenty of others just like her.

I speed up slightly and drive past her, watching her in the rear-view mirror. She's wearing a dark blue jacket, collar pulled up against the rain. A white knitted hat sits on her head, hiding all but a few stray wisps of black hair. Slung over her shoulder is an olive green army rucksack, probably containing everything this girl owns in the world. Her head is bent, eyes on the pavement in front of her trainers.

Her feet must be getting wet. She'll be easy to entice into the car.

I drive on and turn off the road she's walking along and take a few back streets so I end up behind her again. She's still soldiering on in the rain, head bent as if she has a thousand miles ahead of her.

She doesn't; she has only a few more steps left and then she won't have to worry about walking anymore. The past she has run away from will never be able to catch up with her.

The loaded syringe sits in the pocket of my door. I reach down and put it on the seat next to my leg, out of view of the passenger side of the car. As I come alongside the girl, I lower the window and speak to her. "Terrible night."

She doesn't answer, merely continues trudging on with her head down.

"Do you want a lift?"

Again, she ignores me.

"If you need a bed for the night, I know where you can get one. For free."

She whirls on me. There is anger in her grey eyes but also a hint of weakness behind it. "Oh yeah? I bet you do."

"It's nothing like that," I say. "Wouldn't you

rather spend the night somewhere warm and dry than shivering in a doorway somewhere?"

"And what's in it for you?" she asked cynically.

"Nothing. I'd be helping you, that's all. That's what I do; I help people."

She thinks about that for a few seconds while the cold rain hisses down around her. Finally, she says, "Are you one of those religious nutters who's going to try and convert me into your God-squad?"

I shake my head and laugh. "No, not at all. Honestly, I just want to help, that's all."

She turns her head to glance at the street around her and then her gaze shifts to the interior of the car. I can tell she's weighing up the possible danger of getting into the car against the need to get out of the rain. She shrugs. "All right. But you'd better not try any funny business."

"No funny business," I assure her. "Come on, get in."

She reaches out hesitantly for the door handle. When the door opens, she slides the rucksack off her shoulder and climbs into the car. She rests the rucksack on her knees.

"You'd best put your belt on," I say, indicating her seat belt.

"No, thanks."

"You have to put it on or the car is going to be sounding a warning every few seconds and we won't be able to talk." I point at the dashboard where a symbol of a person wearing a seatbelt is illuminated red. If I drive off while the symbol is lit, the car will chime repeatedly.

"I don't want to talk anyway," she says.

"Come on, don't be like that. I'm giving you a lift, the least you can do it talk to me."

She sighs and pulls the belt across her chest. As it clicks home, the symbol on the dashboard dies.

I pull away from the kerb, checking the rear-view mirror. The road is almost deserted and I'm sure no one saw her get into my car. Even if they did, they no one took any notice. This girl is beyond the notice of the world.

"What's your name?" I ask.

She hesitates and then says, "Lily."

"Is that your real name?"

"Does it matter?"

"No, I suppose it doesn't. Where are you from?"

"Does that matter?" Her face darkens slightly.

"No, I'm just trying to make conversation. I'm guessing it's a place you'd rather forget."

"Wow," she says sarcastically, "you must be psychic."

I drive east, towards the outskirts of Manchester. She isn't familiar with the city; she won't even know we've left it behind until we're in the countryside and heading towards Dark Peak.

"Let me guess," I say, "you had an argument with

your parents. They don't understand anything about you or your life."

"You've got that right," she says with a slight sneer. "Only it isn't my parents. I only have one parent, my mum. My dad left when I was two or three or something."

"So you fell out with your mum?"

"Yeah, something like that." She seems to shrink into the seat and puts her arms around the rucksack as if hugging it will make everything better. It won't.

"You can tell me, you know. I won't tell anyone. I don't even know who you are, do I? I bet your name isn't even Lily, really, is it?"

She goes quiet for a couple of minutes and then, probably feeling secure behind the anonymity of a false name, says, "My step-dad hits me. He gets pissed a lot and when he's like that, he's handy with his fists. My mum gets the worst of it but sometimes he has a go at me as well. I told her she should kick him out but she doesn't listen. She's so desperate to have a bloke, she'll put up with a no-good layabout like him, never mind what happens to her daughter. Well, maybe now she'll come to her sense. He'll never hit me again, that's for sure."

"No, he won't," I say. "Did he...do anything else?"

She looks at me and raises an eyebrow. "You mean have his wicked way with me? Yeah, that's happened a couple of times." She shifts her gaze to the darkness beyond the window and her voice becomes low. "I tried to fight him off, you know, but he was too strong. Even when he was pissed, he was too strong."

I know enough about her now. She's exactly the type of girl I was looking for tonight. And the fact that she gave me the name Lily is almost too perfect. It's as if the universe delivered her to me so that I can end her suffering.

"Do you like lilies?" I ask.

She seems taken aback by the sudden change of subject. "What? Yeah, I suppose so. Why?"

"Well, since that's the name you gave me, I thought there might be a reason. I know it's not your real name so I was wondering if you liked the flower."

"I think you're looking at it a bit too deeply," she tells me. "I just said the first thing that came into my head."

"Still, lilies are lovely. Do you know there's a wildflower called the lily of the valley?"

She shrugs.

"It has white drooping flowers. In fact, now that I think about it, you looked like a lily of the valley when you were walking along the pavement with that white hat on your head."

She doesn't say anything but shifts farther away from me in her seat, pressing herself against the door.

I take the syringe in my hand and jab it into her

leg. The needle punctures her jeans and I press the plunger.

Her eyes go wide and her face twists into a mask of horror. "What?" she gasps. Her hands scrabble for the door handle but the drugs are already beginning to course through her system. Her movements are sluggish and her clawing hand fails to find the handle. It drops to her side at the same time as her head lolls back against the headrest.

Her breathing becomes shallow, as if she is in a deep sleep, which, of course, she is.

I put my foot down, feeling suddenly anxious to get to the woods where I have something special prepared for this girl.

Forty minutes later, I pull over to the side of the deserted road in Dark Peak. The rain has stopped and the clouds are parting, revealing the beauty of the stars. They look down on me like a billion shining eyes as I get out of the car breathe in the fresh air that smells of rain-wet grass and tangy pine.

There's a wet field by the side of the road and beyond that, the forest.

I go to the boot of the car and take out the piece of board with its yellow nylon sling and a shovel. I place the board on the ground next to the passenger-side door and lower Lily onto it. Then, I put the sling around my waist and move into the field, the board and its slumbering load sliding along on the wet grass behind me. Even the weather is synchronised with my mission, wetting the grass to make my makeshift sleigh slide easily across the field.

The forest waits.

When I reach the trees, I have to leave the board behind and pick Lily up. She's only a slight thing but it takes me half an hour to get her to the place I have prepared for her. Then I have to go back for her rucksack.

This worries me slightly because I'm not sure how long it will be before the drugs wear off. The concoction is of my own making and its effects aren't consistent.

But Lily is still asleep when I return to the grave.

Within the deep, oblong-shaped hole beneath the trees, a packing crate will serve as her coffin. I'd like to have an actual coffin for her but the crate is the best I can give her in the circumstances. Anyway, it doesn't matter what lies beneath the earth, the grave will look beautiful when it is filled in and the flowers are planted.

I remove the crate's lid, exposing its empty interior. I lay Lily on the edge of the grave and give her a push. She rolls limply into the buried crate. After throwing her rucksack in with her, I replace the lid and use the shovel to pile the earth I dug out of the grave earlier back in. It lands heavily on the crate's wooden lid.

Eventually, I can't see the wood at all, only earth. I continue to fill the grave.

When I'm done, I hear a muffled groan come from within the grave. It sounds so far away, I'm not sure if my ears are playing tricks on me.

"Sshh," I whisper to the newly turned earth. "There's no need to be scared. You won't suffer anymore."

I step back and examine my work. In the black shadow of the night, the grave looks sombre. But in a few days, I'll return here with wildflower seeds and where there is only dark earth at the moment, there will be an abundance of lilies of the valley.

9

THE JOURNAL

It was early Sunday evening when Mitch dropped Leigh off. He parked the Jeep outside her house and went around to the boot to get her case. The weather had stayed fine during their hike on Saturday and also for most of Sunday, only beginning to rain when they'd checked out of the hotel and were about to drive back to Leamington Spa. When they hit the motorway, they left the rain behind as they headed south.

As Mitch was unloading Leigh's things, the door to the house opened and Jess stepped out onto the front step. She offered Mitch a short wave. He returned it and passed the case to Leigh.

"Did you have a nice time?" he asked her.

"A great time." She grinned and added, "Let's go hiking again next weekend as well."

"Sure, if that's what you want to do. I'll find somewhere for us to go."

"We're going away next weekend to see my mum and dad," Jess called from the porch. "I told you about it, remember?"

"Oh, yeah." Mitch had forgotten Leigh was going to see her grandparents in Sussex. "I guess we'll have to make it the weekend after," he said.

Leigh nodded. "Okay, Dad." She hugged him and walked up the drive to her house, the case rolling behind her on its wheels.

"How'd it go in Derbyshire?" Jess asked as Leigh reached the porch.

"It was great. We went on a ten-mile walk and we ate at the pub."

Mitch was glad Leigh hadn't mentioned the break-in or the police. She'd tell Jess about those things later, he had no doubt, but at least they weren't the first things on her mind when she remembered the weekend.

He got into the Jeep, waved at his daughter and ex-wife, and headed across town to his apartment. When he got through the door, he dropped his suitcase, rucksack and walking boots in the hallway and went to the kitchen to brew coffee. While the water was percolating through the coffee maker and the rich smell of ground roasted beans drifted tantalisingly in the air, Mitch remembered the journal in the rucksack.

He went back into the hallway and unzipped the rucksack, taking out the journal from beneath his waterproof jacket. Returning to the kitchen, he flicked through the pages. The handwriting was spidery in places, bolder and more confident in others. The pencil sketches, interspersed among the writing, were of flowers, landscapes, and people.

Mitch stopped at a random page and read the first line. The words had been scrawled in spidery black ink.

Walked along the river to the place where the bluebells grow today. Their bloom has gone. Soon they will be nothing more than blue rot in the shadow of the weeping willow.

He turned to an earlier page.

In the woods near Edge House, the foxgloves blush pink, hiding their secret.

Beneath the words, a foxglove plant had been sketched on the page, drawn in pencil with a high degree of skill.

Mitch knew his father had been artistic. He remembered drawings of birds and landscapes in sketchbooks, made during his father's rambles through the countryside. When he was little, Mitch would sometimes sit at the kitchen table and pore over the books. His father would point at the bird pictures and tell Mitch the name of the species. But as far as Mitch knew, the man had never been interested in plants. Mitch had an interest in flora, of course, it came with the job. But that was something he'd developed during his horticultural training, not something he'd inherited from his father.

The coffee maker gurgled and then beeped when the pot was full. Mitch put the journal down on the counter and got a mug from the cupboard, pondering over the journal and why it had been locked in a safe deposit box. Tilly had said Michael put the journal into the safe deposit box a couple of days before he died. When Mitch opened the box, the journal was the only thing in there, so had the safe deposit box been empty until then? Or had something been taken out at the same time the journal was put in?

He poured the coffee and added milk and sugar before taking the steaming mug and the journal into the living room. Sitting on the sofa and placing the journal on the coffee table in front of him, he ruffled through the pages until he found another drawing. This one was a portrait of a young woman with fair hair held back by a tartan Alice band. Mitch didn't recognise the woman and there was no identifying name in the text on the page. The words beneath the sketch described a walk in the countryside and a visit to a patch of poppies in a field.

The description in the journal was vivid yet generic, detailing the way the grasses in the field swayed in the wind "like hypnotised women waiting for their master's command" and the shape of a nearby fence as "damp with rainwater and bowing like an arched back" but never mentioning actual place names.

Mitch closed the book. It seemed to be nothing more than the ramblings of his father's mind. He remembered Battle's words, that his father's name had come up during the investigations into a number of disappearances. Maybe there was a clue in the journal. Maybe he should hand it over to the police to assist them in their investigation.

He found Battle's business card in his pocket and read it. The card contained a mobile number as well as an office number. The mobile would probably be the best way to get hold of the detective on a Sunday evening. He rang it.

Battle answered after three rings. "DCI Battle."

"Hi, it's Mitch Walker. I was wondering if we could talk some more about what you told me regarding my father. I have something that you may be interested in." He began to flip through the pages of the journal idly.

"Mr. Walker, it's good to hear from you. I sent the fingerprint lads around to Edge House on Friday. They dusted the door and were hoping to get elimination prints from you and your daughter but you weren't there. I sent two officers around today as well but you weren't in then, either. I even rang you on the house phone. No joy."

"I had to come home," Mitch said. "We didn't touch the back door anyway."

"Well it isn't just the door, sir. There's the kitchen, the bannister, your father's office. And the safe, of course. We need your permission to enter the house and dust everything. Also, I'd like the housekeeper to have a look around the house. She might know if anything has been stolen."

"Of course. You have my permission. Do whatever you need to do." Mitch leafed towards the back of the journal, past a sketch of a stone bridge spanning a river, low hills in the background.

"I'd still like a set of your prints, sir, as well. So if you could come into the station sometime, that would be very helpful. Now, you said you had something I'd be interested in?"

Mitch wasn't listening. He'd turned to a page in the journal that caught his attention. He felt his heart pounding.

"Mr. Walker?" The voice sounded distant, faint. "Are you still there?"

"I'm still here," Mitch said.

"You said you had something for me?"

"It's nothing."

"Well, if you could come into the station so we can take those prints—"

Mitch ended the call. He leaned closer to the journal to inspect the page he'd landed on. A sketched portrait of Sarah filled half of the page. She looked exactly as she had the night she'd gone missing, with a plait down the left side of her hair, tied with two blue beads with white stars.

Below the sketch were two lines of writing that made Mitch's blood run cold.

A forget-me-not that never blooms

Might hide and then grow old

But it wasn't the picture or the words beneath it that had caught Mitch's attention. There was something else, something stuck to the page. He reached forward and ran his finger over it.

A strip of clear tape had been laid across the bottom of the page. And beneath the tape lay a lock of chestnut hair.

10

MURDER BOARD

Elly threw the covers aside and got out of bed at nine, welcomed by the view of the moors and distant hills through the window. The day was grey but it wasn't raining, so after going downstairs and making a cup of tea, she slipped her feet into her boots and went out into the back garden. The smell of wet grass and lavender laced the morning air. Elly felt a slight chill but that was only because she was still wearing her cotton pyjamas. Besides, the chill made her feel alive. It was like a splash of cold water in the face after a long, heavy night. It felt invigorating.

As she stood on the grass and sipped her steaming tea, she shivered slightly. She knew it wasn't because of the cool breeze. A sense of anticipation buzzed through her like electricity, making her tremble with its power.

She'd come here on a "fool's errand" as her

mother called it, and if she was honest with herself had only taken the job to get away from the Paul situation. But now that she was in the place where the girls had been plucked from their lives like apples from a tree, she was sure there was some mystery here. And she was determined to reveal its secrets, to shine a light into the dark corners and chase away the shadows that surrounded the fates of Josie Wagner, Sarah Walker, and Lindsey Grofield.

Finishing her tea, Elly went back into the cottage and wiped her damp feet on the mat inside the back door. She put the cup in the sink and went upstairs to get dressed, choosing jeans, an old T-shirt, and a dark green woollen jumper from her case.

She went out to the Mini to get her whiteboard and pens from the back seat. When she got back inside, the propped the whiteboard up on one of the dining room chairs and arranged the magnets down the left-hand side. In the middle of the board, she drew a large blue question mark. The symbol represented the unknown subject of her investigation, or the unsub.

Using the magnets, Elly stuck the three newspaper articles onto the board in chronological order. The murder of Josie Wagner in 1977 in the top left-hand corner, the disappearance of Sarah Walker in 1987 in the top centre, and the disappearance of Lindsey Grofield on New Year's Eve 1999 in the top right.

Beneath the articles on Josie and Sarah, she wrote "Gordon Farley". Farley was a detective whose name was mentioned in both articles. In 1977, Josie Wagner's case had been led by a detective named John Hanscombe, with Farley acting as second-in-command. In 1987, Farley was the lead investigator dealing with Sarah Walker's disappearance.

Farley's name didn't appear in the Lindsey Grofield article. The detective in charge of that case was DCI Stewart Battle, whose name also appeared in the article about the Sarah Walker case. On the whiteboard, Elly wrote "Stewart Battle".

At the bottom of the board, she wrote "Michael Walker" and next to that, she added "Edge House".

Standing back and inspecting the board, she realised she had very little to go on. The names and articles were lone islands floating in a sea of white with no lines connecting anything to anything else. Elly drew a blue line connecting both instances of Gordon Farley's name so there was at least one connection on the board and the whole thing didn't look so nebulous.

The most promising place for Elly to start was to interview Farley, if he was still living in the area, to find out what he knew about the Wagner and Walker cases. Then she should track down Stewart Battle and interview him about Sarah Walker and Lindsey Grofield. That would give her the official police view regarding the murder and the disappearances.

She needed to investigate the areas in each case where the police might have overlooked something. One of those areas was the involvement of Michael Walker. If the police had ignored leads because of Walker's social status or because he had friends in high places, that was where Elly could find something new, something Farley and Battle had missed because they were tied down with red tape.

Edge House was as good a place as any to begin her investigation into Walker. Most serial killers kept trophies of their kills, so it stood to reason that there could be something hidden at the house. She shivered when she remembered that there were also two bodies missing.

Now that Michael Walker was gone, it was possible that the Edge House was empty, waiting to give up its secrets to anyone who had the guts to break in and snoop around.

She went to the table, grabbed her camera and map, and left the cottage. She got into the Mini and started the engine. For a moment, she paused, hands on the steering wheel, the engine idling. Was she really considering breaking into Edge House? If she got caught, the consequences would be serious. Maybe she should go back into the cottage and spend the day on her computer finding out how to contact Gordon Farley and Stewart Battle.

She looked out of the windscreen at the distant mist-shrouded peaks as if they could give her an answer to her dilemma and tell her which path to take. Spend the day indoors or risk everything and become a burglar?

She needed to know what, if anything, was hidden at that house. It might be the key to finding out what happened to the girls. They were relying on her.

She pulled out onto the road and set off in the direction of Edge House.

11

AMONG THE PICTURES

ELLY ARRIVED at Edge House an hour later. The entrance was almost hidden from the road among the trees. She'd expected a wide driveway behind a tall iron gate but the approach to the house was a narrow track leading into the woods behind low stone pillars topped with statues of sleeping lions.

She steered the Mini between the stone pillars and proceeded slowly along the track. The house wasn't visible ahead because the track bent left. Damn it. At least if she could see the house, she'd know if there were vehicles parked outside. This way, she might drive around the bend ahead and find herself in the middle of a garden party or something. She could hardly say she was lost and had turned off the road by mistake; the lion pillars clearly stated where this track led and there'd been a Private Road sign back there too.

Oh well, she'd think of something if she had to. Better not to dwell on it now or she'd find herself turning around and going back to Windrider Cottage without even seeing the place where Michael Walker lived. If she was going to do this properly, she had to get a feel for the man. She relied on intuition a lot in her work and the only way to nurture that intuition was to get close to the subject of her investigation.

The same way she'd gotten close to Leonard Sims, the Eastbourne Ripper.

At least Michael Walker was dead. He wasn't going to fill her head with graphic tales of how he'd killed and mutilated his victims. The things Leonard Sims had told her gave her nightmares most nights.

She turned left, following the track, only to find it turned right almost immediately and revealed Edge House. The sharp S bend seemed to have been put in the track to hide the house from the road, something a straight approach wouldn't have done.

There were no vehicles parked outside the house, no lights on inside. The place seemed dead.

Unwilling to leave the Mini in front of the house where it could be easily spotted, Elly drove around the side of the house and to the rear where the gravel terminated at a high brick wall. She killed the engine and got out.

She was considering scaling the wall and seeing what was beyond it when she noticed the back door was open. A small indentation cratered the wood and the latch was broken. Dark powder, which Elly recognised as fingerprint powder, had been applied along the frame and in various areas of the door.

It looked like someone had beaten her to the house. Was it someone with the same motive as her, or a common thief? She went to the door and pushed it gingerly. It swung open slowly, opening onto a light, airy kitchen.

Elly paused at the threshold, trying to calm her breathing. Her heart pounded and she felt heat prickling up her neck. If she went into the house and was discovered, no amount of smooth-talking was going to get her out of trouble.

She went back to the car, opened the passenger door, and reached into the glove compartment. She kept a pair of black wool gloves in there. Donning them, she grabbed the camera and slung it around her neck. Even if she didn't find anything incriminating in the house, some pictures of the interior would be useful, especially if all of this was going to end up in a book someday.

She returned to the open door and stepped inside. She took two steps into the kitchen and froze when she heard a sound. A tapping sound reached her ears. It took her a couple of seconds to realise it was rain on the window. Now she saw that the brick wall she'd parked near surrounded an overgrown garden.

A walled garden miles away from the closest

neighbour was a private-enough place to do some digging at any hour of the day or night and bury bodies. Was this overgrown, weed-infested garden the final resting place of Sarah Walker and Lindsey Grofield? Elly took a picture of it through the window but the spatter of rain on the glass obscured the garden, blurring it so the camera lens couldn't pick out any detail.

Elly walked across the kitchen as silently as she could, telling herself that only she could hear her rapid breath and the heartbeat that seemed to pound in her ears. She came to an open door that led to a small passageway and, beyond that, the front door and the house's foyer. Treading carefully, she made her way to the foyer and paused there, listening to the house around her. She could hear the rain lightly tapping on the windows and the roof but apart from that, Edge House was quiet.

She wasn't sure where to begin her search so she went through the nearest door and found herself in a living room with a sofa and an easy chair in front of a plain wooden coffee table, fireplace, and flatscreen TV. There were a couple of bookcases standing against the walls but otherwise the room was empty.

She'd expected the interior of such a grand house to be stuffed with pieces of art, antique furniture, and huge portraits. But apart from a few paintings of hunting scenes in the foyer, there seemed to be nothing grandiose about Edge House other than its outward appearance. The interior was purely functional. She took a quick photo but there was nothing interesting about the room.

She went back to the foyer and through the door set in the opposite wall. The room beyond was brightly lit by daylight streaming in through a large window that overlooked the lawn. Except for an ornate stone fireplace decorated with carvings of vines and cherubs, the room was empty. There wasn't even a chair where someone might sit and enjoy the sunlight on a nice day. Elly took a photo but wasn't sure who would be interested in looking at a picture of an empty room.

Despite the brightness, the emptiness of the room was depressing.

Elly returned to the foyer and stood for a moment in silence. There was a lonely atmosphere here that was almost tangible. It was as if the heart of Edge House had withered and died.

Or maybe it had been ripped out when Sarah vanished and Michael Walker's wife and son left him. Walker had been living on his own here for the past thirty years, rattling around in this Gothic box with nothing to keep him company other than his own thoughts. He'd never divorced his wife and remarried, never had any other children. No wonder the place was devoid of plush furnishings.

If he was an innocent man, Elly felt sorry for him. The disappearance of his daughter had torn his family apart and he'd lived out his years alone, within a vast house that was filled with nothing.

She heard a noise outside, like tyres crunching on gravel. She went quickly back into the empty room and peeked through the large window. When she saw a police car approaching the house, she panicked. Had someone seen her enter the house and called the police? Or were there silent alarms that had been triggered the moment she'd stepped inside?

She couldn't get to the Mini and drive away without being seen, couldn't flee on foot because the police would find her car parked at the side of the house and find out exactly who she was. She was trapped. Why had she been so foolish to think that such a large house like this wouldn't be alarmed?

Two uniformed officers got out of the police car and began walking to the front door.

Elly fled upstairs, almost tripping over a Persian rug on the way. She took the wide stairs two at a time until she reached the landing. A long hallway lined with doors ran the width of the house and a second staircase led up to the upper floor. Obeying the flight instinct that told her to get as far away from the threat as possible, Elly bounded up the second staircase.

At the top, another hallway ran the width of the

house. Elly was about to choose a room to hide in when she noticed a trapdoor in the ceiling, presumably the entrance to the attic. A metal ring hung from the door and there was a pole with a hook on it resting against the wall at the far end of the hallway. Elly rushed to grab the pole and hooked the ring, pulling the trapdoor open. She cringed inwardly when a wooden ladder slid down to the floor with a loud clatter.

There was a knock on the front door. Three sharp raps.

Taking the pole with her, Elly ascended the ladder. When she got to the top, she knelt over the open space, reached down with the pole and snagged the ladder, pulling it up after her. The trapdoor closed and she was plunged into darkness.

Faintly, she heard more knocking on the front door.

As her eyes adjusted, she realised she wasn't in total darkness. Two small circular windows positioned under the eaves, one at the back of the house and one at the front, allowed a meagre splash of light to get into the attic from outside. Elly went to the window at the front of the house and looked down at the police car parked on the gravel.

She couldn't see the front door from this angle but she could hear the voices of the two policemen below.

"Looks like no one's home."

"Want to try the back door?"

Elly tensed, willing them not to go around to the back door. They'd find her car. They'd know she was here. It would all be over.

There was a pause before she heard, "No, he's probably gone out for the day. Come on, let's get out of this bloody rain."

She watched them go back to their vehicle and get in. The engine kicked into life and the car drove back to the wooded track before disappearing behind the trees.

Elly let out the breath she'd been holding.

She searched for a light switch and found one on a wooden joist near the trapdoor. Two bare bulbs hanging from the ceiling flickered into life, giving off a sallow glow that hardly illuminated anything.

From what Elly could see in the dim glow, the attic was dusty, festooned with cobwebs, and mostly an empty space like the rooms below. A pair of bicycles, one a girl's pink Barbie bike, the other a boy's black ten-speed racer, were propped against the wall, gathering dust. A green skateboard sat on the floor next to the racer. At the rear section of the attic, half a dozen cardboard boxes had been placed haphazardly.

Elly opened each one, finding old clothes, bedding, curtains, toys, and board games. There was nothing here that could aid her in her investigation.

She finished searching the final box and sat on the wooden floor, sighing in frustration. There was nothing here that implicated Michael Walker or exonerated him.

"What did you expect?" she asked herself. "A signed confession?"

She noticed another box on the far side of the attic, half hidden in shadow. This one was draped with an old pink blanket. When Elly pulled the blanket away, she saw that it wasn't a box that had been hidden beneath the blanket but a small, blue, steel trunk.

Elly lifted one of the handles on the side and pulled the trunk tentatively, testing its weight. It scraped across the wooden floor. She pulled it out of the shadows and into the dim light. Two metal clasps held the lid closed but there were no locks.

Elly steeled herself before lifting the lid. Hearing tales of the mutilation of victims was one thing but what if she opened this trunk and found the remains of such a victim? What if she lifted the lid and saw Sarah Walker's dead face staring at her?

"Come on, Elly," she told herself, "you can do this. It's important."

She unfastened the clasps and lifted the trunk lid.

When she saw what was inside, she let out a breath of relief.

The trunk was filled with photos.

"See?" she said. "It's nothing, you scaredy-cat."

She took out a photo and examined it. It was difficult to see clearly in the low light but it seemed to be an old family snap of a young boy and girl. Elly knew what Sarah Walker looked like from a school photo in the article about her disappearance and was sure it was Sarah in the picture. She held it directly beneath one of the bare bulbs to get a better look.

In the photo, Sarah was sitting on the pink Barbie bike on the lawn in front of Edge House, looking at the camera but not smiling. Her face was set in a defiant expression, her lips tight, eyes slightly narrowed. Now that Elly thought about it, she hadn't been smiling in the school picture either but instead had offered the school photographer that same defiant look.

Elly assumed the boy standing next to Sarah in the bike picture was her older brother, Mitchell. His bike was in the picture too, the black ten-speed, but instead of sitting on it, Mitchell was holding it with one hand while he waved at the camera with the other. He was smiling, face and posture carefree, unlike Sarah's.

Elly pocketed the photo before returning to the trunk, grabbing the handle and dragging it closer to the bulb's pale light. She rummaged through its contents, finding more pictures of Sarah and Mitchell that seemed to have been taken the same day as the bike photo as well as a handful of shots of a woman with long, dark hair Elly assumed to be Margaret Walker, Sarah's mother.

Margaret seemed as carefree as her son in all of the pictures except one. She appeared to have been shot by the camera without her knowledge because, unlike the other pictures she appeared in, she wasn't looking at the camera and smiling. In this one, she was outside Edge House, leaning against the large window of the room that was now totally empty. She had a cigarette in her hand and she was looking towards the woods at the edge of the gravel. Her face was pensive, her arms folded, and her posture seemed defensive.

The room beyond the window Margaret was leaning against wasn't empty, as it was now. There was an artist's easel in there, the canvas resting on it covered by a cloth of some kind. Next to the easel was a small table littered with sketch books, pencils, paint tubes, brushes, and an artist's palette.

Elly shoved the photo into her pocket along with the bike picture.

She wanted to find an image of Michael Walker himself to add to the whiteboard. But it seemed he was more comfortable behind the camera than in front of it because most of the pictures were of Margaret, Sarah, and Mitchell.

Digging deeper into the trunk, she grasped a handful of photos from the bottom and brought them into the light. These were much older and were black and white. The first picture Elly looked at showed two dark-haired boys playing in a stream. They were holding nets on long poles and seemed to be attempting to catch fish. Elly guessed their ages at ten and eight. Sitting on the bank behind them was a girl who was maybe four or five years old. She wore a light-coloured 1960s style broadcloth dress and stared vacantly into the water, her face mostly obscured from the camera by her long dark hair.

Elly slid the photo into her pocket. She had no idea who the children were but guessed she might be looking at a young Michael Walker and his siblings.

The next picture showed the same three children standing outside Edge House, although some features of the house were different. The front door, beside which the children were standing, had a large knocker in the shape of an eagle's head. Elly hadn't seen that eagle's head on the front door when she'd driven past the door earlier. She was sure there'd been a lion's head, not an eagle's.

The window that Margaret Walker had been leaning against in her photo also looked different. The lead work criss-crossing the panes was spaced farther apart in the older picture.

The two boys were standing with their arms around each other's shoulders, smiling at the camera. The girl had a tight-lipped expression on her face, an expression that was mirrored by Sarah Walker in a photograph taken years later.

Flicking through the other photos in her hand, she found one that was in colour. The image showed the two boys, now young men. The eldest was in his early twenties while his younger brother looked around eighteen. The photograph had been taken in a village on what looked like a warm summer day. The young men sat at a table outside a pub, pints of beer sitting before them. From the wide shirt collars the two wore and the flared jeans Elly could see on the people in the background, she guessed this picture to be from the seventies. Part of the pub's name was visible in the photo, painted on the wall above the young men's heads. MAID. There was no sign of the girl from the previous photos. Maybe she'd taken the pic, pointing the camera at her brothers with that same tight-lipped expression she and Sarah Walker shared.

Elly put the photos into her pocket, along with the others. She had no doubt that one of the boys was Michael Walker. An Internet search should tell her which one, since there were bound to be pictures of Walker on the net. She should also be able to find out more about his brother and sister. It was even possible she could be able to track them down and interview them.

As she reached into the trunk again, a sound from within the house startled her. Somewhere, a phone was ringing. It was the strident ring of an old-fashioned phone, the type with a bell inside the casing.

Elly waited for it to stop. When it finally did, she breathed a sigh of relief and resumed digging through the trunk.

The phone rang again. When it finally stopped after fifteen rings, Elly felt unnerved. Whoever was ringing the house obviously expected someone to be here. That someone could be on their way here now. Or the caller, who was obviously insistent based on the length of time they'd stayed on the other end of the line while the phone was ringing, might come to the house.

She couldn't risk being here any longer. Maybe she'd come back another time and leave the car parked somewhere else, somewhere it wouldn't look out of place. She could sneak through the woods to get to the house, come after dark and bring a torch.

"Oh God, what's come over me?" she asked herself. Less than seventy-two hours ago, she'd been sitting in the Belanger with Glenister discussing Derbyshire as if it were nothing more than a concept, and now here she was breaking into a house and stealing photos.

She closed the trunk and slid it back to its resting place in the shadows. It left a trail in the dust on the floor but there was nothing she could do about that unless she swept the entire attic and she didn't have time for that. She suddenly felt as if she had no time at all.

After checking that the attic looked more or less how she'd found it, she opened the trapdoor in the floor. As the ladder clattered to the floor below, she turned off the lights. When she got to the foyer, the phone started ringing again, making her heart leap into her mouth. She could still hear its insistent call as she got into her car and started the engine.

She pushed the Mini as fast as she dared along the track through the woods and didn't relax until she was on the main road, driving south aimlessly, not ready to return to the cottage yet because she felt as if she were on fire with adrenaline.

A minute later, she reached the village of Relby and hit the brakes when she saw the pub. She took the photos from her pocket and found the one of the two young men sitting at a table with their beers in the seventies. She held it up to the car window and checked the pub. This was the place. The MAID visible in the photo was part of the pub's name, THE MERMAID.

There might be patrons here who remembered Michael Walker, who could tell her about his younger days as well as his later life.

After all, the seventies was when Josie Wagner had been murdered. Elly might be able to find some information that placed Walker at the scene of the crime or suggested he knew Josie.

She looked at the photo in her hand and wondered if it had been taken while Josie was still alive or after her naked body had been discovered at Blackden Edge.

Elly looked at the faces of the two young men in their wide-collared shirts and wondered if she was looking into the eyes of a future killer or those of one who had already done the deed.

12

INTO THE WOODS

Mitch arrived at Edge House on Monday morning and parked the Jeep in the early morning sunshine that had burned the mist off the moors and promised a warm day ahead. He got his suitcase out of the boot and placed it by the front door before returning to the Jeep and getting the house key and the journal from the passenger seat.

He'd spent a couple of hours after getting off the phone with Battle last night going over the words and pictures in the journal, searching for any mention of Sarah. But apart from her portrait and the lock of hair, which was probably hers, there was nothing else.

Most of the book seemed to be written in some sort of linguistic and pictorial code, with names and drawings of flowers signifying something other than flora. Some of the walks detailed in the book mentioned flowers that could not have been seen by the writer at the times described because the flowers would have been out of season. A walk along a snowy riverbank, for instance, mentioned a visit to a patch of columbine plants. Mitch knew that the columbine, also known as aquilegia, bloomed in late spring and early summer, not in winter.

In another passage, flowering winter heliotropes were mentioned in a part of the journal that was clearly written during the summer, based on the descriptions of the weather. Winter heliotropes did not flower later than March.

Mitch believed these anomalies were not errors on the part of the journal's author but that in some cases the flower names represented something other than flora.

He'd considered taking the journal to Battle but dismissed the notion every time. According to Battle, the investigation into Sarah's disappearance hadn't been conducted properly because it may have been obstructed by senior members of the police force. If Mitch handed the journal over, who was to say the same thing wouldn't happen again? Besides, apart from the lock of hair taped to one of its pages, the journal was nothing more than a book of sketches and recollections of walks in the countryside.

If he had any chance of finding out what happened to Sarah, he had to crack the journal's code himself. If his father had played some part in what had happened on December 21st, 1987, Mitch was sure there would be proof hiding behind the flower metaphors. He just had to figure out the code.

He'd chosen to stay at Edge House while he tried to find the truth behind his sister's disappearance. This was where she'd lived all her short life. It was where their father had continued to live after she was gone. If there were any clues that would help Mitch decipher the journal, they were most likely in this house.

This was his best shot at finally finding out what happened to Sarah, after thirty years of not knowing. So he'd arranged to be here for as long as it took. After finding the lock of hair in the journal, he'd rung Ed Yardley, a gardener who worked for Mitch during busy times, and asked him to take over the business while he was away. He told Ed he had "family problems" and didn't know how long he'd be gone.

"Family problems," Mitch muttered to himself as he opened the front door of Edge House and stepped into the foyer. "That's putting it lightly."

The first thing he had to do was fix the back door. He went into the kitchen and took a ring of keys from the hook on the wall. Somewhere among them was a key to the garage, which was where he'd expect to find some tools. He went out through the front door and over to the side of the house where the garage was situated. It sat towards the rear of the property, next to the wall that surrounded the garden.

The garage had two doors: a large metal door that slid up to allow vehicular access and a wooden side door. Both were painted dark green. Mitch searched through the keys on the ring and found one with the same manufacturer's name stamped in it as was in the large door. He tried it and the door unlocked. Mitch slid it up, letting daylight into the interior of the garage.

There was a dark green Land Rover Defender parked in there, sitting among workbenches and tool racks. Mitch found a hammer and various screwdrivers, which he threw into a half-empty toolbox that was sitting on a shelf. He took the box, along with a couple of lengths of wood that had been discarded beneath the shelf, around the house to the back door and began nailing the door shut from the inside. He affixed the lengths of wood and screwed them into place, barricading the door.

With the door secured, he took the tools back to the garage and locked it up. As he was walking back around the front of the house, a police car came crunching over the gravel and stopped by the Jeep. Two uniformed officers, one a blonde woman, the other a dark-haired man, got out and came over to him.

"Morning, sir," the female officer said, showing him her warrant card. "I'm Officer Preston, a Scenes of Crime Officer from the Buxton station, and this is my colleague, Officer White. We've come to dust your house for fingerprints following the break-in you reported on Friday. DCI Battle said we had your permission to enter the house and get to work."

"Yes, of course," Mitch said. "Go ahead."

"We were going to let ourselves in through the back door," she said. "DCI Battle said you'd returned home to Leamington Spa."

"I changed my mind," Mitch told her. "I'm going to stay here for a while. I've sealed the back door, so I'll let you in the front."

"Thank you," she said as he let them into the house. "I'll let DCI Battle know you're here. I believe he wanted to have a word with you. Will you be here for the next hour or so?"

Mitch nodded.

She told Officer White to get started in the kitchen and she took her phone outside for some privacy. Mitch heard her say, "Mr. Walker is here, sir."

When she came back in, she said, "He'll be here shortly," and went to join her colleague in the kitchen.

Mitch explored the rooms that opened off the foyer. The first was empty of any furnishings whatsoever. The second, the room DS Morgan had taken Leigh into to watch TV, was a modestly-furnished living room.

He went in, sat on the sofa, and began leafing through the journal. He was certain the code could be cracked. Although the images and words looked innocent to the casual reader, his father must have feared that someone would see through them and discover whatever truth they were hiding because he'd locked the journal away in his safe deposit box. Doing that had been a mistake. If he'd left it in plain view—on one of the bookshelves in the living room, for instance—no one would have looked at it twice. It was only its presence in the bank vault that had told Mitch it was no ordinary journal of walks and sketches.

Michael Walker had drawn attention to the one thing he obviously wanted to hide. Of course, he hadn't known he was going to die a couple of days after depositing the book at the bank, or that Mitch was going to come along and find it.

Mitch knew he needed to find the locations written about in the pages. The sketches would help if he had any knowledge of the Peak District but he had none. He didn't recognise any of the places in the sketches. Some of the writings mentioned caves, waterfalls, rivers, and bridges, locations he could eventually pinpoint although it would take a lot of time. There was only one passage he'd read that mentioned a specific place.

In the woods near Edge House, the foxgloves blush pink, hiding their secret.

It was both specific and maddeningly vague. The house was virtually surrounded by woods and there would be wild foxglove plants everywhere. Also, foxgloves weren't perennial plants; they didn't recur every year. They were biennial, taking two years to grow and then dying off. They were known to reseed themselves abundantly but the stand of pink plants mentioned in the journal would be long gone, if it ever existed at all and wasn't just a figment of the writer's imagination.

He left the journal on the coffee table and went outside to prove his own theory correct, that the woods around the house would be full of foxglove. He walked to the edge of the gravel and stared into the sun-dappled woods. As expected, he saw patches of wild foxglove scattered here and there. The reference in the journal was meaningless.

"Looking for something specific, sir?"

The voice came from behind him. Mitch turned to see Battle approaching. The detective's green Range Rover was parked next to the police car but Mitch hadn't heard it arrive because he'd been so wrapped up in his thoughts.

"You got here quickly," Mitch said.

"Well, I was on my way as it turns out. I was bringing Mrs. Jenkins to have a look around the house. You did say that was all right. She's in there now. We'll soon know if those thieves took anything. What are you doing out here? Find anything interesting?"

"Just admiring the woods," Mitch said.

"I don't blame you," Battle said. "This is a lovely part of the world, if a bit wild in places. Those moors for instance,"—he gestured to the drop-off behind the house and the sunlit moors beyond—"you could hide a body in there and it might lie there undiscovered for decades, perhaps forever. This land keeps its secrets."

"Very poetic," Mitch said.

"Not really. I don't like secrets, Mr. Walker. It's my job to uncover the truth. Although God knows that's difficult sometimes."

Mitch nodded. "It must be rewarding sometimes as well, though."

"It can be," Battle said. He pointed at the woods. "Care for a stroll?"

"Sure." Mitch wasn't sure why Battle had rushed over here to talk to him but now that the detective was here, there were a few things Mitch wanted to ask him regarding his father.

They stepped off the gravel and into the trees, following a trail that had been made by boots treading through the undergrowth. Mitch wondered if this was a route his father had walked often, his footfalls creating the trail over time.

"When you rang me last night, you said you had something I might be interested in," Battle said. He wasn't looking directly at Mitch but instead gazed up at the sunlight filtering through the branches above them.

"I told you, it was nothing," Mitch said.

"Still, if you have any information pertaining to an ongoing criminal investigation—anything at all—you should hand it over to me."

"An ongoing investigation?" Mitch asked. "You told me yourself that my father wasn't being investigated for anything. Your superiors made sure of that."

"I did," Battle admitted, "but that doesn't mean I'm not trying to uncover the truth about what happened to those girls."

"Those girls?" Mitch asked.

Battle trailed his hand through a stand of tall grass as they walked. It seemed to Mitch that the detective was trying to discern any secrets the woods might hold through his senses of sight and touch.

A secret that makes the foxglove blush pink, Mitch thought, paraphrasing the damned journal. He wondered if Battle knew something about these woods, if he suspected that there might be something here that Michael Walker was trying to hide.

"Of course, you don't know about the girls," the detective said, as if reminding himself. "It's common knowledge around here but your mother took you away when you were nine. You wouldn't know anything at all about it. How silly of me."

"I wouldn't know anything about what?" Mitch asked. As they walked, his eyes were drawn to every stand of pink foxglove they passed. There must be hundreds of them in these woods. The sight of them made him angry. The one clue in the journal that mentioned a specific place was actually no more helpful than any of the vague ramblings found elsewhere in the book.

"When your sister went missing in 1987, she wasn't the first girl to vanish from this area. She wasn't the last either. We've had our fair share of mysterious disappearances over the years and they don't always make the national news. Those that did were soon forgotten by the rest of the world. Disappearances don't sell papers, you see, not like murder anyway. Not gruesome enough. It's all too vague to be a good news story. Now, if there's a body, then there's a good story for your average newspaper reader. A body is something tangible. Bodies sell papers because the readers can picture them in their minds."

Mitch was surprised to hear that Sarah's disappearance was just one in a long line of vanishings. "How many girls have gone missing? You must have suspects if this has been going on for a while."

"The length of time this has been going on for is part of the problem. It's difficult for me to convince my superiors there's a link between a girl going missing in 1974 and the same happening in 1999. The extended time period also makes it harder to investigate the links. The police force's personnel changes over time, of course, so by the time the next girl disappears, the officers who worked the previous case have all retired or moved on to pastures new. Not to mention witnesses moving away from the area or dying. It makes it hard to follow up leads that might prove a connection."

"It's been going on that long?" Mitch asked. "Since 1974?"

Battle nodded. "In the winter of 1974, two sisters, Evie and Mary Hatton, went missing from Blackden Edge. Evie was ten, her sister eight. Do you know Blackden Edge, Mr. Walker?"

Mitch shook head. "I'm not from around here, remember?"

"It's in the Dark Peak area. That's an area mostly north of here. The landscape is wilder up there and there's a lot millstone grit in the soil, which means the land gets saturated in winter and becomes bogs and moors. Evie and Mary lived in one of the villages in the Dark Peak area and one winter's evening, they went out after tea and were never seen again. The police never found their bodies. A couple of weeks later, some weekend ramblers were walking along Blackden Edge and one of their party found an earring in the shape of a star. It was brought to the police station and confirmed by the girls' mother to have been Evie's."

Battle looked up at the sky through the overhead branches. "The girls vanished without a trace apart from that earring. That was thirty-four years ago, and to this day no one knows what happened to them."

"The police didn't have any leads?" Mitch asked.

"There were some rumours in the village that the girls were being sexually abused by their father so he was looked at very closely but he had a cast iron alibi for the night of their disappearance. He was sitting in a cell in the local police station after causing a drunken disturbance in the pub. So that all came to nothing. And then, just a year later, another girl disappeared from the same area. I'm surprised you don't already know about it but you'd only have been three years old at the time and I suppose your parents weren't exactly bursting to tell you the news while you were still a child. It isn't the kind of thing that comes up at the family dinner table."

"I don't know what you mean," Mitch said.

"In 1975, another girl went missing from the Blackden Edge area. Her name was Olivia Walker." Battle paused and then added, "She was your aunt."

13

ONE OF THESE THINGS

"My aunt?" Mitch couldn't believe what he was hearing. As far as he knew, he didn't have an aunt. His mother had no siblings and his father only had a brother, Silas.

"Your father's sister," Battle said. "Olivia. I take it from the look on your face that you've never heard of her."

"Never," Mitch said.

"She was the youngest of the three siblings," Battle told him. "Two years younger than Silas, five years younger than your father. By all accounts, Olivia was a quiet child. From the witness statements I've read, it seems that she kept herself to herself. In 1975, when she was sixteen, she left Blackmoor House, on a winter's night just like the Hatton sisters, telling her mother that she was going to a schoolfriend's house. She never returned. Despite the thorough investigation that was carried out at the time, the schoolfriend Olivia mentioned was never tracked down. According to everyone the police interviewed, Olivia had no friends. The girls at school thought she was strange and avoided her."

"Nobody ever told me about her," Mitch said. "I never knew she existed."

"Well, perhaps now you understand why your mother did a runner when Sarah disappeared. First your father's sister goes missing, then his daughter. She probably thought she was next."

Mitch remembered the way his mother kept them constantly on the move, never staying in one place for more than a year, avoiding contact with the neighbours, keeping him off school. Was she trying to protect them because she believed Michael Walker would come after them if he knew where they were?

"The police found Olivia's jacket hanging on a fence post near Blackden Edge," Battle said. "So, of course, you can imagine what happened next. Everyone started talking about the Blackden Edge Murderer. With Evie and Mary going missing the year before, it was inevitable that rumours of a serial killer would spread from village to village. No one dared go out after dark. They believed a bogeyman wandered Blackden Edge, waiting to snatch young girls."

"Did the police have any suspects?" Mitch asked.

"No. They checked the known criminals in the

area, particularly sex offenders, but nothing came of it."

"What about my father?"

"The entire family was looked at closely but nothing came of that either. The police had no reason to believe the boys or their parents were involved."

"But that doesn't mean they weren't," Mitch said.

"No, it doesn't," Battle conceded. "And you have to remember that the family was extremely wealthy and held a lot of sway in the community. Frank Walker, your great-grandfather, was good friends with anyone who held any power—political or otherwise, and that included people at the highest levels of the police force."

"So you think there was corruption involved?"

Battle spread his hands. "I don't know. I wasn't even a copper then so everything I'm telling you now is what I've read in the case files. I do know that when Josie Wagner was murdered in 1977, the detectives handling the case were told there was no reason to include the Walker family in their investigations. As far as the then-chief was concerned, the Walkers had been cleared of all wrongdoing and that was that."

"Murdered," Mitch said, feeling as if he'd fallen down a rabbit hole and was in an alternate world. Why had his mother never told him about any of this? She must have known. It was as if she'd been lying to him his entire life for not revealing important information that could be linked to Sarah's disappearance.

"Josie Wagner was a young nurse who went hiking along Blackden Edge," Battle said. "She wasn't from the area, so she'd probably never heard anything about the killer. Besides, it was two years after Olivia's disappearance and everything had been quiet since then. Josie's naked body was discovered at the Edge. She'd been strangled."

Mitch felt sick. If the person who'd abducted Sarah was the same one who'd murdered Josie Wagner, did that mean Sarah had been strangled too? And if Josie Wagner had been found naked... "Had she been raped?" he asked.

"No," Battle said, "there was no evidence of rape. Josie's killer wasn't motivated by lust but by something else. Sexual frustration, perhaps. Or anger towards women."

"What do you mean?"

Battle stopped walking and turned to Mitch. "Are you sure you want to know?"

Mitch thought about it. "Do you think the person who murdered Josie Wagner is the same person who took Sarah?"

Battle nodded. "I think it's possible, yes."

"Tell me," Mitch said, steeling himself for whatever Battle was going to say next.

"Josie hadn't been raped but she had been sexually mutilated. A knife had been used on her breasts, stomach, and between her legs."

"I see," Mitch said flatly. He couldn't let his thoughts go to the dark place to which they were travelling. If the same person who'd taken Josie Wagner had also taken Sarah...

"After Josie Wagner, everything went quiet," Battle said quickly. Maybe the detective had sensed the direction of Mitch's thought process and was trying to pull Mitch out of it. "For ten years, at least. Tales of the Hatton sisters' disappearance and Josie Wagner's murder persisted, of course, but in time the Blackden Edge Murderer passed from reality into local folklore. Parents told stories of the murderer to keep kids away from Blackden Edge at night, that sort of thing. The police continued their investigation but no arrests were made."

"But they must have had suspicions" Mitch said.

"Not really. They rounded up the same people as they'd done in the case of the Hatton sisters the previous year but no one was implicated in the killing."

"And ten years later, Sarah vanished," Mitch said.

Battle nodded. "I worked on your sister's case. You probably don't remember me coming here and asking questions. It was my guv'nor, Gordon Farley, who was the lead detective on the case. I was just a young Detective Constable working my first case for the CID."

"I remember very little from that time." Mitch was going to say more, about how memories sometimes flashed into his head that had very little meaning to him but seemed to suggest a troubled childhood, but his eyes had seen something next to the trail that made his breath catch.

"Are you all right, Mr. Walker?" Battle seemed genuinely concerned. He put a hand on Mitch's shoulder.

"I'm fine," Mitch said, turning away from what he' seen so Battle wouldn't realise what it was.

He was too late. Battle's eyes followed the direction Mitch had been looking and he said, "What lovely flowers." Stepping off the trail, he went over to the patch of foxglove and touched one of the flowers. "Digitalis, I believe."

"You know your flowers," Mitch said. "Most people call it foxglove."

"I probably don't know as much about them as you do, Mr. Walker, given your profession, but I know that the crushed-up flowers of this little beauty are used to make heart medicine. And I've read enough Agatha Christie novels to know that too much of it is a poison that stops the heart completely." He looked closely at the stand of flowers he was touching and at the others in the area. "These look different to the others. I expect that's why they caught your attention."

He looked at Mitch with a searching expression. Battle wasn't stupid; he knew seeing these flowers had affected Mitch.

Mitch cursed his own overreaction. He'd been casually inspecting each stand of foxglove they'd passed, looking for something that might indicate which stand was the one mentioned in the journal. When he'd seen these flowers nestled in the shade of a wych elm, the certainty that these were the foxgloves from the book had startled him.

"They're a hybrid variety," he said. "Not wild like the others. That's why they have that unusual yellow stripe on the petals."

"I see," Battle said, stroking a flower with the tip of his finger. "They're very vivid, deeper pink than the wild ones." He stood up, frowning. "I wonder how they got here."

"The only one way a hybrid species could be here," Mitch said, sure he was telling Battle something the detective already knew, "is if someone planted them here."

"Seems an odd thing to do," Battle said. "Your father wasn't much of a horticulturalist judging by the state of the garden at the house, so why would he plant flowers out here in the woods?"

"If my father planted them," Mitch said. "It could

have been anyone." He had no doubt that his father *had* planted them but he didn't want Battle to become too suspicious about the foxgloves. He was sure that there was something buried in the earth beneath the hybrid flowers and he needed to be the one to discover it.

If Battle started digging around and found something odd, the entire police force might come swooping into the woods and either cover up evidence or start a half-assed investigation. Mitch couldn't let either of those things happen. He was determined to find out what happened to Sarah himself, without interference from people who might be trying to protect his father.

"Yes, it could have been anyone," Battle said, staring at the foxgloves. "But these woods are part of the Edge House property so it would be strange for someone else to be planting flowers here." He continued to stare at the flowers, seemingly considering something. Then, he snapped out of his reverie and looked at Mitch. "Shall we head back to the house? I'm sure the officers will have dusted everything they want to dust and are probably waiting to take your fingerprints."

As they retraced their steps, Battle said, "Mr. Walker, are you sure there isn't something you know that could aid my investigation?"

Mitch wanted to trust Battle because the detective obviously had a keen mind and would be a big help in finding out what happened to Sarah. But

Battle was working against a huge disadvantage; he was tied down by red tape. If Mitch told him about the journal, it would probably end up locked away in an evidence room somewhere and he'd have no chance of cracking its code. He couldn't relinquish the journal until he knew its secrets.

"There's nothing," he told the detective.

Battle sighed. "Very well. If you change your mind, you know where to find me."

FIFTEEN MINUTES LATER, Battle and the officers had left, along with Mrs. Jenkins, a pale woman in her sixties who had insisted that nothing was missing from the house and she had no idea what Mr. Walker had kept locked away in the safe.

Mitch strode along the trail that led into the woods, this time with a shovel in his hands.

As soon as he reached the stand of hybrid foxgloves, he started to dig. The ground was still damp from yesterday's rain and the shovel blade sank easily into the earth. As he dug, Mitch felt both elation and trepidation. After thirty years, he was finally doing something proactive in his search to discover what had happened to his sister. But he was also aware that what was unearthed here could be her body.

If that happened, if he found her remains here

beneath the wych elm, he would call the police. His search for her would be over and he could give her a proper burial. He'd still need to find out why her life had been cut short after only seven years and he'd still need to know who had killed her.

The answer to that last question would be obvious, though. If Sarah was buried in the woods near Edge House, in a grave marked by a stand of foxgloves mentioned in the journal, it was obvious. But why would Michael Walker kill his young daughter? It didn't make any sense. The only answer Mitch could come up with was that his father had been mentally unstable. Some of the rambling passages in the journal certainly supported that theory.

After carefully digging up the hybrid foxgloves, Mitch placed them to one side. If he found something here that wasn't Sarah's body but a piece of a puzzle that meant he had to keep searching, he would replace the foxgloves so it looked like they'd never been disturbed. He knew Battle was suspicious of this place and he didn't want the detective to know he'd been digging here. Battle would begin asking questions he didn't want to answer.

With the flowers out of the way, Mitch put his back into the work, removing shovelfuls of earth quickly. He had to dig around the elm's thick roots when they got in his way but other than that, the ground succumbed easily to the shovel blade as it sliced into the soil.

Sweat formed on Mitch's face. He fell into a rhythm, a rhythm he was used to from thousands of hours of digging his clients' gardens. Working the shovel efficiently, he concentrated on his task and not what he might find in this hole. He'd deal with that when he had to. A swarm of gnats attacked his face, some drowning in beads of his sweat, others swatted by a quick hand. He dug until the hole was deep enough that he could stand in it. When he stood in it, he was waist-deep in the earth. Still, he continued to dig.

Then he found something.

The shovel slid into the earth. Mitch lifted the load of soil and flicked it out of the hole. As it landed on the ground, he heard a dull metallic clang. He scrambled out of the hole and rushed over to the discarded earth. A small, square metal tin lay on the ground. Its surface was pitted and rusty. It was closed.

He picked it up and turned it over on his hand. There was something metallic inside, rattling around as the tin moved.

It was an old tobacco tin. The label was a faded orange colour and the words *Grand Cut* and *2 oz. Net Weight* were visible. Around the edge of the lid were the words "Insert Coin in Slot Below Lid Here and Twist to Open." An arrow pointed to a slot in one of the rounded corners of the tin, directly below the lid.

Mitch fished in his pocket for a coin, found one and inserted it into the slot. When he twisted it, the lid popped off and fell to the ground, leaving Mitch with the tin and its contents.

The inside of the tin had been sealed and looked shiny and new. A delicate gold chain rested inside, long enough to be a necklace. Attached to the chain was a flat, gold emblem in the shape of a heart.

Mitch didn't recognise it and was sure Sarah had never owned such a necklace. So this must have belonged to one of the other girls. Maybe one of the Hatton sisters had worn it, or Josie Wagner, or the aunt Mitch had never known about.

There was one thing Mitch was sure about: the piece of jewellery he was looking at had once adorned the neck of one of the victims of the Blackden Edge Murderer.

14

FAMILY MATTERS

Elly's investigation had been cut short on Sunday because when she'd returned to the cottage, she'd found she had no Internet connection and no phone signal. She'd supposed that was a regular occurrence in this area and had spent the rest of the day pottering around the cottage doing nothing more than watching TV and sitting in the garden.

When she padded downstairs in her cotton pyjamas on Monday morning, she noticed her phone had a signal and was telling her she had two new voicemails.

One of those alerts had been on there since Friday night but she'd been ignoring it because she was sure she knew who the message was from.

Sure enough, it was Paul's voice on the line. "Hey, hun, I was just wondering where you are. I came round to see you but you're not here. Your car isn't here either so I guess you've gone out somewhere. Call me."

Elly deleted the message. She was glad she'd decided to come to the Peak District on Friday and wasn't at home when Paul had come round. What had he come to the house for on Friday anyway? He'd said he was coming on Saturday to collect his stuff. And why the hell was he calling her hun? Maybe his relationship with his personal assistant wasn't going so well. Maybe there was trouble in paradise. Whatever, it wasn't her problem. Paul had made his bed so now he could lie in it.

The next message was Paul again, this one left on Saturday. "Hi, Elly, it's me, Paul. I'm at the house like we arranged but you're still not here. Is everything okay? Call me, I'm worried about you."

"Is everything okay?" she asked the phone incredulously as she deleted that message too. "No, everything isn't bloody okay! Go back to your bit of fluff and leave me alone."

She made herself a cup of tea, concentrating on her actions to put thoughts of Paul out of her mind. Then she went to the dining table and booted up the laptop. The Internet connection had returned so it was time to get to work.

The photos she'd stolen from Edge House were fixed to the whiteboard with magnets. Elly had arranged them across the top of the board in what she assumed was their chronological order: the three children at the stream, the same children in front of Edge House, the two young men in front of The Mermaid pub, Margaret Walker looking pensive by the window through which an artist's easel could be seen, and finally the photo of Sarah and Mitchell standing on the lawn of Edge House with their bikes.

It didn't take a genius to figure out that the women in the Walker family weren't happy. Elly wondered if it was just general malaise or if it could be linked to something more serious, like abuse.

Sitting at the table, she used the laptop to search for information about the family. She got a number of hits and placed the results into separate tabs. Then she put the tabs in chronological order, the same as the photos on the board.

Most of the articles came from a site that held archived articles from a local newspaper called *The Peak Observer*. This was the same newspaper that had printed the headline BLACKDEN EDGE MURDERER STRIKES AGAIN! above its write-up of the Josie Wagner murder.

The first article was from 1948 and was headlined GOTHIC MANSIONS SOLD. It was a short piece, stating that two Gothic-styled mansions designed in the nineteenth century by architect Julian Frey had been sold to a Frank Walker and his wife Gwen Walker (née Jones). The couple had moved into the area from Porth Y Nant in Wales and were wealthy due to Gwen's family owning a successful granite quarrying business in Gwynedd.

Edge House had stood empty since 1916, when the previous owner's son had been killed in World War I and the father had taken his own life by wandering on the moors until he died of exposure. Blackmoor House had been owned by a wealthy grocery shop magnate who had decided to move to London where his businesses were situated.

Elly sectioned off a corner of the whiteboard and wrote "Frank Walker" and "Gwen Jones", connecting them with a blue line. Beneath their names, she wrote "Blackmoor House." She had no idea why the couple needed two houses but it was a testament to their wealth, and perhaps that was the point; they moved to the Peak District and let everyone know how well-off they were. Money and status meant a lot back then and a display of both was a way to gain power in social circles.

The next article on the laptop was from the same newspaper but at a much later date, 1962. This was a piece that mentioned Frank Walker's purchase of a limestone quarry in the Dark Peak area and the formation of his new business venture, Walker & Sons Aggregates. The article informed readers that the sons referred to in the company's title were Michael, aged eight, and Silas, aged five. Frank said he'd started the new company because he wanted to build a future for the boys. The article also mentioned that Frank had a three-year-old daughter named Olivia.

Elly looked at the photo of the children playing in the stream. So the eldest boy was Michael, the younger boy Silas, and the girl on the bank Olivia. She wrote Silas' and Olivia's names on the whiteboard.

The picture Elly had assumed was taken outside Edge House, with the children standing by the front door, was probably actually taken at Blackmoor House. That explained why the door knocker was in the shape of an eagle and not a lion.

The next article on the computer had a headline that read OLIVIA WALKER MISSING. Apparently, the poor girl had left the house one evening and never returned. Her jacket had been found at Blackden Edge where, according to the article, two sisters named Mary and Evie Hatton had vanished the previous year.

So that explained the "Blackden Edge Murderer Strikes Again" headline that had intrigued a wannabe detective at Wollstonecraft Publishing. By the time Josie Wagner's body was found at Blackden Edge in 1977, three girls had already gone missing from the area.

Elly turned to the photo of Michael and Silas sitting outside The Mermaid pub. Glenister had told her that Michael might be the Blackden Edge Murderer but why not Silas? It was suspicious that

Michael's sister and daughter both went missing but equally so that the two vanished girls were Silas' sister and niece.

"Which one of you did it?" she asked the smiling boys in the photograph. She thought about it some more and then added, "Maybe you both did."

The next article on the computer was the one Elly already had on the murder board, the article from 1987 headlined SEVEN-YEAR-OLD GIRL GOES MISSING IN PEAK DISTRICT, detailing the disappearance of Sarah Walker. She'd been walking in the woods with her brother, Mitchell, and had vanished virtually from under his nose. It sounded suspicious to Elly. She didn't think Mitchell, who'd been nine at the time, had killed his sister, although God knew things like that happened, but wondered if he'd taken Sarah to meet someone else in those woods. Uncle Silas, maybe?

The last search result she'd put into a tab on the laptop was a brief article dated 1989 that stated that Michael Walker had sold his share of Walker & Sons Aggregates to his brother. Silas had said that he was pleased to take over the family business and would eventually pass it on to his son Jack to keep Frank Walker's dream alive.

No reason was given for Michael Walker leaving the company. Maybe the loss of his family had killed his passion for the business and he'd just decided to get out. There was a picture of the two brothers shaking hands. Michael was leaning over his younger brother because Silas was in a wheelchair.

Elly wondered how long he'd been in the chair because it would be a stretch to believe he could be the Blackden Edge Murderer while wheelchair-bound.

She typed on the laptop again, this time putting "Silas Walker" into the search engine. She got some of the same results from the previous search and a couple of new ones. One of the new results caught her attention straight away.

QUARRY ACCIDENT INJURES OWNER'S SON

Elly clicked on the link. The first thing she saw was a black-and-white photo of a quarry with a caption underneath it that read: "Walker & Sons Aggregates quarry, Derbyshire." The article was dated June 12th, 1977. It said that Silas Walker, 20, son of the owner of Walker & Sons Aggregates had been at the limestone quarry on the night of June 9th and had been involved in an accident that had left him with extensive back injuries. It wasn't known why he'd been at the quarry in the dead of night.

The article was frustratingly brief. Elly returned to the search page to see if she could find anything else about the accident but there was no more information. The only other new information she could find regarding Silas was a wedding announcement from 1975, saying he'd married a girl named Alice

Davies from the village of Leath in North Derbyshire. The wedding had taken place at St. Paul's Church, Relby, and the newlywed couple would be living at Blackmoor House, one of two estates owned by the Walker family.

Elly wrote the name "Alice Davies" on the white-board and connected it to Silas' name with a blue line. Then she drew a second line to connect them to Blackmoor House.

The board was filling up but the identity of who the large question mark in its centre represented was still an enigma. At this point, Elly would put her money on Michael or Silas, but Silas' wheelchair probably ruled him out.

She gulped down her tea and went to the kitchen to put the cup in the sink. She looked out at the sunlit moors and distant hills. She needed to get outside. Returning to Edge House wasn't an option right now because the police were interested in the place and might show up at any time. Maybe she'd go back there later in the week when the heat on the place had died down.

In the meantime, she'd track down Gordon Farley, the retired detective who'd been second-in-command in the Josie Wagner murder case and lead investigator in Sarah Walker's missing person case. She also needed to speak to Stewart Battle, who'd been involved in the Sarah Walker case and had been in charge of the hunt for the missing journalist Lindsey Grofield.

But there was somewhere else she wanted to visit first. The article about Silas Walker's marriage had mentioned a St. Paul's Church in Relby. It stood to reason that the church's graveyard would be where Michael Walker was buried. Elly felt a burning need to see the grave. She wasn't sure why she felt that way until she happened to glance at the faces of the girls in the photos. If Michael Walker was the man responsible for destroying the lives of these women, then Elly needed to see his grave so that she knew he could never hurt anyone ever again.

On a conceptual level, she knew he couldn't cause any more pain to any other women but to see his final resting place with her own eyes would give her a sense of closure.

She went upstairs to get dressed. It was time to pay a visit to the dead.

15

SILAS

Mitch was sitting on the lawn in the sunshine with the journal in his hands. After finding the necklace, he'd tried to sit on the sofa and read the journal but had felt as if the walls of the living room were closing in on him, squeezing the air from the room and entombing him within Edge House. Leaving the tobacco tin and necklace on the coffee table, he'd come outside for some fresh air. It wasn't until he'd reached the lawn that he'd felt far enough away from the cloying atmosphere of the house to be able to breathe normally again.

Now, he knew that the writing in the journal was written in a secret language that led to the secrets of the past. It was the language of murder.

Discovering the necklace had convinced him that the journal could be decoded but now he desperately needed to find a clue to decipher some other cryptic passages within its pages. The landscape sketches were the obvious place to start but if he wanted to find out where these places were, he was going to have to show the sketches to someone else, someone who knew the Peak District well.

He didn't want to do that, so that brought him back to attempting to decode the words, the secret language that appeared on the surface to be nothing more than recollections of walks in the countryside but beneath the surface veneer spoke of tragedy and death.

He looked up from the book when he heard a car coming up the track. Thinking it might be Battle again, he went inside and slid the journal, along with the tobacco tin, under the sofa before going back outside to greet whoever was driving to the house.

The car that emerged from behind the trees was a large black SUV. Mitch didn't recognize the man behind the wheel but the woman in the passenger seat looked familiar. He seemed to think that when he'd known her before, the hair that was now white had been blonde. And the expression that was at the moment set into a hard scowl had been softer, kinder.

The SUV stopped and the engine died. The driver got out and nodded to Mitch in a manner that was polite but certainly not friendly. "Mitch," he said, "it's been a long time." He went around to the rear of the vehicle and removed a wheelchair from the boot. He unfolded it before assisting a large, dark-haired, bearded man out of the back seat of the SUV and into the chair.

Now Mitch knew who his visitors were. The man in the wheelchair was his father's brother, Silas. The woman with the hard face was his Aunt Alice, which meant the driver was Jack, their son. Mitch hadn't seen Jack since he'd been nine and Jack seven, so it was no wonder he hadn't recognised him.

Jack took the handles of the wheelchair and wheeled it towards Mitch. Alice got out of the SUV and stood by her husband's side with a face like thunder.

"We haven't seen you around here for a while," Silas said, offering a smile that he didn't seem entirely invested in. "How are you, lad?"

"I'm fine," Mitch said. He didn't know what else to say. This wasn't exactly a happy family reunion. The atmosphere seemed almost as oppressive as it had felt in the living room. Mitch wasn't sure why but his skin began to prickle and he felt the fight-or-flight instinct kick in. He forced himself to remain calm.

"We're not staying long," Alice said, tight-lipped. "Silas just wants a word with you." She put a hand on her husband's shoulder, as if prompting him to get on with whatever he'd come here to say.

"I'll get right to it," Silas said. "Mercer and Robinson tell us that you want to sell Edge House. So I've come here to do you a favour. The house needs a lot of work doing to it before you can sell it. I can save you the bother. I'll give you a good price for it in the state it's in now. You won't get a fairer offer than that."

"The house isn't for sale at the moment," Mitch told him.

"What do you mean it isn't for sale? Of course it is. The solicitors told us you don't want it."

"How do they know what I want?"

"Because you told John Mercer you wanted to sell."

"I've changed my mind." Mitch didn't like the idea that Mercer had been speaking to Silas about their meeting. What else had the solicitor told Silas about? Had Silas known when Mitch would be in Matlock? He thought of the slashed tyre on his Jeep. Silas didn't know what vehicle he drove but if he'd waited around outside the solicitor's office and seen Mitch arrive...

Now he was being paranoid, wasn't he?

"My parents bought that house," Silas said, stabbing his finger towards Edge House. "It belongs in the family."

"I *am* family," Mitch said. He realised he was making an argument to keep a house he hated and if Silas had made this offer a couple of days ago, Mitch would have handed over the keys there and then. But things were different now. He'd already discovered one of the journal's secrets in the grounds of Edge

House and for all he knew, there could be others. If he was going to find out what had happened to Sarah, he needed the house just as much as he needed the journal.

"Call yourself family?" Alice scoffed. "We haven't seen hide nor hair of you in thirty years."

"That isn't my fault," Mitch said. "My mother took me away from here. I was only a child at the time."

Silas nodded. "That's right. But you're in control of your own actions now, aren't you? You must have built a life for yourself somewhere else so why don't you go back there and leave Walker family business to those of us who've been loyal to your father all his life?" Before Mitch could answer, he added, "Michael didn't ever get over you leaving, you know. He was never the same man after that. You and your mum destroyed him and we were here to pick up the pieces."

"I'm sorry for that," Mitch said, "but I already told you, it wasn't my choice. After Sarah disappeared, my mum—"

"Don't bring your sister into it," Alice said. "We don't need to be reminded of all that again."

Mitch wheeled on her. "I'm sure it would be convenient for you to just forget Sarah but she was my sister and I can't forget."

Alice narrowed her eyes, full of fury. "You come back here after all this time saying you can't forget a dead girl but you soon forgot your father while he was alive, didn't you? I'll bet you haven't even visited his grave. All you're interested in is his money, like a vulture picking apart a carcass."

"That isn't true," Mitch said with conviction. He was here to find out what had happened to Sarah and those other girls who'd died by a madman's hand. But he couldn't say that because he sure as hell didn't trust anyone standing in front of him right now. Instead, he turned to Silas. "You know what it's like to lose a sister. Have you forgotten Olivia?"

He expected Silas to react to Olivia's name but the severity of the reaction shocked him.

Silas grasped at his chest. His eyes bulged in his skull. He pointed at Mitch and gasped, "Don't you mention my sister."

Jack and Alice bent over to attend to him, trying to calm him with soothing words. Jack shot Mitch a disgusted look and wheeled Silas back to the SUV. Silas seemed to have calmed down from his panic attack, or whatever it had been, and was now sitting quietly, staring at the ground. Mitch noticed a tear, glistening in the sunshine, rolling down Silas' cheek.

Alice glared at Mitch, shaking her head. "You've been back here five minutes and already you're causing trouble. Just go home and leave us in peace." She turned to the SUV and got in the passenger side, staring at Mitch through the windscreen while she waited for her son to get into the driver's seat.

When Jack finally put the wheelchair into the boot and got into the SUV, he gunned the engine and spun the vehicle around fast enough for the spinning tyres to spray gravel. When the vehicle reached the track and disappeared behind the trees, Mitch breathed a sigh of relief. He could hardly remember Silas and Alice from his childhood but something about what he *did* remember gave him the creeps, even though he couldn't pin that feeling on a specific event or time.

When the sense of relief was gone, guilt rushed in to replace it. Alice had been right about one thing: Mitch hadn't even visited his father's grave. Whatever he thought of the man, he felt it was his duty to at least see his father's resting place. He guessed the grave was located at the church in Relby.

He needed to get away from the house for a while, anyway. The suffocating atmosphere he'd felt in the living room seemed to be seeping through the walls and reaching for him like a slithering shadow.

The keys were already in the Jeep, so he climbed in and started the engine. He turned the vehicle more leisurely than Jack had done but when he was pointing away from Edge House, he put his foot down.

He didn't intend to stay long at his father's grave, only the bare minimum to perform his duty as a son. If his father was the Blackden Edge Murderer, did he even deserve to lie in a grave while his victims' remains languished in places unmarked?

They're marked with flowers, he told himself as he reached the main road. *But in places that are secret.*

Those girls were as lost to the world as broken petals scattered on a cold winter breeze.

16

FORGET ME NOT

St. Paul's Church was the largest structure in Relby, looming over the other buildings from its elevated position on a slope at the northern edge of the village. A small car park was situated near the church. Mitch parked the Jeep near a blue Mini, the only other vehicle there. He pushed through the wooden gate and ascended the stone steps to the church.

He remembered coming to Sunday School here with Sarah, Tilly, and Jack. He couldn't recall anything else about that, not even if he'd enjoyed it or found it boring. He just remembered that he'd come to this church regularly when he was young.

Like Edge House, the church had been built in the neo-Gothic style, with flying buttresses, a tall steeple, and traceried windows. The churchyard was overgrown, with grass, weeds, and brambles covering some of the older, fallen gravestones. Some of the newer graves seemed to be still tended by loved ones and these had been cleared of over-enthusiastic plants and mowed. Instead of snarls of brambles and tangles of weeds, these graves were adorned with neat bunches of bright flowers in pottery vases.

Mitch had no idea where his father's grave was located but didn't mind if it took him all day to find it. He needed to stay away from the house for a while, even if it meant he couldn't read through the journal again and look for clues until he got back.

The memory of fleeing along the track and looking over his shoulder to see one lighted room still haunted him. He felt that something terrible had happened in that room where the light burned and he had witnessed it. Yet he couldn't remember anything other than running.

Maybe he needed a break from the journal too. Finding the necklace had been exhilarating at first because it had proved the journal was authentic and could be decoded. He'd felt one step closer to finding Sarah.

But then reality had set in. The necklace had belonged to a girl who was now dead. His self-assigned mission to break the journal's code wasn't going to save anyone; the path he was following led only to the remains of those lost girls. The best that could be hoped for was some sense of closure for their families.

He felt unsure that he could decode any more of the journal. The one clue he'd managed to solve had mentioned a specific location but the others didn't. He had no idea where to even begin trying to decipher the other passages.

Mitch felt that Sarah was as far away as she'd ever been and his chances of finding her were non-existent.

He searched a section of newer graves, reading the names on the stones that stood as sentinels over the dead. None of the names inscribed into the stones were familiar to him.

Farther along the stone path that wound between the graves, Mitch could see a woman standing in the long grass. She wore jeans, a dark green T-shirt, and a dark green baseball cap. From beneath the cap, shoulder-length red hair flamed in the sunlight.

She had a camera in her hands and constantly adjusted her position in the grass to capture the best angle of whatever she was photographing. Mitch followed the direction of her lens. She was pointing the camera at two graves that lay side by side in the shadow of the church.

Abandoning the section of graveyard he'd been searching, Mitch set off up the path towards her. She might know the churchyard well and maybe she could tell him where the newest graves were situated. Even if she didn't know and was just here to photograph a relative's grave for some reason, it would be a refreshing change to speak to someone who wasn't a long-lost relative or a member of the police force.

She was so absorbed in what she was doing that she didn't notice Mitch even when he was almost standing next to her. Crouched in the long grass, she continued snapping pictures. When she was done, she checked the screen on her camera and, seemingly satisfied with her handiwork, stood up. It was then that she noticed Mitch.

"Morning," she said. "Lovely day."

"It is." Mitch gestured at the graves around them. "Do you come here often?"

She laughed and raised an eyebrow. "I haven't heard that one before. Not in a graveyard, anyway."

"Sorry," Mitch said, "I didn't mean it like that." Now that he could see her up close, her face looked familiar. And her eyes were searching his face as if she recognised him, too. She'd probably turn out to be some long-lost relative after all, he mused. "I meant do you know the graveyard well? I'm looking for the area where they put the newest graves."

"I think that's down there," she said, indicating the area Mitch had just been searching. "They've got the most recent dates on them, anyway. Unless the grave you're looking for is part of a family plot, then I guess it could be anywhere." She paused and then said, "Oh, I'm sorry, have you recently lost a member of your family?"

"No," Mitch said, "Well, yes. It's complicated."

"Sorry to hear that," she said.

"It's fine," he said. He was sure he knew her face from somewhere and searched his memory to remember where. When no answer presented itself, he said, "This isn't a line, I swear, but do we know each other?"

She looked sheepish. "No, I'm pretty sure we don't. You may recognise me, though. I wrote a bestselling book a few years ago. *Heart of a Killer*."

Now Mitch knew where he'd seen this woman. He'd seen her on TV. Her book had been the bestselling true crime book in a long time. "The Eastbourne Ripper," he said.

"Yes, that's me." She looked uncomfortable for a second and then added, "I mean, I wrote the book about the Eastbourne Ripper. Elly Cooper." She held out a slender hand.

Mitch shook it. "Mitch Walker. So what are you doing here?" he asked. "Are you working on a new book?"

She didn't answer him immediately. Her face had paled, making the red hair framing it seem even more vibrant. The searching look that had been in her eyes transformed to one of realisation. "You're the boy with the bike," she whispered, almost to herself.

"I'm sorry?" Mitch asked.

"No, no, I'm sorry," she said, coming to her

senses. "I should have realized who you were. You're Mitchell Walker. Of course you are."

"It's Mitch. I haven't been called Mitchell since I was a kid."

"Mitch," she said, as if confirming his name to herself. "I think I know where you'll find the grave you're looking for." She pointed at the two graves in the shadow of the church, the ones she'd been taking photos of.

Mitch walked through the long grass to the gravestones. Each was square-shaped, fashioned simply from black marble with gold lettering etched into the stone. Both graves had been tended to recently and were clear of grass and weeds.

The first grave Mitch came to was his father's. Its inscription read:

Michael Walker

Beloved Brother

1954 - 2017

The matching gravestone closer to the church had an inscription that made Mitch's breath catch in his throat.

Sarah Walker

June 17th 1980 - December 21st 1987

Taken too soon

Mitch had never considered the possibility that Sarah would have a grave. Now that he thought about it, it made sense, but it had never crossed his mind until now.

A stone vase sat on the headstone. A bunch of forget-me-nots poked up from it, their blue-petalled heads waving slightly in the warm breeze.

A forget-me-not that never blooms might hide and then grow old.

He felt a chill run through his body. The forget-me-nots on the grave were fresh and had been placed there recently, certainly after his father had died.

"Are you okay?" Elly asked. Her eyes held a look of worry.

"Yeah," Mitch said. But he didn't feel okay. He was unable to take his eyes off the cut flowers or stop the thoughts whirling around in his head. Who had placed these here? Was it someone who knew he'd read the journal? Had the flowers been left here as a taunt?

"You don't look okay," Elly said.

"I...I just didn't know my sister had a grave here," he said. But it wasn't the grave that disturbed him so much, it was those flowers. He wanted to tell Elly about the flowers, about the journal, about everything, even though he didn't know her. Or maybe it was *because* he didn't know her that he wanted to bring her into his confidence. She wasn't connected to the case in any way, had never known Sarah, and wasn't a suspect. Mitch felt that if he didn't tell someone soon about what was going on, the oppressive atmosphere at Edge House was going to swallow him up and he was going to go crazy.

He knew madness could be hereditary. When he finally unravelled the tangle of this mystery, perhaps he would be left with nothing but a single thread of insanity that ran through his family.

But he didn't tell Elly about the flowers, or the journal, or the fact that his father was probably a murderer who had killed several women. Because he remembered what Elly had been doing when he'd first got here.

"You were taking photographs of his grave," he said. "And Sarah's."

She nodded. "Yes, I was."

He looked at the graves and then back at Elly, understanding why she was here. "Are you writing a book about my father?"

"Technically, no," she said. "But I'll be honest with you. I was sent here by a publisher to look into some cases of abduction. My research may become a book someday."

"You're researching my family," he said.

"I'm following a number of leads."

"But why my family in particular?"

She frowned, as if deciding whether to share something with him. "Mitch, how much do you know about your father? Your mother took you away when you were nine, so you may not know what's been going on around here."

"You've been researching me?" he asked incredulously.

"Look," she said, reaching into her pocket and taking out a business card. "I have some information you may be interested in. Call me if you want to discuss it."

He took the card but now he was sure he would never confide in her. Rather than being uninvolved in the events surrounding his father, she was working for a publisher that wanted to profit from them.

"I can't discuss anything with you," he said. "You want to turn the tragic deaths of young girls into entertainment. I won't have any part of that."

Coming to the graveyard had been a mistake. He'd thought that seeing his father's grave might give him some sort of closure but instead, old wounds had been opened. Seeing Sarah's grave had reminded him that he'd been with her when she'd been taken, that he could have done something about it.

The sight of the blue forget-me-nots nodding in the breeze slammed home the fact that he had to decode the journal. He hadn't saved Sarah and he couldn't save any of those other girls but if their bodies were found, then at least the world that had forgotten them would remember again. He could bring them back from the lonely world of the lost.

He turned on his heels and walked back along the stone path towards the gate.

"It isn't like that," Elly called after him. "I want to do what's best for Sarah. For all the girls."

Ignoring her, Mitch descended the steps and

pushed through the wooden gate into the car park. He had no intention of returning to Edge House just yet but he needed to get away from here. He needed to put Relby in his rear-view mirror and drive to somewhere far enough away that no one had ever heard of Michael Walker, the missing girls, or the Blackden Edge Murderer.

As he climbed into the Jeep, he saw Elly at the top of the church steps. She shouted something to him but he couldn't hear her through the window. She descended the steps quickly and came running over towards the Jeep.

Mitch put the vehicle into gear and drove out of the car park. He saw her in the rear-view mirror. She shouted again, and this time, he heard her.

She was shouting, "The killer might still be out there."

17

THE LETTER

Elly watched the Jeep drive away and sighed in frustration. "That could have gone better," she told herself.

The thing that really frustrated her was that she was usually good at getting the measure of people and judging the best way to talk to them. She could usually get them to open up and confide in her. She'd mistakenly judged the best way to handle Mitch Walker was to be honest with him. He seemed like the sort of person who dealt with life in a straightforward manner and would appreciate honesty.

He probably was but he'd caught her taking photos of his dead sister's and father's graves and it was always going to go downhill from there.

It was just bad timing, she reassured herself, opening the Mini and getting in, wondering if she should follow Mitch and try to explain that she wasn't trying to profit from tragedy at all. She just wanted justice for those girls.

Better leave him alone for a while. She could try to contact him in a few days and see if he was more receptive then. She wasn't sure how helpful he would be anyway. He hadn't been here for years and probably knew less about his father's involvement in the girls' disappearances than Elly did, if he knew anything at all.

She needed to speak to someone who had inside knowledge of the case. That meant retired DCI Gordon Farley or DCI Stewart Battle.

She decided to try Battle and called the Buxton police station after finding the number on her phone.

"Derbyshire Police," a female voice said after four rings.

"Hi, could I speak to DCI Stewart Battle, please?"

"Do you have a case number?"

"Umm, no, I'm calling to speak to him about an investigation he worked on some time ago."

"Could you give me some information about the case?"

"The disappearance of Sarah Walker," Elly said.

"If you leave your name and number, someone will call you back."

Elly left her name and mobile number, wishing she'd spoken to Battle himself. She might have been able to persuade him to talk to her if she'd asked directly but if he just got a message on his desk that someone had called about a case from 1987, he'd probably ignore it.

She spent five minutes searching on her phone for retired detective chief inspector Gordon Farley and discovered that he lived in Bakewell. His exact address wasn't listed anywhere but there was an article about him that included a photo of him standing outside his house.

The article was a human-interest piece about the retired policeman who now lived by the river in Bakewell and spent his time tending his garden instead of catching criminals. Farley supplemented his pension by selling flowers to florists in town.

Elly got the SatNav out of the glove compartment and set it for Bakewell town centre. Somebody there would know the house in the photo, or even know Farley himself and tell her where he lived.

She may have screwed things up with Mitch Walker but she wouldn't make the same mistake with Farley. She'd handle him with kid gloves. As she started the car, she wondered if she'd lost her edge when it came to interviewing. She hadn't interviewed anyone for six years.

"Yeah, but that was a serial killer," she told herself as she left the car park and drove through Relby. "The Eastbourne Ripper, no less. If I could handle him, I can handle a retired copper."

But had she actually handled Leonard Sims, the

Ripper, or had he played with her the way a cat plays with a mouse it's about to kill and devour?

Trying to distract herself from that question, she put the radio on. She usually listened to a station that played eighties and nineties hits and right now it was playing "Sweet Dreams" by the Eurythmics. Elly sang along as she left Relby behind and drove along the tree-shrouded road.

An hour later, she was standing in front of Gordon Farley's house by the river in Bakewell. Actually, she was standing behind it because the house's rear gardens backed onto the river and Elly had guessed that the most likely place she'd find Farley on a warm day such as today was in his garden.

She was right. As she'd walked along the wide, cemented riverbank along with the many locals and visitors to the town who were out for a stroll, enjoying the sunshine, she'd spotted Farley working on a flowerbed with a trowel, digging into the soil beneath a spray of pink and white flowers.

He was easily recognisable. He looked exactly the same as he did in the photo, right down to his loose blue shirt and white panama hat.

Elly approached the wooden gate set in the low stone wall surrounding Farley's garden and cleared her throat to get his attention. He looked up from his work. He was in his sixties but looked lean and fit. When he saw Elly, he gave her a nod and smiled. "Afternoon. Can I help you?"

"I was wondering if I could talk to you," Elly said. "My name is—"

"I know who you are," he said. "I've read *Heart of a Killer* three times. I may be retired but I can't seem to shake my fascination with criminals. Don't feel you have to stand outside the gate. You can come in if you like." He waited until Elly had opened the gate and entered the garden and then said, "Now, what would you like to talk about, Miss Cooper?"

"One of your old cases."

He grinned. "They're all old. I've been retired for seventeen years."

"Yes, I know," Elly said. "You retired on New Year's Eve 1999."

"That's right. The night that poor Grofield girl went missing from the pub not far from here. Is that what you want to talk to me about?"

"No, I want to discuss a couple of your earlier cases, if that's all right. The murder of Josie Wagner and the disappearance of Sarah Walker."

Farley's face darkened slightly. "They were bad ones. What had been done to Josie's body didn't bear thinking about, and as for Sarah, just seven years old and never seen again. It makes me shudder to think what might have happened to that poor girl."

"Yes," Elly said. She tried not to think about what might have happened to the girls after they disappeared. "I'd like to discuss Michael Walker," she told Farley.

He nodded slowly. "I've known for seventeen years that someone would come to me wanting to talk about Walker. I suppose I should have realised it would happen after his death. You'd better come in. I'll put the kettle on." He set the trowel down and opened the back door to the house, leading Elly into a bright farmhouse-style kitchen that smelled faintly of eggs and bacon. A small wooden table with two chairs sat in one corner.

"Please, take a seat," Farley said, filling the kettle and taking two mugs from a cupboard.

Elly unslung the camera from around her neck and placed it on the table before sitting down.

"What would you like to know about Michael Walker?" Farley asked. "I don't know all that much because we were warned away from looking at him too deeply."

"How did his name crop up during the investigation of Josie Wagner's murder?" Elly asked.

While he waited for the kettle to boil, he stared out the window at his garden and the river beyond. But Elly was sure he wasn't actually looking at what was in front of his eyes but was instead staring through a window into the past.

"I was only twenty-three when Josie Wagner's

body was found," he said. "A junior detective on his first case, wanting to make an impression. John Hanscombe was in charge of the detectives in those days and John was a big bull of a man, old-school in every way. He liked cases to be solved early, all of us did. But John was fanatical about it. He was always talking about putting cases to bed and considered any case that dragged on for weeks to be a personal failure. So when we arrived at Blackden Edge, John said to me, 'Let's put this one to bed early, Gordon. I know who did this and we're going to get the bastard'."

Farley went quiet for a moment and Elly wondered if he was remembering the condition Josie Wagner's body had been found in. The kettle clicked off, bringing Farley back to the present. He put tea bags into the mugs and poured boiling water over them.

"Was John talking about Michael Walker?" Elly asked.

"Yes, he was," Farley said, stirring the tea bags in the water. "He'd had some dealings with the Walkers already, when Olivia disappeared a couple of years earlier. John was sure Michael Walker was involved in Olivia's disappearance."

Farley finished making the tea and came over to the table with the mugs. He set one in front of Elly, along with a pint of milk from the fridge and a sugar dish.

"Thanks," Elly said. "So why did John think Michael Walker was guilty?"

"John suspected the father at first. As soon as the investigation began, it became clear that Olivia Walker had been the victim of some kind of abuse before she disappeared. Everyone the police interviewed said they suspected something wasn't right about that family. The boys seemed like normal kids but Olivia was shy and withdrawn."

"That doesn't necessarily indicate abuse," Elly said, stirring sugar and milk into her tea.

"No, it doesn't. But there were other indicators too. Two nights before she disappeared, Olivia was found wandering along the road near Blackmoor House by a passing motorist. She was in her nightgown, half-frozen, and covered in scratches and bruises. She got into the motorist's car and begged him to take her far away and not make her go back home. He took her to the nearest police station where she repeatedly told officers she couldn't go back home. When asked why, she went silent. There was nothing anyone could do other than send her home. Her father, Frank, picked her up from the station."

"Didn't the police ask him why his daughter ran away and was begging not to go home?" Elly asked.

Farley shrugged. "Frank Walker was a very influential man and this was a long time ago. The world was different then. Olivia didn't utter a word against her father so the officers had no choice other than to send her home."

"And two nights later, Olivia vanished," Elly said.

"Yes, and at first, John went after Frank Walker. He'd read the report about the night Olivia was found wandering in the road and he'd decided that Frank had doled out some kind of physical punishment on Olivia, gone too far, and killed her. But Frank had a rock-solid alibi. He was drinking in The Mermaid pub on the night Olivia disappeared. He was there all night, along with Silas and Silas' wife Alice. They were seen there by many independent witnesses. The pub was having some kind of disco night and was busy."

"But Michael wasn't there," Elly said.

"No, he wasn't.

"What about Frank's wife, Gwen?"

"She died from emphysema in 1969."

Elly took a sip of tea. The Walker family had certainly experienced its fair share of tragedy. The women, especially, seemed to meet an early demise. If Frank, Silas, and Alice had nothing to do with Olivia's disappearance, the question mark on her whiteboard was starting to point in one direction only. "Where was Michael that night?"

"He said he was out walking along the fells."

"At night? In winter?"

Farley nodded. "I admit, it sounds implausible.

The weather up on those hills in winter is no joke. But Michael was a keen artist and he said he was out walking that night with his sketchbook. He had sketches in the book that he said proved it but they didn't really prove anything. He could have drawn them at any time."

"But he was never arrested," Elly said.

"No. He was questioned on a couple of occasions but nothing really came out of it.

"Were there any other suspects?"

"No, there was nobody else John Hanscombe even remotely liked for the crime. He was sure it was Michael. His theory was that Olivia had been abused but the abuse had come from her brother, not her father. There was no actual evidence pointing to Michael but his lack of a real alibi was enough for John."

Farley took a swallow of his tea. "And, you see, if Michael Walker had abducted Olivia at Blackden Edge, then he was also responsible for the abduction of Mary and Evie Hatton the year before. The fact that the girls all disappeared from the same area was impossible to overlook. And Michael didn't have an alibi for that night either. Apparently, he'd been driving around in his Triumph Stag. No destination in particular, just tooling around in his sports car. When asked if he'd driven up to the Dark Peak area, he said he couldn't remember."

He threw up his hands in a questioning gesture.

"So did he do it? We'll never know because the Chief told John to leave Michael alone. John was livid. He was sure Walker was guilty and thought he was eventually going to crack him in the interview room. But the word came down from on high that the Walkers were out of bounds. All of them. We knew why, of course. The Chief and Frank Walker played golf together. It may even have gone deeper than that; there could have been financial incentives from Frank for the Chief to look the other way where his family was concerned."

Elly thought about what Farley had just told her. There was no evidence that Michael had committed any crime at all, yet there was evidence that other people who would have been suspects were definitely not involved in the disappearance of Olivia Walker. In her mind, she conjured up an image of the whiteboard in the cottage. She mentally erased the names of Frank, Silas, Alice, and Gwen. That left Michael Walker. Unless the Blackden Edge Murderer was just a murderer taking random women and girls. But what were the odds of Michael's sister and daughter both being taken by chance by the same serial killer?

"Then there was the Sarah Walker case," she prompted Farley.

"Yes, the Sarah Walker case." His eyes took on a faraway look, as if they were looking into the past again. "That was 1987. John Hanscombe had left the force by then. Retired in 1982 and died of a heart attack only a couple of months later. I was lead detective on Sarah's case, assisted by a fresh-faced DS named Stewart Battle." He chuckled. "Poor lad was thrown in at the deep end just like I'd been with the Josie Wagner case. We had it tough, too. On the one hand, our superiors were telling us to tread carefully around the Walkers and on the other, Michael was begging us to pull out all the stops to find his daughter."

"Was he?" Elly asked, surprised. "That doesn't sound like the action of a guilty man."

"I agree. Because I'd been on Olivia's case, I suspected Michael as soon as I heard Sarah Walker was missing. But everything I saw in that man's body language told me he was genuinely distraught. I believe he was innocent based on that alone. Unless he was capable of pulling off an Oscar award-winning performance, Michael Walker had nothing to do with his daughter's disappearance."

Elly finished her tea and put the empty mug on the table. If Farley's assessment of Michael Walker was correct and he was innocent of any wrongdoing in the case of his daughter, could he still be guilty in the case of his sister? It seemed a stretch to think that he'd killed his sister in 1977 and then someone else had killed his daughter ten years later but the two events could be linked. Maybe she should reinstate the names she'd mentally erased from her mental whiteboard.

"I'll be honest with you," Farley said, "the Sarah Walker case ended my career. I retired twelve years after she disappeared because my confidence as a detective, my confidence in myself, was shaken. I'd seen a young woman cut to pieces on Blackden Edge and then tried to find a missing seven-year-old. Seven, for God's sake. It was too much. I felt like I'd failed both those girls, especially Sarah. It hit me hard and I started drinking. When I left the force on New Year's Eve 1999, I'm sure the senior officers weren't just celebrating the new millennium that night, they were probably happier to see me leave than they were to see 2000 arrive."

"New Year's Eve 1999," Elly said. "The night Lindsey Grofield went missing."

Farley gave a sardonic smile. "Yeah, I woke up on my first day of retirement to discover another girl had gone missing and there wasn't a damn thing I could do about it. Perhaps, if I'd still been on the job, I could have found her." He looked down at the table with eyes that held a mix of regret and sorrow. "Well, as it turned out, no one found Lindsey Grofield. Her name just got added to the list with all the other missing girls."

Elly found it easy to believe the other disappearances were connected but Lindsey Grofield seemed like the odd one out. She'd gone missing from

Bakewell, not Blackden Edge, and her disappearance had occurred twenty-five years after the Hatton sisters went missing.

"Do you think Lindsey's name belongs on that list?" she asked. "It seems unlikely that her disappearance is connected to the others."

"Well, officially, *none* of them are connected," Farley said. "The police have always maintained that each disappearance, and Josie Wagner's murder, are totally separate crimes perpetrated by different people. They didn't want a media circus, you see. They justified their decision by the fact that the only evidence linking the crimes is circumstantial. There was no matching DNA at every scene or calling card left by the killer that links the girls' abductions together."

"Do you believe that? That none of them are connected?"

"Of course not," he scoffed. "And neither do you. Otherwise, you wouldn't be writing a book about it. I assume that's what you're doing here."

"Probably," she said.

"Good. It's about time those girls got some kind of justice. We were silenced at the time, of course, and from what Battle tells me, the police are still sticking to their story that there's no connection between any of it. Maybe your book can make people question that. The cases need to be re-opened, new investigations carried out. I'd do it myself but I told you, I'm tired. If I got involved in all that again, I think it would kill me."

He looked at her closely, considering something. "I'll make you a deal. If you sign my copy of *Heart of a Killer*, I'll show you something the police received a few weeks after Lindsey Grofield's disappearance. It might be a letter from the killer. Or it might be nothing. Nobody's sure exactly what it is. The original is sitting in an evidence locker but I've got a photocopy of it here in the house."

"Of course," Elly said immediately.

Farley got up and went into the living room. He came back less than a minute later with a hardback copy of *Heart of a Killer* and a folded sheet of paper. He passed the book to Elly along with a fountain pen.

When she opened the book to the title page and brought the pen to the paper, she found her hand was trembling slightly. If the sheet of paper in Farley's hand was an actual photocopy of a letter from the Blackden Edge Murderer, it could contain the answer to everything.

She told herself to calm down. The police had had this letter for eighteen years. If there were any clues to the killer's identity in it, they'd have acted on them by now. Or maybe not. Maybe the protection that seemed to surround the Walkers prevented the police from doing anything.

Was that why Farley was showing her the letter?

Because he knew she could act on its contents where the authorities wouldn't?

She signed the book, *To Gordon, A fellow seeker of truth*, and signed it. The signature didn't look anything like her usual one. She put the cap on the pen with a shaky hand.

"Thank you," Farley said. "Now, I can see you're excited about seeing this letter. First, let me explain why it might be nothing more than the work of a crackpot. It was received at the Buxton police station after Lindsey Grofield's disappeance. The word URGENT was printed on the envelope in capital letters. According to the postmark, it had been posted in Matlock."

Elly asked, "Do you mind if I make notes?"

"Of course not."

She searched her pockets for something to write on and came up with a grocery receipt. She picked up the fountain pen again and wrote "letter posted in Matlock" on the slip of paper.

"Do you want some better paper?" Farley asked. "I've got a notebook in the living room."

"No, this is fine. Go on, please."

"When Battle read the contents of the letter," he said, "he had the lab analyse the paper and the envelope for DNA, fingerprints, and chemicals. Everything came back negative. The paper and envelope were Basildon Bond, a common brand. As I said, the original is locked up but Battle had some photocopies made."

Elly looked at the paper in Farley's hand. She wanted to see it now.

"At first, Battle tried to keep me in the dark. He knew how the Wagner and Walker cases had affected me and he wanted me to enjoy my retirement. So, instead of telling me about the letter, he came to me and asked me to teach him about flowers.

"I thought that was a strange request since he'd shown absolutely no interest in flowers all the years we worked together. Then I thought it was his excuse to come and visit me, keep an eye on me and make sure I was all right.

"It turns out, I was wrong. He only seemed to be interested in certain flowers, all of them wildflowers. But there didn't seem to be any rhyme or reason behind his choices. Finally, I confronted him and asked him why he really wanted to learn about these particular flowers. He told me he'd received a letter that may be nothing or may be from the Blackden Edge Murderer."

"I don't understand the connection," she said. "To the flowers, I mean."

"You will. Anyway, I made Battle show me a copy of the letter and he gave me this. Unfortunately, when you read it, you'll understand why it could be nothing at all."

He slid the paper across the table to her.

Elly opened it. The photocopy was of good quality. The original letter had been folded in two places to make it fit into the envelope but the folds didn't interfere with the writing, which was neat and blocky. As soon as Elly read it, she realised why this letter hadn't exactly blown the case wide open and led to an arrest of the Blackden Edge Murderer. It was a poem about flowers.

Two bluebells lie in the willow's shade
Does anybody care?
Don't look in the woods or in the glade
The pimpernel's not there
A cuckoo flower that meets its doom
Loses its heart of gold
A forget-me-not that never blooms
Might hide and then grow old
For whom the bell tolls at year end
Only the daisies know
The question you should ask, my friend
Where do the flowers grow?

Elly looked from the paper to Farley. "I assume the flowers represent the girls."

He nodded. "Some of it seems to fit, some of it appears to be nonsense. The reason Battle took it seriously is because of the line about the cuckoo flower losing its heart of gold. Lindsey Grofield was wearing a gold heart necklace when she was murdered but it was never found. It was never mentioned to the press. But the writer of the poem seems to know about it."

Elly held up the receipt and said, "This won't fit on here. Could I have a sheet of paper, please?"

"You can have that," Farley said, indicating the photocopy. "I know it by heart, anyway."

"Thanks," Elly said, getting up and putting the camera back around her neck. She slipped the sheet of paper and the receipt into her jeans. "If you remember anything else that might be useful, here's my card." She put the card on the table.

Farley looked at her closely again. "I can see you want justice for those girls, just as much as I did when I worked their cases, maybe even more. Be careful because you might never find that justice. I couldn't find it for them and it ruined my career. Don't let the same thing happen to you. You have to accept that they might be lost forever."

Elly opened the back door and stepped out into the garden. She turned to Farley and said, "I can't accept that. I have to find them."

18

FLOWER GIRLS

After leaving Farley's house, Elly found a cafe in Bakewell and ordered a baked potato, a salad, and a cup of coffee. She placed the photocopy of the letter on the table along with the receipt she'd written on earlier and a pen she borrowed from the waitress.

She read the flower poem again, the pen poised over the back of the receipt.

Two bluebells lie in the willow's shade

Does anybody care?

The two bluebells obviously referred to the Hatton sisters, Mary and Evie. On the receipt, Elly wrote, the words "bluebells" and, next to it, "Hatton Sisters."

The next victim of the Blackden Edge Murderer was Olivia Walker. So it was logical to assume the next part of the poem referred to her.

Don't look in the woods or in the glade

The pimpernel's not there

Elly wasn't sure if there was a flower called a pimpernel but the poem seemed to paraphrase a quote from the book *The Scarlet Pimpernel.* Elly had read the book as a child and knew the quote but checked on her phone to ensure she was remembering it correctly.

They seek him here, they seek him there

Those Frenchies seek him everywhere

Is he in heaven or is he in hell?

That damned elusive Pimpernel

After checking the quote, she typed "pimpernel flower" into the search engine. There *was* a wildflower called a Scarlet Pimpernel. So the killer was taunting the police, saying Olivia was as elusive as the Scarlet Pimpernel and that they'd never find her. She wrote the word "Scarlet Pimpernel" on the receipt and Olivia's name next to it.

The next two lines obviously referred to Josie Wagner and mentioned the heart locket that was a secret known only to the police and the killer.

A cuckoo flower that meets its doom

Loses its heart of gold

Elly wrote on the receipt again. The words "Cuckoo flower" and "Josie Wagner" joined the list she was building.

A forget-me-not that never blooms

Might hide and then grow old

Elly put Sarah Walker's name next to "forget-me-not." She supposed the "never blooms" part of the poem meant Sarah would never bloom into womanhood. As she thought that, her fingers tightened on the pen. The line about hiding and growing old didn't seem to make sense. She'd have expected it to say "never grow old." Maybe the wrong word had been written in the poem, "then" instead of "never."

For whom the bell tolls at year end

Only the daisies know

This was why Farley knew Lindsey Grofield belonged on the list with the other girls, despite not being taken from Blackden Edge. *For whom the bell tolls at year end* obviously referred to New Year's Eve, when she went missing.

The last two lines of the poem were simply a taunt.

The question you should ask, my friend

Where do the flowers grow?

Elly looked at her new list of flowers next to the girls' names. Why had the killer chosen these particular flowers for each girl? Was it random or was there some kind of reasoning behind it? She knew next to nothing about flowers, especially wild ones. Paul bought her roses on Valentine's Day and sometimes a bouquet of colourful, unidentified blooms, but that was the extent of her contact with the world of flowers. If there was some reasoning behind the choice of flowers, she supposed Farley would have figured it out by now since he was an expert.

There was still no sign of her food so she decided to check the photos she'd taken at the graveyard. It had been sunny when she'd taken them and too bright to see the screen properly.

Turning the camera on, she scrolled back to the first photos she'd taken at the graveyard. She had a couple of shots of the church and a few establishing shots of the graveyard taken from the top of the steps. The next four shots were of Michael Walker's grave, taken from various angles. There were six pictures of Sarah's grave, also taken from different angles. These were the photos she'd been taking when Mitch Walker had showed up. Everything looked fine. There was no need to go back to the graveyard and retake the pictures.

She was about to turn the camera off when she remembered the blue flowers on Sarah's grave. Finding the picture that showed the flowers the most clearly, she enlarged that part of the photo. The flowers were blue with yellow centres but that was as far as Elly's flower knowledge went.

The waitress came over with her baked potato and salad. She placed the plate on the table and said, "There you are, my love, a jacket potato and salad. Enjoy your meal."

"Thanks. Do you know anything about flowers?"

"Flowers? No, not really, duck. Why?"

It wasn't the first time Elly had heard the term "duck" used as an address since arriving in Derbyshire. It seemed to be a local term of endearment.

"I was just wondering what these are," she said, showing the waitress the enlarged image of the flowers.

"Oh, I've got some of those in my garden," the waitress said, her face brightening as she obviously realised she could help this customer. "Those are forget-me-nots."

"Thanks," Elly said, feeling suddenly cold. It had to be more than coincidence that the killer's letter likened Sarah to a forget-me-not and those exact flowers were on her grave.

But who had put them there? Not Mitch Walker. He hadn't even known his sister had a grave at all.

She remembered his reaction to seeing the grave, the way he'd stared at it in disbelief.

What if he hadn't been staring at the gravestone at all, but at the flowers?

That was unlikely. For the flowers to upset him so much, he'd have to know that the killer referred to Sarah as a forget-me-not. That wasn't possible, was it?

The more she thought about it, the more sure she was that Mitch *had* been staring at the flowers on the grave. She needed to contact him, to find out what he knew. She was under no illusions that he would contact her, despite having her card. He'd made his thoughts about her quite clear.

She guessed he'd be at Edge House. His father was dead so it stood to reason that Mitch had inherited the place. Of course, it was possible that Michael had left the house to his brother, Silas, but Elly doubted it. In the article about Michael selling his share of Walker & Sons to Silas, it had mentioned that part of the deal was that Michael took sole ownership of Edge House, which had presumably been a communal family property before. Elly got the impression that the brothers had eventually grown apart, maybe even fallen out with each other over something.

So, assuming Mitch was at Edge House, all she had to do was find the number of the phone that had rung when she'd been there. Assuming the phone number was listed, she could get that from directory enquiries. Before she rang Edge House, though, she was going to plan her opening gambit. Mitch might hang up on her unless she got his attention straight away.

She searched directory enquiries for Edge House, Relby, Derbyshire, and got a number, which she put into her phone with the contact name "Edge House." She rang the number, deciding she was going to open the conversation by saying something about forget-me-nots. That would get his attention.

She waited while the phone on the other end of the line rang, imagining the strident bell sounding throughout the Gothic house.

There was no answer.

Deciding to try later, she put her phone down and started eating her potato.

A couple of minutes later, her phone rang. She thought it might be Mitch but felt disappointed when she saw Jen's name on the screen. "Hi, Jen, what's up?"

"Elly, I've been talking to Mum and she's very worried about you." Jen sounded stern and upset.

"She's always worried about me," Elly said. "Mainly because I'm not you."

"Don't be so obnoxious. That isn't true and you know it. And now I've been pulled into your little game."

"What are you talking about?" Elly held the phone between her ear and shoulder and continued eating her potato.

"You've got Mum so worried with all this talk about serial killers that she's convinced Dad to drive up there and make sure you're all right."

"What? You can't let him do that. Dad can't drive very well at the best of times. I can't imagine what he'd be like on a motorway. What the hell is Mum thinking?"

"I don't know," Jen said, "but she's on a mission to save you from yourself. She's determined and you know what she's like when she gets like that, there's no talking her out of it. I can't let Dad come all the way up there so now I have to drive all the way to the bloody Peak District."

"No," Elly said firmly. "No, you don't. No one does."

"It's me or Dad," Jen said.

"But you've got the kids to think about. You can't just leave them."

"Trevor's going to take a couple of days off work. Even he can manage to get them dressed in the morning and take them to school. At least I think he can."

"You've already discussed this with him?"

"Yes, what else could I do? I tried to convince Mum you were fine and just having one of your little episodes but it just started an argument. And then Dad got involved and was ready to put his coat on and drive to Derbyshire there and then. So I told them I'd do it."

One of her little episodes? What was that supposed to mean? Elly didn't know what to say. She was an adult who could look after herself. Why couldn't her mum respect that? She knew that if she didn't let Jen come up for a day or so, her dad would be tooling up the motorway in his Astra. He wasn't in good health, having had a minor stroke a year ago. She let out a sigh of resignation. "All right. Come up here for a day. We'll go for a walk in the hills or something. The scenery here is incredible. Then you can go home and assure Mum and Dad that I'm absolutely fine."

"All right," Jen said. "I'll be there tomorrow. It might be late in the day because I should probably get the kids to school in the morning. At least I'll be able to show Trevor what to do."

"Fine," Elly said. "I'll text you the address of the cottage and the combination for the key safe. I'll leave the key in there if I go out, so just let yourself in when you get there." Without waiting for Jen's reply, she ended the call.

That was all she needed, for her sister to be under her feet while she was trying to work. Jen wasn't exactly the type of person who could keep her nose out of the things going on around her. She liked to interfere. No prizes for guessing where she got that from.

Elly finished her meal and left the cafe, reminding herself to go to the Co-Op and get a bottle of wine for when Jen arrived. They could go hiking during the day and relax with a glass of red in the evening. Might as well make the most of it.

As she walked through Bakewell, she rang Edge House again. Still no answer. Maybe Mitch wasn't there after all and the house was still empty. If that was the case, she was tempted to break in again and search the place some more.

I didn't break in, she told herself. *I just walked in*

through an open door. She wasn't sure if a judge would call that breaking and entering or not and she didn't want to have to find out.

Still, her investigation wasn't exactly going places at the moment. She'd eliminated a few names from the suspect pool and was left with Michael Walker as the most likely candidate for being the Blackden Edge Murderer.

She knew it couldn't have been Michael who'd put forget-me-nots on Sarah's grave but did those flowers really mean anything? It could just be a coincidence that the flowers were the same type the killer associated with Sarah in the poem.

She wanted to know more about Michael Walker. She didn't just want to prove that he was the Blackden Edge Murderer, she wanted to know why. Why had he killed his sister and daughter?

More urgent than the desire to know these things was the burning need she felt to discover what had happened to the missing girls. Where were their bodies? In what secret places had Michael hidden them?

Where do the flowers grow?

The answer to that question had to be at Edge House.

19

OLD GHOSTS

Mitch returned to Edge House in the late afternoon. After leaving the church, he'd driven around aimlessly for a while before getting hungry and stopping at a pub for steak and chips and a pint of Doom Bar. By the time he'd eaten the meal and finished the beer, he'd decided it was time to go back to Edge House.

He got out of the Jeep and faced the house. *It's just a house*, he told himself.

Even if it had been inhabited by a killer, the house itself was nothing more than bricks and mortar. Bricks and mortar shaped into an eerie Gothic mansion, sure, but nothing more than that. There were no ghosts that prowled the hallways at night, no spirits entombed within the walls. The only phantoms were in his head.

He went inside and straight upstairs, taking the

steps two at a time until he was standing on the top-floor landing. Striding to the door of the room that featured in his dream-memory, the room with the light burning behind the traceried windows, he took a deep breath. By the time he let the breath out, he was in the room.

It was a small room compared to the others in the house, the type of room that might be used as a nursery or small child's bedroom. Mitch couldn't remember what had been inside this room when he was young so he reasoned that it hadn't been anything interesting. Yet he remembered running barefoot along the track to the road and looking back at this particular window.

He went to the window and looked out through the leaded pane. From this vantage point, he should be able to see the track.

But he couldn't. The trees were in the way.

In the dream-memory, he had looked back over his shoulder along a track that led straight to the house from the road. But the track wasn't straight at all; it had that twist just beyond the lawn. That curve had been put there so that the house *couldn't* be seen from the road. It was a privacy measure.

So the dream-memory was purely a dream and not a memory at all. That twist had always been in the track. Mitch had owned a green skateboard when he was seven or eight and he remembered riding it around that bend. One time, he hadn't turned sharply enough and had ended up hitting the grass at the side of the track and sprawling headlong into the undergrowth. He'd grazed his elbow and knee. He still had the scars.

Shaking his head at the tricks his own mind was playing on him, he left the room feeling relieved and relaxed. The dream-memory had frustrated him, making him think that if he could only remember what he was running from, he might be able to solve an enigma from his childhood.

But there was no enigma. The flight along the track and the glance back over his shoulder at the house had never happened. It was impossible.

When he got back downstairs, he went to the kitchen and made a coffee, reminding himself as he looked out the window that he needed to sort out the garden sometime.

Taking his coffee to the living room, he took the journal and tobacco tin from beneath the sofa and put them on the coffee table. He opened the journal to a random page and read a passage that described a walk across windswept moorland to a "grave of daisies in a glade watched over by the Ladies."

Mitch wondered if his father had been high when he wrote the journal. It was all nonsense.

He had to keep believing he could somehow make sense of these rambling thoughts put to paper. He picked up the Grand Cut tobacco tin. It was real and solid and in his hands thanks to the journal. It was proof that he could find answers in the words that were right there in front of him. He had to believe. Without his belief, Sarah was lost forever.

He reread the description in the journal.

I looked upon a grave of daisies in a glade watched over by the Ladies.

Mitch frowned. Was his father saying there were women buried beneath a grave of daisies in a glade? It was infuriatingly obscure.

He repeated the passage over and over in his head. It didn't give up its secrets.

Mitch slammed the journal shut. He wouldn't give up, couldn't give up, but he needed to leave the words alone for now and come back to them again with fresh eyes tomorrow.

He heard a noise outside and went to the window to see a blue Mini park next to the Jeep. It was the same Mini he'd seen at the church and it was Elly Cooper who got out of it.

He sighed. He thought he'd made it clear to her what he thought of a publisher trying to profit from the tragedies of the missing girls. He went to the front door and opened it. She was already just outside it, her hand reaching for the lion-head knocker.

"Hi," she said with an uneasy smile.

"I told you at the church, I'm not interested in helping you write your book," he said. "I can't stop you doing whatever you think you have to but I'm not going to be a part of it."

"Forget-me-not," she said.

"What?" He'd heard what she'd said, he just wasn't sure he could believe it.

"Forget-me-not. That's what the killer refers to your sister as. A forget-me-not that never blooms. I can see from your face that you know what I'm talking about."

"I...yes, I know what you're talking about. But how do you—"

"So, are you going to invite me in?" she asked, pushing past him.

He turned to face her in the foyer. His mind was reeling. How did she know what was in the journal? It had been locked away in a bank vault. Was there another copy somewhere and had she read that? Did it have different clues to his version?

"You've read the journal?" he asked.

"Yes, I—" she began, then looked confused. "What? No, I've read the letter."

"What letter?"

She paused, narrowing her eyes. "What journal?"

He sighed. Maybe it was time to show someone else the journal. He wasn't getting anywhere with it on his own. And if Elly had a letter that mentioned Sarah and forget-me-nots, maybe it was the key to deciphering the journal.

"I'll let you see the journal if you show me the letter," he said.

She shot him a wicked grin. "I like the sound of that. You first."

"Follow me," he said, leading her into the living room.

"Is that it?" she asked, pointing at the journal on the coffee table.

"Yes, that's it."

She reached into her back pocket and took out a folded sheet of paper. She held it up. "I think we have a lot to talk about. A cup of tea would be nice." She gave him the sheet of paper.

"I'll be back in a minute," he said, heading to the kitchen, unfolding the paper on the way. While he made a cup of tea for her, he read the poem. He'd seen most of these lines in the journal. The others were probably in there too somewhere, he just couldn't remember them.

He was disappointed that this letter didn't contain any new information. But it did seem to be more focused than the journal because these lines were scattered throughout the journal yet when put together, they formed a poem about the girls. There was even a line about the heart necklace he'd found.

"Shit!" He ran from the kitchen to the living room. The necklace was sitting on the coffee table right next to the journal.

When he opened the door, Elly was sitting on

the sofa. The tobacco tin was open on the table and the necklace was dangling from Elly's hand, the gold heart swaying slightly.

"This is Josie Wagner's necklace," she said. "You need to tell me everything."

20

TWO HANDS

An hour later, Elly stood by the living room window, looking out at the lawn of Edge House while Mitch made more drinks in the kitchen. The clouds were beginning to darken, promising rain. Mitch had told her how he discovered the journal in Michael Walker's safe deposit box and how he'd later followed a clue from it and found the heart necklace.

In exchange, she'd told him everything she knew from her research. He hadn't known any of the Walker family history and had listened with interest.

She'd flicked through the journal while Mitch was speaking and had seen the landscape and botanical sketches, as well as the portrait of Sarah Walker and the lock of hair taped to the page. She'd read some of the descriptions of walks in the countryside and visits to certain flowers.

Those passages had been written with a deliberate vagueness. The writings were so obscure that even if Michael Walker were still alive and arrested for his crimes, the journal would never stand up as evidence in a court of law. And that was probably the point of writing them in such a manner.

The lock of hair taped to the page didn't actually prove anything, even if it turned out to be Sarah's. Lots of parents kept locks of their children's hair.

The foxglove line had led Mitch to Josie Wagner's necklace but the other sections of the journal, the ones that led to the bodies of the victims—if that was what they actually led to—were wilfully obscure.

The journal's outward appearance of innocence bugged Elly. Not because of its coyness in describing actual places, although that annoyed the hell out of her, but because the manner in which Mitch had found it didn't make sense.

"What I don't understand," she told Mitch as he came back into the room and handed her a second cup of tea, "is why the journal was locked away. It was obviously written in such a way that it wasn't a signed confession or anything. So why did your dad lock it in a safe deposit box?"

"I don't know," he said. "According to my cousin, who's the manager at the bank, he seemed perfectly normal when he took it into the bank. She didn't say he seemed nervous or anything so I don't think he was afraid of someone finding it. He probably just thought the bank was a safe place for it."

"Your cousin? Are you related to everyone in this area?"

"It seems like it sometimes. When I saw you at the graveyard, I wondered if you might be some distant relation."

She laughed. "A red-headed stepchild, maybe."

Mitch grinned. It was the first time Elly had seen him grin and she liked it. He seemed to be wound up most of the time so it was good to see him relax, if only for a second.

Before the journal was taken to the bank," Mitch said, becoming serious again, "I think it was locked away in the safe upstairs. The house was broken into recently and the thieves seemed particularly interested in the safe. But it turned out to be empty. According to the housekeeper, nothing is missing from the house so it looks like the safe was the target."

"Oh," Elly said, turning back to the window so he wouldn't see in her eyes that she already knew about the break-in, that she'd entered the same way as the thieves. "It sounds to me like someone was trying to get their hands on the journal. Someone who wanted to use it against your dad. Maybe they wanted to blackmail him."

"But the break-in happened after he was already dead," Mitch said.

Elly sipped the hot tea and wondered why someone would want the journal badly enough to break into Edge House. How had they known about the journal in the first place?

"Wait a minute," she said, going over to the coffee table where the photocopied letter and the journal sat side by side. She opened the journal to a random page and looked from it to the letter and then at Mitch. "The handwriting's different. Whoever wrote the journal didn't write this letter to the police. Look, they're totally different."

He picked up the letter and ran his eyes over it. "Maybe he disguised his handwriting when he wrote the letter?"

"No, it isn't that," Elly said. "It's a different person altogether. Okay, new theory." She paced the room while she thought it out. "Your father had an accomplice. The journal was kept here under lock and key and after your father died, the accomplice feared that someone—namely you—would eventually open the safe and get their hands on it. So he broke into the house to get it."

Mitch seemed to be thinking it through. He gazed at the journal and at the letter. "It seems unlikely, two murderers working together like that. How would they have met? They wouldn't have just bumped into one another in a coffee shop. 'Hi, I'm a murderer.' 'Oh, cool. So am I.' It doesn't sound plausible."

"It happens all the time," she said. "Myra

Hindley and Ian Brady. Fred and Rosemary West. These people are drawn to each other."

"So why did the accomplice send this to the police in the year 2000?" Mitch asked, holding up the letter.

"Maybe he slipped up. He wanted to gloat about their crimes, so one day, just after they killed Lindsey Grofield, he wrote the letter and posted it."

Mitch looked unconvinced. "No, I don't buy it. It's possible but it just doesn't sound right. And it doesn't explain why my father moved the journal from the safe to the bank vault. By moving it there, he was essentially giving it to me because he'd named me as his beneficiary."

"But he wasn't planning to die," Elly said. "He probably thought it would languish in there for years."

"Well, he was wrong about that," Mitch said. "He died two days later and now here it is back in the house."

"What do you mean two days later?"

"My cousin told me my father took a manila envelope to his safe deposit box two days before he died. It had to be the journal because that's all there was in the box and it was inside a manila envelope."

Elly groaned inwardly. Why hadn't she been told this before? The timing was too perfect to be a coincidence. "He knew someone was coming after the journal," she said. "That's why he put it in the bank. And that's why he died two days later."

"What are you talking about?"

"Don't you see? It all makes sense. Your dad put the journal in the safe deposit box because he knew someone wanted it and he needed to keep it out of their reach."

Mitch frowned at her. "Or maybe he just thought the bank was a better place to keep it."

"And then, two days after thinking that, he died?" she asked. Pointing at the foyer beyond the open door, she said, "What if he didn't fall down those stairs? What if he was pushed?"

"By the accomplice?"

"Maybe they had some kind of argument. The accomplice might have wanted to send another letter or gloat about their crimes in some other way. There was a clash of personalities. Your dad was more reserved, killing quietly and keeping everything under wraps. The accomplice was more hot-headed, seeking notoriety for his crimes. What if that clash escalated into murder?"

Mitch was nodding slowly. "It sounds possible."

"So one of the Blackden Edge Murderers is still out there somewhere," Elly said. She looked through the window at the shadows beneath the trees that surrounded the house and shivered. "We need to make sure no one knows we have that journal.

Because somebody wants it badly enough to kill for it."

THE REDHEAD who arrived at Edge House in a blue Mini has a face I recognise. She stands just inside the window, looking out over the lawn, unaware that I'm out here in the shadows beneath the trees. I try to remember where I've seen her before. She's not from around here, that much I know. So why does she seem familiar?

When the question begins to frustrate me, I push it aside and instead assign her a flower. Because of her red hair, a field poppy comes to mind. But I don't know anything about this woman and the comparison seems weak because it is based purely on physical appearance. The flowers I choose for my girls are carefully selected in a way that goes beyond mere hair colour.

The Hatton girls were bluebells in every aspect of their being. Heads hung in shame, eyes on the ground beneath their feet, never looking up to the sun.

And Lindsey Grofield was a daisy because she was just the opposite. Instead of keeping her head down, she was always snooping into other people's business. So the daisy is apt because it looks like a wide open eye. Lindsey's eyes were open at the end, just like daisies, staring in surprise.

Josie Wagner was a cuckoo flower, of course. What else could she be after what she did?

My hand has clenched so tightly that my nails dig into my palm. I open my fingers slowly and look down at the crescent-shaped marks in my flesh.

Forcing myself to breathe slowly and deeply, I calm the emotions boiling up inside me. I need to keep my focus steady. Mitch's arrival has already unnerved me and the appearance of this unknown yet familiar woman makes me nervous. The fact that they are both in Edge House only makes me more anxious.

I shrink back into the shadows when the front door opens and the redhead leaves, keys jangling in her hand as she heads towards the Mini. Mitch stands at the open door, watching her go. As the woman climbs in behind the wheel, she gives him a little wave. He waves back at her like a schoolboy waving at his first crush.

The redhead starts the car and drives away, a slight smile on her lips. If Mitch is anything like the other Walker men, that smile will soon be slapped away for good.

Perhaps he isn't like the others. Perhaps this redheaded woman will never fear the unreadable expression that crosses a man's face before he clenches his fists into twin battering rams. Or the sneer of cruelty that curls his lip just before he takes what he wants by force.

I laugh at myself for even considering that Mitch could be different. The rage and need are in his blood. They flow through the family tree like bile drawn up from the roots.

He goes back into the house and closes the door.

I wait in the shadows a little longer before turning my back on Edge House and making my way along the trail that leads through the woods. The air is fragrant, scented by the wildflowers that thrive here. My own addition to the abundance of flora lies farther along the trail, growing beneath a wych elm. I've tended the plants there for years, replanting when necessary and nurturing the seeds until they grow into the bright pink abundance of flowers that mark the place where I buried Josie Wagner's heart.

It isn't her real heart, although that would be poetic. It's the necklace she wore the night she went to Blackden Edge. The moment I saw it, I knew it would be my trophy. Unlike my other girls, Josie didn't deserve to be buried beneath a covering of flowers. I left her body where the police would find it and took only the tiny gold heart to remember her by.

The foxgloves are the flowers I visit the least often. Remembering Josie Wagner is painful and I only come to the place where I buried her necklace when I want to think about what I did to her. Sometimes I need to remember.

When I see the wych elm, I hurry along the trail, but as I get closer to the site, I can tell it's been disturbed. The foxgloves have been dug up and moved. They sit on a pile of freshly-dug soil while the place where they were—where the heart was—is nothing but a hole.

This time, I don't calm myself when I feel the anger boil inside me. I dig my nails into my palms, squeezing my hands into tight fists. It has to be Mitch who has done this. He's found the heart and taken it.

That means he has the journal.

That thought arrives with cold clarity. Mitch has the journal.

Has he talked to the redhead about it? Has he called the police? Perhaps the redhead is a police officer and she's taken the journal to the station.

This won't do. This won't do at all.

I turn away from the hole and make my way through the trees to the place where I parked my car by the side of the road. It's over half a mile away because I didn't want to park too close to Edge House, but the journey gives me time to think.

I need to find out who the redhead is.

I need to know where the journal is.

By the time I get to my car, I'm still boiling with rage. The sky is beginning to darken with storm clouds. I get into the car as the first spots of rain begin to fall.

I don't want to go home yet.

I start the engine and drive. At first, I drive aimlessly, turning in a random direction when I come to each intersection. But after twenty minutes, it becomes clear where I'm going.

I'm heading north into Dark Peak.

The landscape on either side of the road gradually changes from woods and rolling farmland to high peaks and rain-sodden moors. The ruggedness of the land excites me. Anything could happen in these wild places. A person could wander into this landscape and never be seen again.

The road gets steeper as it ascends a hill. Up ahead, I see someone walking by the side of the road, head bowed against the rain, working hard to trudge up the incline. As I get closer, I see it's a girl. Her jacket is bright red, her walking trousers black, the same as her damp hair, which I can now see is plastered to the collar of the jacket.

She wears a blue-and-grey rucksack and in her right hand is a walking pole. She sinks it into the grass by the roadside with each step she takes before flicking it ahead of her, ready for the next. She needs to take extra care because the grass slopes away sharply on either side of the road. If she fell, she'd end up on the moors with a broken leg or neck.

As I come alongside her, I slow the car and open the window on the passenger side. Her hair is stuck to her face so she brushes it away to look at me. Her eyes are blue and friendly, without a trace of fear.

"Terrible weather," I say, as if she hasn't noticed. "Have you got far to go?"

She offers me a sheepish smile. "I'm not sure. To be honest, I'm a bit lost."

Yes, you are, I think. The image of the empty hole in the woods by Edge House has been stuck in my mind the entire time I've been driving, making me seethe with anger. I manage to keep the emotion out of my voice and smile at the girl. "Where are you trying to get to?"

"I'm trying to find the Little Nook B&B. Do you know where that is?"

I nod. "It's four or five miles up the road. Do you want a lift?"

She frowns, weighing up the risk of getting into a stranger's car against the discomfort of walking four or five more miles in this weather. I lied to her about the distance. The Little Nook B&B is two miles back. I passed it a couple of minutes ago.

The answer to her dilemma seems to come easily to her. "If you're sure you don't mind," she says.

"Of course not. Jump in."

She takes off the rucksack and climbs into the passenger seat, putting the rucksack on the floor and holding it steady between her legs. "Thanks."

I put the car into gear and set off up the hill. "Don't mention it. I couldn't leave you back there in this weather, it wouldn't be right. What are you doing out here on your own anyway?"

She sighs. "I was hiking with my boyfriend, Mike, but we got into an argument so I went one way and he went the other."

"Oh dear, that doesn't sound very good. Do you argue a lot?"

"No, not really." She glances at the side mirror as if expecting to see her boyfriend on the road behind us. "To be honest, when I went storming off, I thought he'd follow me and try to smooth things over." She takes her eyes from the mirror and looks straight ahead. "But he didn't."

I don't say anything but shake my head in disapproval of her boyfriend's actions. Now she's in the warm car, out of the rain and confiding in someone, and I can tell she'll keep talking without any prompting.

"It isn't like I even enjoy walking," she says. "This holiday was all Mike's idea." She pauses and then folds her arms. "He's probably sitting in a pub somewhere with a pint in his hand."

"He doesn't sound like a very good boyfriend," I tell her.

She shrugs. "I seem to attract the wrong type of men." A horrified look crosses her face and she adds, "Oh, God, I shouldn't be telling you my problems. Forget I said that."

We pass the brow of the hill and begin the descent down the other side. "Don't worry about it," I say. "It's easy to confide in someone you don't know.

You can tell me whatever you like." I take my eyes off the road for a second and look at her. "I get the feeling Mike is just one in a long line of bad boys."

A slight smile curls the edge of her mouth but her eyes drop in shame. "Yeah, I guess I'm attracted to the wrong type of men. Mike's problem is that he's too hot-headed, you know? The slightest thing makes him fly off the handle. Then he goes and does something stupid, like leaving me alone out here."

I nod slowly in understanding. "What else does he do? People who have a short fuse like that are capable of a lot of things."

She shrugs again and looks out of the window, dismissing the question.

"A friend of mine was like that," I say softly. "When he lost his temper, he sometimes lashed out. Physically, I mean. His wife ended up with a few bruises."

"Oh no, Mike isn't anything like that," she says, clearly mortified that I might think he might be. "He's never laid a finger on me. He wouldn't hurt a fly."

She isn't making this easy for me. In my head, I've already picked a flower for her, a field poppy based on the red jacket. It's a snap decision based on physical appearance, which I already berated myself about in regard to the redhead at Edge House. But I don't have time to get to know this girl and choose a more appropriate flower. This isn't how I choose my girls. I don't pick them up randomly at the side of the road. My resolve begins to falter.

"Are you all right?" she asks. She sees something in my face, something which brings the first tinge of fear into her eyes.

"Yes, I'm fine. What did you say your name was?" I direct the conversation onto herself and away from me.

"I didn't. It's Penny Meadows."

Penny Meadows. It's almost too perfect. But at the same time, it isn't. I should never have picked her up. I can't just kill a random girl; it isn't right. The others were chosen so carefully.

A memory comes to me. I'm fifteen years old and standing outside our house in the village, waiting for my dad to come home. Before he left for work on the farm this morning, he told me the puppies that the farmer's dog had are old enough to go to new homes. He's promised he'll bring one home. I told him I want a girl and that I'm going to call her Jenny.

Mum is in the kitchen making liver and onions. The smell drifts out of the open windows and onto the street, making my mouth water. I want to go into the kitchen where the delicious smell is stronger and I can watch Mum getting everything ready for Dad's return, but I can't move from this spot until I see my new dog.

After what seems like an eternity of waiting, I see him coming up the street with a small cardboard box under his arm and I go running towards him, my heart lifted by the sight of the box. "You got her," I say when I reach him.

He smiles and crouches, opening the box just a little to let me see the black-and-white bundle of fur inside. The dog lets out a yap that sounds both frightened and happy at the same time.

When we get into the house, Mum comes from the kitchen to see the newest family member. Jenny springs out of the box and goes from Dad to Mum and then me, wagging her tail and sniffing us. I stroke the soft fur between her ears.

"You like her?' Dad asks.

"She's the best dog ever!" I say.

The memory skips ahead two years. Jenny and I have been inseparable ever since she arrived at our house. I take her out on her lead every evening. We walk through the village and into the countryside, roaming along Blackden Edge. There's a brook there and Jenny likes to play in the water while I saunter alongside and let my thoughts drift. I like it out on the Edge, away from the village and our house. I feel free, wandering beneath the open sky on a wild landscape that seems to stretch into the distance forever.

On this particular evening, there's a January chill in the air and snow clouds in the sky. Jenny and I are wandering along the Edge when I see two girls in the distance. They're throwing sticks into the water. As we get closer, I recognise them as Evie and Mary

Hatton. I see them around the village, usually with their heads down as they walk to and from school. They don't speak much and seem to only be friends with each other, which is sad.

"Evening," I say when I get close enough for them to hear me.

Evie, the oldest, looks at me and waves. Her eyes brighten when she sees Jenny frolicking in the water. "Can we stroke her?"

"Sure," I say. I call Jenny over and she obediently runs over to us, tail wagging, water dripping from the fur on her belly and legs.

"Look, Mary," Evie says to her younger sister, "you can touch her. She won't bite." She pets Jenny on the head.

Mary looks over and I see tears on her cheeks and in her eyes. Her lips are trembling.

"What's the matter?" I ask.

"She'll be all right," Evie says. "She's just a cry-baby."

"No, I'm not," Mary protests. "You'd cry as well if it happened to you."

"No, I wouldn't. And it does happen to me. I don't cry over it like you. You need to grow up, Mary."

"Cry about what?" I ask. "What happened?"

"It's our dad," Mary says through her tears. "He—"

"Sshhh!" Evie hisses. She looks at me and says, "It's nothing."

I've heard rumours about the Hatton family. In a little village like ours, they spread like wildfire. From what I've heard, the girls' father is a pervert. That's what I heard at school a couple of years ago, anyway. Tess Goodall told me in the playground that she'd heard her dad telling her mum that John Hatton molested his girls. Since then, I'd heard the same thing again a couple of times just by eavesdropping on hushed conversations in the village. The rumours were spoken in whispers but you could hear them if you listened hard enough.

"You can tell me," I say. "I won't tell anybody. And Jenny won't either."

"I want to stroke the doggy," Evie says, moving to Jenny and stroking her back.

"Are you going to tell me why you're crying?" I ask softly. I'm not really sure why I want to know. In fact, I'm not even sure that I want to know at all. The thought of John Hatton molesting his daughters disgusts me. There's a chance the rumours could be wrong, but if one of the Hatton girls tells me about it, then it must be true. That would mean I'd have to do something about it. You can't have that kind of knowledge in your head and not do something about it.

Evie looks at me closely, her fingers still running

through the fur on top of Jenny's head. "If I tell you something, will you promise not to tell anyone else?"

"Yes," I say. "I promise."

She hesitates, then says, "You've probably heard about our dad." She says the words with a heaviness in her voice.

I nod.

She shrugs as if trying to make light of the situation. "Well, whatever you heard is probably true."

"Oh," I say.

Mary's tears begin anew as she continues stroking Jenny.

"He drinks," Mary says, as if that explains everything. But it doesn't. It doesn't explain anything at all. The two girls in front of me are broken. Nothing can explain that and nothing can fix it.

"You promised not to tell," Evie reminds me.

I nod solemnly. "Yes, I did. And I won't tell."

But later, after I leave the girls and I'm walking home, I realise that I now know something that can't just be ignored. I have to do something for those girls. I just don't know yet what that is.

When we reach the road that leads to the village, I bend down to put Jenny's lead back on but she sees something moving in the hedgerow and scampers away after it.

"Jenny," I call after her, "come back!"

She runs across the road as a bright red car comes speeding around the corner. The driver sees her and

I hear the squeal of the tyres on the road. Then there's a heavy thud as the car strikes Jenny. The impact throws her at least ten feet before she lands in a heap in the road.

"Jenny!" I race over to her, tears already stinging my face. She isn't moving and there's blood seeping out of her. It surrounds her like a dark red puddle.

I crouch next to her. She's alive, her eyes staring at the hedge at the side of the road. I try to pick her up. If I can get her home, Mum and Dad will know what to do. But as I begin to lift her, she whimpers and then squeals.

The driver of the car is saying something but I can't hear his voice. It sounds jumbled in my ears. I stroke Jenny's head and her eyes roll up to look at me. She whines softly.

"You're going to be all right," I tell her. "It's going to be okay."

The next thing I know, my dad is there. He's holding a large cardboard box. It reminds me of the box he brought Jenny home in two years ago, but this one is much larger.

"Let's get her into this," he says gently, crouching down next to me. "Then we can get her home."

I'm still sobbing but I help him slide Jenny into the box. She cries out in pain when we move her but once she's in the box, she's quiet again. Dad picks her up and we walk back home. But instead of going inside, he takes the box around the side of the house to the back garden.

I follow, still crying. Jenny and I had been so happy, enjoying the crisp winter evening as we roamed over Blackden Edge. How could it all change in an instant? I feel wretched. If I'd put the lead on her when we were still in the fields, none of this would have happened.

Dad places the box down on the ground gently. I can hear faint whimpers from inside.

"Is she going to be all right?" I ask. I already know the answer. I know it because of the way Jenny had lain in the road and the amount of blood that had pooled around her. But I still hope and pray that Dad will say, "Yes, of course she will."

He doesn't say that. He looks at me with pity and sadness. "I'm afraid not. We can't let her suffer like this."

I feel like I'm going to be sick. My hand flies to my mouth and my stomach convulses but nothing comes out of my mouth except a whimper that echoes Jenny's.

Dad puts a hand on my shoulder. "Jenny is hurting. The suffering will just get worse. The kindest thing we can do for her is to end it."

I shake my head, tears blurring my vision.

"You stroke her and talk to her. I'm sure she'll like that. Say goodbye to her. I'll be back in a minute." He goes inside the house and I hear him telling Mum what has happened. Her face appears at the kitchen window, shock in her eyes.

I sit on the cold ground next to Jenny and stroke her head. She doesn't look at me. Her eyes are fixed on the side of the cardboard box.

"I don't want to say goodbye," I say.

Dad comes outside again, carrying his shotgun beneath his arm. "You go inside with your mum," he says. "You don't want to see this."

I get up off the ground and look at Jenny one last time. I can't bring myself to say goodbye to her. Mum comes out of the back door and takes my hand, leading me inside, into the kitchen where there's a smell of bacon in the air.

She pulls me to her. There's bacon grease on her apron.

A sudden bang outside makes me jump. It isn't loud but it carries a heavy note of finality.

A couple of minutes later, Dad comes inside and puts a hand on my shoulder again. "Come on, we'll bury her in the garden. You can choose the place. And you can choose the flower."

"The flower?" I ask, sniffing.

"Of course. You choose a flower and we'll plant it where we bury Jenny. We'll have to wait until spring to do that, though. And then, when you go to that part of the garden and look at the flowers, it will remind you of Jenny and all the nice times you had with her."

"But we didn't have enough nice times," I bawl. "There should have been more."

"I know," he says, "but sometimes bad things happen. A bad thing happened to Jenny but we did right by her by making sure she didn't suffer. If she could have thanked us for that, she would have. You were a good friend to her."

He takes me outside into the cold night. The cardboard box is closed now and I don't want to open it. "Where do you think is a nice spot for her?" he asks.

I think about it and then point at the apple tree. It's bare and spindly now but in summer, it produces so many apples we have to give some to our neighbours because we can't eat them all.

"That's a good place," Dad says. "I'll go and get my spade from the shed. While I do that, you go inside where it's warm. There's a botanical book on the bookshelf. Have a look through it and choose a flower for Jenny. Then, in spring, we'll get some seeds and plant them."

I nod and go inside. In the living room, I find the book, a large hardcover with colour plates, and take it to Dad's armchair by the gas fire. As I begin leafing through the pages, the colours of the various flowers grab my attention. Concentrating on their shapes and names takes away a little of the pain I feel. I want to choose the best flower for her and watch it grow beneath the apple tree.

It's warm in front of the fire and I curl up in the chair, discovering new flowers with each turn of the page. When I've been through the entire book twice, I settle on sweet violets for Jenny. They are named for their sweet scent but I choose them for Jenny's sweet nature.

A week later, I'm walking along Blackden Edge for the first time since Jenny died. I haven't been able to face coming here without her until now and walking along the brook is bittersweet. I close my eyes and imagine I can hear splashes as Jenny frolics in the water.

After walking for half an hour, I decide to turn around and head home. This place just isn't the same without Jenny, and I make a decision to never take my evening walks here again. The Edge feels lonely.

Just as I'm about to turn around, I hear a splash farther along the brook. I squint against the darkness and see two figures throwing sticks into the water. I wonder if it's the Hatton sisters. I've been thinking about them a lot since the night we buried Jenny.

I trudge along the brook towards them. As I get closer, I can see that it is Evie and Mary. And just like the last time I saw them here, they're alone.

"Evening," I say, waving at them.

They both look up, startled. They were so busy in their game of stick-throwing that they didn't hear me approach. This time, it's Evie who has tears rolling down her cheeks. Mary isn't crying but she has a sad look on her face.

"Hello," Evie says, wiping at her face. She looks along the brook behind me. "Where's your dog?"

"She died," I say flatly. "She was hit by a car."

Now Mary begins to cry. Evie puts a comforting arm around her sister's shoulder and that gesture breaks my heart.

"It's all right," I say. "She isn't suffering anymore. And in the spring, we're going to plant sweet violets where she's buried."

"That sounds nice," Evie says, "but I don't know what they are."

"They're beautiful flowers that have a sweet smell. I chose them because Jenny was a sweet dog. If you know about flowers, you can choose the right one for any person."

"Really?" Mary looks astonished. "Could you even choose one for me?"

"Of course. I think you two are like a pair of bluebells."

"I know what those are," Evie says.

"Yes, they grow in the woods," I tell her. "And they're very pretty. And they look down at the ground beneath where they grow, like you and Mary are always looking down at your feet when I see you in the village."

Evie shrugs. "People say mean things about us

and about our dad. They don't think we know what they're saying but we do."

I frown. "But you told me those things are true."

She shrugs and looks down at her feet.

"Are they true?" I ask.

"Yes, but people don't have to be mean about it."

"I'm sure they're not being mean," I say.

"They are. They wouldn't like it if it was happening to them. It's horrible." She begins to sob. Mary is crying as well and I'm not sure if it's still because of Jenny or because of what their dad does to them. These girls are broken. They're suffering.

When I last saw them, I knew that I couldn't just do nothing about what they'd told me. Now I know what I have to do.

"I bet you'd do anything to not have those horrible things happen to you anymore," I say.

Evie nods, tears streaming down her face. The false bravado she displayed last time is gone. There isn't a shred of it left.

"I know what might cheer us up," I say.

"What?" they both ask in unison.

"You see those woods over there? I bet we can find some bluebells in there."

Mary frowns and shakes her head. "I don't like the woods. They're dark and scary."

"Don't be such a baby," Evie tells her.

"Come on," I say. "We'll be fine." I take their hands and lead them towards the dark woods. There aren't any bluebells there at the moment, of course, because it's winter. But next spring, I'll make sure there's a special patch of bluebells in these woods, a patch selected specially for these two girls.

As we reach the trees, I repeat a single sentence over and over in my head.

No more suffering.

"Do you know how much farther it is to the B&B?" Penny Meadows asks from the passenger seat. There's a note of concern in her voice and a worried look on her face. I wonder how long I've been silent while remembering the past. The anger I felt earlier hasn't vanished, but remembering Evie and Mary Hatton has made me feel a little calmer.

It has also made me realise what I must do now.

I slam on the brakes. The car skids to a stop. I forget to put my foot on the clutch and the engine stalls. The dashboard glows with warning lights.

"Is everything okay?" Penny asks.

"Get out," I say.

"What? Listen, if I said something to offend you—-"

"Get out. Now."

"Okay, okay. I'm going." She opens the door and slides out, taking the rucksack with her. As soon as the door closes, I start the engine and drive away, leaving her by the side of the road.

After following the road for another four or five miles, I pull over again and let out a long breath. I had almost let my stupid impulses destroy the purity of what I'm doing. The bluebell grave and the daisy grave are a testament to my work and those buried in them. Penny Meadows is not in the same league as my girls. The flower graves are earned through pain and suffering, something Penny Meadows probably thinks she knows something about but does not.

I put the car in gear and resume following the road through Dark Peak. The rain becomes torrential and batters the car and the surrounding moors like tears of the gods.

21

NIGHT CALL

DCI Stewart Battle woke up fast when his phone started to vibrate on the bedside table. He jabbed the screen and brought the phone to his ear quickly, whispering into it so as not to wake Rowena, who was sleeping next to him.

"Battle."

"We've got a body, guv." It was DS Morgan.

Battle could hear the wind blowing on the other end of the line as well as outside his bedroom window. Each gust blew a thousand raindrops against the glass. "Have you called the SOCOs?"

"I called you first. I thought that considering where the body is, you'd want to be the first to know."

He felt a sinking feeling in the pit of his stomach. "It's at the Edge." It wasn't a question, merely a statement of fact.

"That's right, guv."

"Right, text me the exact location and call the SOCOs." He hung up and climbed out of bed, dressing quickly in the dark.

Rowena stirred. "What's happened?"

"There's a body at Blackden Edge," he told her as he buckled his belt.

She sat up in bed. "Oh no, not another one. Is it connected to the others?"

"I don't know. I don't know anything yet. If it is connected, then hopefully the bastard will have slipped up this time and we'll get him." He glanced at the rain-battered window. "Although judging by the weather, it's likely that any evidence will have been washed away."

"You be careful," she told him. "It's treacherous enough up there without gale force winds and rain."

"I'm always careful. You go back to sleep and don't worry about me." He went around to her side of the bed and kissed her before leaving the bedroom.

"You know I always worry," she called after him.

When he got downstairs, he turned on the kitchen light and checked the clock on the wall. Three thirty. Bloody hell, he needed a strong coffee. But there was no time for that so he opened the fridge and took out a can of Coke. At least there was some caffeine in it and he could drink it on the way. Before he closed the fridge, he took out a second can for DS Morgan.

His Range Rover was parked in the garage, which was connected to the kitchen by a door so he didn't have to go out in the rain and get soaked before even going anywhere. Thank heavens for small mercies. He'd have plenty of time to get wet later when he was out on the Edge looking at the body.

Grabbing his coat and hat from the stand by the front door, he went through the kitchen to the garage and loaded everything into his vehicle. He climbed in and hit the button on the remote control that opened the garage door. As it slid up, it revealed the dark, rainswept street. Some of the neighbours had put their wheelie bins out for tomorrow's recycling collection and at least three had blown over, spilling their contents. The wind blew empty bottles and cans over the road.

Battle drove onto the road carefully, avoiding a scattering of glass where a bottle had been blown into the kerb and had shattered.

Once he was on the road that led north through the Peak District to Dark Peak, Battle opened one of the Cokes and sipped it. The sugar-hit woke him up a little but he'd give anything for a decent coffee or cup of tea right now. He had a forty-minute drive ahead and then a trudge over wet grass and rocks in the type of weather that killed people in the wild places.

Maybe the body at the Edge was a hiker who'd been blown off one of the ridges that surrounded the ravine. Or somebody who'd died of exposure. God knew it was possible up there in that terrain.

He pushed those thoughts away. DS Morgan wouldn't have called him if it were a hiker who'd lost their way or a climber who'd been foolhardy. There was a girl at the Edge and she'd been murdered. That much he was sure of.

His phone dinged. Battle pulled over to the side of the road to read the text. He'd seen the consequences of drivers not paying attention to the road; he wasn't taking any chances. This body could hold a clue to the identity of the Blackden Edge Murderer and he could hardly apprehend the killer if he were in a hospital bed, injured by his own stupidity.

The text from DS Morgan was brief but told him everything he needed to know. *Two uniforms will meet you at Leath.*

Battle put the phone down and got back on the road. He realised his theory that Michael Walker could be guilty of the Blackden Edge murders might have to be thrown out. There was no way Walker committed murder from beyond the grave. That put Battle back to square one. He sighed and took another sip of Coke.

Forty minutes later, when he turned off Snake Road and onto the road for Leath, he spotted two police officers in hi-vis jackets standing at the side of the road. A number of police vehicles were parked nearby, including the white van the SOCOs used.

Battle parked the Range Rover in front of the line of vehicles, struggled into his coat in the confines of the car, and got out. He left his hat on the passenger seat. There was no way it was going to stay on his head in this wind. Slipping DS Morgan's Coke into his coat pocket, he walked around to the back of the Range Rover and opened it to get his walking gear.

Working the Peak District meant carrying the proper equipment at all times. Battle had walking boots, spare clothing, and even vacuum-packed meals stowed in the boot of the Range Rover. He put on a blue waterproof poncho before changing his shoes for a pair of Karrimor walking boots and donning a black knitted watch cap in lieu of his usual tweed hat.

After taking out a walking pole, he strode over to the uniformed officers, whom he recognised as Badwal and Stern. Badwal was a Sikh and wore a black turban instead of a hat. Stern wore the bowler style female officer's hat with her dark hair pinned up beneath it. The hat was pressed down hard onto her head in an effort to keep it from blowing away. Stern still had to hold it with her hand. Both she and Badwal looked wet and miserable.

"Right," Battle said when he reached them. "Let's get going."

They led him through a gate and into an overgrown field through which a path led to a low wall on the opposite side of the field.

"How was the body found?" Battle asked.

"A man and a woman were camping at the Edge," Stern said. "When the weather closed in, they decided to abandon their campsite and head back to their car. During their travels, they stumbled over the victim. They legged it to the village and dialled 999 from the phone box there. They hadn't taken their phones onto the Edge with them. Wanted to get away from it all, apparently."

"Tell me about the couple." Battle was surprised at how out of breath he sounded. They'd hardly walked halfway across the field. This bloody case was going to be the death of him yet.

"Officer Badwal took their statement, sir," she said.

"James and Marie Mitchener," Badwal said. "From Nottingham. She's a computer analyst and he's a website designer. They fancied a couple of nights in the wild."

"Does their story check out?"

"They're being taken to the station to be interviewed now, sir, but I didn't get any bad vibes from them."

"Bad vibes? Is that what policing has come to now? If only it were that easy. What do we know about the girl?"

"Girl, sir?" Stern asked.

"The victim. Unless our killer has changed his MO, it's a girl. It's always a girl."

"They haven't identified her yet, sir. DS Morgan is at the scene, along with the SOCOs."

They reached the low stone wall. Beyond it, the trail led down to Blackden Brook and then alongside the brook into the ravine that was Blackden Edge. There was a public right of way here, so a narrow gap had been left in the wall to allow access. Battle squeezed through, followed by Stern and Badwal.

"We need more uniforms," he told them. "I want a fingertip search of the area. I don't care how many officers have to be pulled out of bed, I need them here while the scene is still fresh."

"Yes, sir," Stern said.

When they reached the brook, Battle could see lights farther along the path. As he got closer, he saw the white square tent that had been erected around the body. Its sides trembled in the wind. There were lights inside, powered by a generator that some poor sod must have lugged all the way here from the van. Two SOCOs were outside the tent, dressed in white protective clothing and masks.

The tent and the officers looked out of place in the countryside, as if they were aliens who had landed in the middle of nowhere to examine humankind and had found only death.

Blue-and-white crime-scene tape fluttered in the wind, stretched between two metal poles on either side of the path. A uniform in a hi-vis jacket stood sentry by it. When he saw and recognised Battle, he lifted the tape and said, "Sir," with a slight nod as Battle passed beneath it.

DS Morgan stood outside the tent, the light suffusing through the PVC walls giving her face a ghostly pallor. Like Battle, she wore a blue waterproof poncho and a black watch cap.

"What have we got?" Battle asked.

"Female in her twenties," she said. "No ID yet. If she was up here walking, she wasn't dressed appropriately."

"Cause of death?"

"Looks like strangulation."

"Same as Josie Wagner," he said, pulling back the flap of the tent and stepping inside.

The girl lay on her back, blue eyes staring at the roof of the tent. She wore jeans and a black sweater but the jeans had been slashed in the area of her upper thighs and the sweater had been slashed in the breast area. She wore white Reebok trainers that were barely mud-stained. In contrast, her long black hair was splayed out around her head and covered with mud. A dark bruise stretched from one side of her throat to the other. The harsh glow of the portable lights bleached her flesh a garish white but even so, Battle could see she was pretty.

He felt a stab of pity for the girl. No one should end up like this, discarded in the mud like a piece of trash.

Two SOCOs were removing fibres from her

clothing with tweezers and placing them in clear plastic evidence bags.

Battle didn't need to see a lab report to understand what had happened here. The Blackden Edge Killer had struck again. There were some differences between the state of this body and that of Josie Wagner—the only other victim left in the open for the police to find, but the MO was the same.

He left the tent and stepped back out into the wind and rain where DS Morgan waited.

"What do you think, guv?" she asked.

"It's clear enough," he said. "Our boy has come out to play again."

"You noticed the different slash wounds, though," she said. It was a statement, not a question. She knew he'd noticed the differences between the slashes on this victim and those on Josie Wagner.

Battle nodded. "They're weak, hesitant. There's none of the ferocity he expressed when he caused Josie's wounds."

"You think it's a different person?"

"We can't rule it out. But remember, Josie's murder took place forty years ago. The killer is older now, weaker."

"Not too weak to strangle Jane Doe in there."

"No, and not too weak to move her body here either. She wasn't killed on the Edge. Not unless the killer removed her coat and put those Reebok trainers on her feet. There was barely a speck of dirt on them.

She was killed somewhere else and then carried here. So if he had the strength to do that, why the weak slashes?"

DS Morgan shrugged. "I don't know, guv."

The tent opened and one of the SOCOs poked his head out. "Detectives, we've turned the body over. You may want to see this."

Battle and Morgan went back inside. The victim now lay on her stomach. The other SOCO was moving around the body, taking photos from various angles.

When Battle saw what was lying in the mud where the Jane Doe had been positioned, his thoughts went to the letter the police had received eighteen years ago, the one with the damned flower poetry on it.

Embedded in the mud, illuminated by the stark lights, was a single red rose.

22

FROM THE SHADOWS

A NOISE WOKE MITCH. He sat up in bed, listening, unsure if the sound had been a part of his dreams. When no further sound came, he slipped out of bed and padded over to the window.

Outside, the moors glowed a ghostly silver beneath the gibbous moon. The gale drove sheets of rain over the landscape and against Edge House. Mitch told himself that what he'd heard had been nothing more than something outside blowing over in the wind, but now that he thought about it, hadn't it sounded as if it had come from inside the house?

He looked down at the walled garden beneath the window. The gate was open. It was the gate that led to the moors, the one he and Sarah had walked through that fateful night thirty years ago. Had it blown open? No, it couldn't have; he'd seen a hasp and padlock attached to the gate earlier and it had been locked.

His mind began to race. If someone was going to try and break in, the back door wasn't really an option now that he'd secured it. Was the sound he'd heard come from a window breaking? He scanned the room for a weapon but found none. The room he'd chosen to sleep in had been empty except for a bed, a bedside table upon which stood a lamp, and a wardrobe that held nothing except empty clothes hangers.

With nothing else to hand, Mitch unplugged the lamp and wielded it like a club. He wasn't sure how much damage he could do with it—the base and stem were made of light wood and the shade was cream-coloured fabric—but he couldn't face the intruder unarmed.

If there is an intruder, he told himself. *The padlock on the gate could have been so old and rusty that it broke when the wind blew against the gate.*

But even as he tried to convince himself of that possibility, he knew he was kidding himself. Someone had broken onto the property from the moors. It could be the same person who had broken in before and tried to find the journal, in which case it was his father's accomplice, if Elly's theory was correct. The man Battle was looking for, a man connected in some way with the murders of at least six girls—including Sarah—was in the house.

Mitch needed to get to his phone and call the police. But it was sitting on the coffee table in the living room, charging up. And sitting next to it was the journal.

Mitch couldn't let the journal slip through his fingers and end up in the hands of the man who may have murdered his father.

He slipped out of the room and onto the landing. Moonlight slanted in through the windows, lighting the landing with the same ghostly glow it had lent the moors. Mitch listened to the house around him. Everything seemed quiet. Had the intruder heard him get out of bed? Was he waiting in the darkness downstairs, ready to strike if Mitch blundered down there?

Mitch walked to the top of the stairs and peered at the dark foyer below. He held the lamp tightly but knew that if he had to use it to hit someone, it would probably just break. Standing here in his pyjamas, the flimsy lamp in his hand, he felt exposed, vulnerable. He was standing in the exact spot his father had been standing when he fell—or was pushed—down the stairs.

Reflexively, Mitch checked the landing he was standing on, half-expecting to see a dark figure rush out of the shadows towards him, hands spread, ready to topple him over the edge of the top step. But there was no one there. Mitch let out a long, low breath.

The living room door stood ajar, the way he'd left

it when he'd come to bed earlier. In the darkness beyond that door was his phone. He needed to reach it and call the police.

And what exactly would he tell them? That he'd heard a noise while he was asleep and the garden gate was open? Would that bring Derbyshire's finest racing to Edge House, sirens blaring? He wasn't even sure the gate had been locked in the first place. He thought he'd seen a padlock but he couldn't swear to it.

Maybe he was imagining things. A bit of wind and rain and an unknown noise in a lonely Gothic house on the moors had sent his mind into overdrive. There was no intruder and the noise he'd heard had probably been the gate blowing open and slamming against the garden wall.

He hadn't turned on the lights because he hadn't wanted whoever was possibly lurking downstairs to know he was aware of their presence, but now he laughed inwardly at himself. Wasn't stumbling around in the dark what every character in a horror movie did and didn't he always mentally berate them for acting in such an unrealistic way?

He found the light switch on the landing and flicked it on.

The lights stayed off.

Okay, no need to panic. Maybe the wind blew down a power line.

Still, he'd be happier if he didn't have to go downstairs in the dark. Telling himself he was letting his imagination get the better of him and that he shouldn't be so foolish, he stepped onto the stairs. As he descended slowly, he listened to the house but heard nothing other than the wind howling in the eaves and the rain beating against the windows.

When his bare feet touched the Persian rug, he paused and tightened his grip on the lamp. He just had to cross the foyer and he would be in the living room. Once he had his phone in hand, he could use its flashlight app and check the windows and doors. He was sure he would find everything as it should be. No shattered window where an intruder had climbed in, no broken door hanging off its hinges.

He stepped forward off the rug and onto the smooth wooden floor. The floorboards creaked under his weight. Just a dozen or so paces and he'd be in the living room. Then he'd have his phone and wouldn't feel so isolated.

He took two steps. A sound reached his ears. It came from the back of the house. Mitch turned to face the corridor that led off the foyer but saw nothing other than the moonlit kitchen. What he'd heard had sounded like a hesitant footstep, like the sole of a boot scuffing on the floor, as if someone had gone to make a move but then changed their mind and stepped back into the shadows where they were hiding.

Mitch froze. He had no doubt now that someone was in the house. He was only a couple of steps from the living room door. He tried to remember if that door had a lock on it, like so many other doors in the house. There was a keyhole below the handle but he couldn't remember if there was a key inserted into it on the other side.

If so, he could lock himself in there and call the police. If not, he was screwed. He was going to have to rely on the lamp in his hand versus whatever weapon the intruder was wielding.

Maybe they'll run away, he told himself. *That footfall didn't sound too sure of itself. If they know I'm down here and that I've called the police, they might make a run for it.*

But a part of him didn't want the intruder to leave. The man in the kitchen probably knew what had become of Sarah, could even be responsible for abducting her, or at least have played a part in her disappearance. If Mitch could overpower him and keep him restrained until the police got here, he might be able to finally solve a thirty-year-old mystery.

But the lamp in his hand wasn't going to cut it as a weapon. He had to find something heavier, something he could use to threaten the intruder even if he didn't have to use actual physical force.

He slipped into the living room without touching

the door at all, sliding his body sideways through the gap that was already there. When he was in the room, he crept to the coffee table to get his phone.

It wasn't there.

His phone and the journal had both been taken from the table.

Mitch's blood ran cold. The intruder in the kitchen already had what he'd come here to steal. If he got away now, he'd take the journal with him and might never be heard from again. Mitch would never know what had happened to Sarah.

His fear forgotten, he grabbed the pottery vase from beside the fireplace and rushed from the room, heading for the kitchen. His plan, only half-formed in his mind, was to knock the intruder unconscious and use the house phone to call the police. He was counting on the element of surprise to give him the upper hand. There was no way the intruder would expect Mitch to be on the attack.

He reached the kitchen and heard—and felt—the chilly wind blowing through the room. The windows weren't broken. The back door was still secure. The door that led to the walled garden was wide open, though. The floor tiles were slick with rainwater, glistening in the moonlight that poured in through the opening. It seemed the intruder had already fled.

His phone was on the floor, probably discarded there when the intruder realised it required a passcode. Mitch picked it up and keyed in the code. He found his contact list. After he checked outside, he'd call Battle.

He went outside, into the overgrown garden. The wind threw rain into his face. He held up his arm to cover his eyes and went to the open gate, trying to see the intruder on the rain-swept moors. But the rain blinded him. He couldn't see anything.

Turning away from the gate, he retraced his steps across the garden to the house. As he reached the open door, a dark shape came rushing out from the shadows in the kitchen. Mitch had no time to react. The intruder threw him towards the doorway. Mitch's head connected with the frame and he wasn't sure if the cracking sound he heard was the wood or his own skull.

The world tipped crazily and his vision became blurred. He squinted down at the phone screen, intending to press his thumb on Battle's name and call him, but the screen was hazy and indistinct, like the rest of the world. Mitch pressed the screen anyway, unsure who the phone was now dialling, hoping that it wasn't his doctor's office or the garage where he took the Jeep to be serviced.

The man who had pushed him was a shadow on the garden path, suddenly moving forward towards Mitch.

Mitch stepped back instinctively, tripping over

his own feet and falling backwards onto the garden path. The intruder lunged at him and Mitch felt something sharp pierce his gut. He let out a surprised yelp as pain lanced through him.

He landed heavily, his head striking the rain-slick stone.

The intruder stood over him, a blood-stained knife in one gloved hand, the journal in the other. Mitch couldn't turn his head far enough to see anything else.

Blood and rainwater dripped from the knife blade. A faraway voice in Mitch's head told him that blood was his own and he might die now. If the knife had punctured anything vital in his body, he didn't have much time left. If the man decided to stab him again, there wasn't much he could do about it.

He couldn't die without knowing who had killed Sarah. Gathering up as much strength as he could, he said, "Who are you?" The words came out as weak as a whisper.

The man with the knife let out a low chuckle. It was the confident sound of a man who not only held all the cards but was in control of his opponent's hand as well as his own.

Mitch realised he was still holding the pottery vase. Somehow, it hadn't shattered when he'd fallen to the ground. He wondered if he had the strength to lift it and smash it against the intruder's leg. It might be the final act of his life but at least he'd die doing something for Sarah.

With a grunt of effort, he swung the vase at the man's knee. It connected with a crack. Mitch hoped it was the sound of bone cracking and not just pottery. The vase fell apart in his hand. The man cried out and dropped the knife. It clattered to the path by Mitch's feet.

As the man bent to retrieve it, Mitch acted in desperation, kicking the knife along the path and into the tangled undergrowth.

The man limped after it. When he saw the limp, Mitch enjoyed a moment of satisfaction. But instead of savouring it, he turned his body towards the door and dragged himself into the kitchen, sliding on his belly over the cool tiles. His arms and legs were working but he couldn't stand up. He didn't have the strength for that. His skull felt as if it had been filled with concrete.

A woman's voice came from his phone. She sounded tired, confused. "Mitch? Do you know what time it is?"

He tried to place the voice but couldn't. It wasn't Jess or Leigh. And it wasn't the woman he'd been speaking to earlier about the murders. Elly, that was her name. It wasn't Elly on the other end of the line.

"Need help," he whispered into the phone. He hadn't meant to whisper, wasn't trying to be quiet, but the words didn't have enough strength behind them to be anything other than a soft susurration.

"Mitch? What's wrong? Where are you?" She sounded alert now, worried.

"Help," he whispered before blackness blotted out everything. "Need...help."

23

THE MOORS

Elly was sitting in front of the murder board in the living room of Windrider Cottage, attempting to intuit a hidden connection between the various elements in front of her but failing miserably. The fact that Olivia and Sarah Walker were both abducted seemed to point at Michael Walker, but where did Josie Wagner and Lindsey Grofield fit in?

Could it be that Michael killed his sister and daughter but someone else was responsible for what happened to Josie and Lindsey? The accomplice theory was beginning to seem more and more likely. As far as she was concerned, the most likely candidate was Silas, Michael's brother, simply because he also had connections with Olivia and Sarah.

Her phone rang, the screen displaying Glenister's number. Elly debated whether or not to answer it. He was obviously ringing for a situation report and she had nothing to tell him. The deeper she delved into the case, the more confusing it became.

Well, Glenister was just going to have to understand that. Besides, she'd only been here four days so he couldn't expect miracles.

There was one part of the mystery she may have untangled. A phrase in the journal read:

I looked upon a grave of daisies

in a glade watched over by the Ladies.

According to the poem that had been sent to the police, daisies referred to Lindsey Grofield, so Elly had assumed the grave of daisies meant the place where Lindsey's body was buried. The fact that the word Ladies was capitalised in the journal had intrigued Elly and she'd Googled the word, along with the word Derbyshire. She'd discovered that there was a place called Stanton Moor a few miles south of the cottage and there was a Bronze Age stone circle there called the Nine Ladies. It wasn't much to go on but it was something. Still, not anything concrete enough to tell Glenister until she'd done some more investigation.

She answered the phone and said, "Hi, Jack," through gritted teeth.

"Elly, I assume you've seen the news today?"

She wasn't expecting that. "No, I haven't. Why? What's up?"

There was a long sigh at the other end of the line. "Put BBC One on."

"Okay." She went into the living room and used the remote to put the TV on and find BBC One. A newsreader was saying, "*It's believed the woman was strangled. The Derbyshire police are expected to give a statement later today.*" In the corner of the screen, a video showed two scenes of crimes officers bringing a body bag on a stretcher out of a field and onto a road where an ambulance waited. The ambulance was parked in a village, along with police vehicles and a white crime-scene van.

Villagers watched with interest and talked amongst themselves as the body was loaded into the back of the ambulance.

"*The body was found near Kinder Scout, a moorland plateau in the Peak District,*" the newsreader said.

"In an area called Blackden Edge," Elly muttered.

"That's right," Glenister said in her ear. "Blackden Edge. So I assume you're on top of this? This book isn't just a retrospective investigation anymore, Elly, it's become a living, breathing thing. Wollstonecraft rang me this morning when the news broke. They're excited because you're right there, in the thick of it. But it seems to me you've been scooped by the local reporters."

"I wasn't watching the news," Elly said with a defensiveness that made her angry at herself. "The person I was sent to investigate is dead and the last disappearance was eighteen years ago. Why would I be watching the news?"

"Because you're a journalist."

"Not anymore," she said.

He ignored her. "So, if Michael Walker wasn't the murderer, I assume you have some other leads?"

She considered telling him about her Nine Ladies lead but decided against it. "I'm working on it."

"You need to find out what's going on and how it fits in with the other murders. Bloody hell, Elly, you don't know what's happening right on your doorstep. What have you been doing all day?"

"Working," she said. She wanted to add that he was her agent, not her boss, but held her tongue.

"Well, ring me when you have something. This murder is going to bring a lot of media attention. Make sure someone else doesn't steal your thunder." He hung up.

Elly sighed and threw the phone onto the sofa. She could do without Glenister breathing down her neck but he was right about one thing: this new murder changed everything. There was a killer in their midst.

She wondered if Mitch had seen the news. Maybe she should call him. They'd exchanged phone numbers yesterday before she left Edge House, promising to let each other know if they discovered anything new. Elly felt for Mitch. She was doing this to try and get her career back on track, but he had a huge personal stake in identifying the killer. He might be able to finally know what had happened to his sister thirty years ago.

"Speaking of sisters, don't forget Jen's coming today," she reminded herself. If she went out, she had to remember to leave the key in the key safe by the door.

Deciding to ring Mitch and tell him about the stone circle and how it might relate to the passage about Lindsey Grofield, she picked up the phone and dialled his number. No answer. She hung up when his voicemail kicked in.

She hoped he wasn't out tracking down some clue or other. Last night, they'd agreed to share all the information they had with each other. After finding Lindsey Grofield's necklace, Mitch said he'd come to a dead end as far as the clues in the journal were concerned. So if he was carrying out his own investigation at the moment and that was why he wasn't answering his phone, he'd already gone back on their deal.

She shouldn't be surprised, of course, she hardly knew the man. Yet something in his eyes had told Elly that he was trustworthy.

"And I'm the expert when it comes to trusting men," she muttered to herself. Sarcasm might be the lowest form of wit but at least it cheered her up a little.

A knock at the door startled her. She went to it and opened it to find her sister on the doorstep. Jen was shaking rain off a Hello Kitty umbrella while she peered up at the grey sky with an expression of disdain. Unlike Elly, Jen had blonde hair and, also unlike Elly, she had it styled professionally every couple of weeks. Rain was her worst enemy.

"Jen, I thought you weren't going to be here until later? Come in." Elly took the pink hard-shell weekend case from her sister's hand and brought it inside.

Jen followed, her eagle eyes inspecting the interior of the cottage as soon as she set foot in the hallway. "It's quite quaint, I suppose. I'd have thought your publishers would put you up somewhere nicer than this, though. Surely a bestseller like you deserves a four-star hotel, at least."

Elly wasn't sure if that was a jibe at Wollstonecraft or herself. Probably both, knowing Jen.

"There's a lovely view of the moors out the back," she said.

Jen smiled but it seemed forced.

"Look, Jen, we talked about this. You didn't have to come here."

"Yes, I did. As usual, you've got Mum worried. And, as usual, I have to put her mind at ease." She stepped into the living room and spotted the murder board. "Well, I'll leave out the bit about you turning the place into a police incident room."

"It's just some notes." Elly put Jen's weekend case down in the hallway. "How about a cup of tea? You can tell me all about Trevor and the kids." Anything was better than having Jen quiz her about the investigation. Elly didn't want to reveal that the case she was working on—the "imaginary serial killer", as her mum had put it—was connected to a murder that had occurred last night or that the killer was anything but imaginary.

There was no need to worry Jen and worry her mum further. She intended to spend a day or two exchanging pleasantries with her sister before sending her home with the news that everything was okay and then getting stuck into the case again. In the meantime, she had to keep an eye on the news. The police hadn't identified the victim yet, or at least hadn't released her identity to the public. Once they did, Elly could explore any connections that might exist between her and the other girls.

Jen rolled her eyes. "Well, they break up from school in a couple of weeks so I'm going to be run off my feet. And Trevor tries his best, bless him, but this morning he didn't know that Wendy had to take her PE kit to school or even that William doesn't like cheddar on his sandwiches, only cheese slices. God knows how he's going to cope tomorrow morning without me there."

"Come in the kitchen and I'll put the kettle on," Elly suggested, wanting to break Jen's dispirited mood. The view of the moors should have the same effect on her as it had on Elly when she'd arrived here. She took the Hello Kitty umbrella from where it was dripping on the hallway carpet and placed it by the back door. "Come and see the view, Jen."

Jen followed her into the kitchen and looked out of the window at the moors and the distant hills while Elly filled the kettle.

"Well, what do you think?" Elly asked.

"It's all right if you like that sort of thing, I suppose."

"Bloody hell, Jen, what does it take to impress you?"

Jen frowned. "I'd rather see shops out of my window. This is all so"— she shrugged as if searching for the right word— "uncivilised."

Elly shook her head in disbelief. "Right, you and I are going on a hike this afternoon. We're going to get out there in the fresh air and see some natural beauty. Life isn't just about shopping and hairstylists and cheese slices, you know."

Jen peered dubiously at the sky. "It's raining."

"That's not going to stop us. I've got plenty of waterproof clothing and a spare pair of boots you can borrow. Come on, it'll be fun."

Jen pursed her lips and frowned. Elly knew this was the face her sister made when she was trying to think of a way out of something. Right now, that something was going for a walk. Finally, Jen said,

"Fine, we'll go. I suppose it'd be a shame to come all this way and not see the *natural beauty.*" She accompanied the last two words with a roll of her eyes.

"Great," Elly said, trying her best to ignore her sister's snarky attitude. "And when we get back, I'll make a lasagne and we can have it with some red wine." She forced a smile onto her face.

"When you say you'll make a lasagne, do you really mean you'll make it or just put it in the microwave?"

Elly struggled to keep the smile on her face. She felt it slipping. "Microwave. Some of us work, Jen. We can't spend all day cooking and being Mother of the Year."

"Oh, that's what you think, is it?" Jen said, whirling on her. "Well, let me tell you something. I'd rather spend my days cooking than searching for serial killers. You've got everyone worried sick. Before you go insulting me for trying to be a good mother, perhaps you should take a good look at yourself and your track record as a daughter."

"I'm only living my life the way I want," Elly argued.

"Well, so am I," Jen retorted.

"All right," Elly said, holding up her hands in surrender. "Point taken." Elly wished they could put this discussion behind them but it was one they'd had many times before and would probably have many times in the future. Elly agreed that both she and Jen should be able to live their lives how they wanted. She didn't want the lifestyle Jen led and Jen didn't want the lifestyle she enjoyed. The difference was that Elly kept her nose out of Jen's business but didn't get the same courtesy in return.

Jen didn't seem to want to end the discussion just yet. Her eyes still held the embers of smouldering anger. "It's just that you always—"

"I'll get the boots and walking gear," Elly said, ignoring her. "If we leave now, we should be able to beat the thunderstorm that's forecast for later."

"Thunderstorm?" Jen's expression shifted from anger to concern. "We can't go out if there's a storm coming."

Elly laughed. She had no idea what the weather forecast was for later. There had been a storm last night but as far as she knew, there wasn't one on its way today. She'd just wanted to wind her sister up.

Jen saw the look of mischief in her sister's eyes and realised Elly was kidding. "Oh, right, very funny." She began to laugh as well.

"You should have seen your face," Elly said.

"Well, it's hard to tell when you're joking. You're always so sombre."

"Sombre? Really?" That took Elly by surprise. She'd always thought she was a fairly carefree person. Yes, she'd had some problems lately but she was generally happy, wasn't she?

"Yes, really," Jen said. "Come on, if we're going to

do this, let's get going. We can have that cup of tea when we get back."

"You're eager—I like that," Elly said, going into the dining room and getting the map off the table.

"Not eager, just desperate to get this over with." Jen snatched the map off Elly. "And I'll decide where we're going, okay? If it was left up to you, we'd end up on a twenty-mile trek."

"No," Elly said. "I know where we're going. And don't worry; it isn't a long walk at all. I'll drive there and you can navigate. You do know how to read a map, don't you?"

"Oh, please," Jen protested. "If our time in Girl Scouts taught me anything, it was how to read a map."

"And how to kiss a boy," Elly said. "Do you remember that time we went camping in Wales and you hooked up with that local boy? What was his name?"

"Robby Jones," Jen said. "Ugh, don't remind me. And I didn't hook up with him. It was just a friendly kiss goodnight."

Elly laughed. "Okay, whatever you say. I'll go get the stuff from the car." She went outside and walked around Jen's black SUV to get to her Mini. She found the spare boots and jacket in the boot and bundled them under her arm.

The rain had eased off and was now no more than a light drizzle. Last night, Windrider Cottage had earned its name. Elly had barely slept and had lain in bed listening to the gale buffet the cottage from all sides. Whoever had built the cottage had obviously predicted the kind of beating it would get from the weather and had used the strongest building materials available. This morning, there wasn't so much as a roof tile out of place.

Elly went back inside, determined to have a good time with her sister despite her differences.

Jen had the map spread out on the kitchen counter and was inspecting it doubtfully. "Look, Elly, I don't think I can manage a hike up a hill. I'm already exhausted just thinking about hiking."

"No hills," Elly promised. "We're going to be walking across a moor. Nice flat terrain. And there's a stone circle. We can just walk to that and then back to the car."

"All right," Jen said, "As long as it isn't too far."

Ten minutes later, they were both dressed in walking gear and in the Mini. When Elly started the engine, the radio came on. When she'd arrived in the Peak District, she'd tuned it to Peak FM, the local station. Now, she switched it off. She desperately wanted to hear the news in case there were any developments in the case of the body on Blackden Edge but she didn't want Jen to hear about the body and get worried.

If Jen knew the serial killer was still at large, she'd

probably refuse to leave the cottage until Elly returned to Birmingham with her.

"Can't we have some music on?" Jen asked.

"You need to concentrate on the map."

"I can multitask, you know."

"Here, find some music on my phone. It's Bluetooth." She turned the stereo back on and hit the button that connected the stereo to her phone.

Jen eyed her suspiciously for a moment. But then she turned her attention to the phone and scrolled through the music.

Elly started the car and reversed onto the main road before heading south.

Jen looked up from the phone. "Elly, you do know there are albums which were recorded since the eighties, right?"

Elly shrugged. "I like what I like."

Jen sighed. "Let's put the radio on." She reached forward and pushed the Radio button. Peak FM filled the car. Elly didn't recognise the music. As Jen had pointed out, her musical tastes were stuck in the past. Jen seemed to recognise the song and sang along absent-mindedly as she checked the map on her lap.

The radio stations broadcasted the news every hour on the hour. According to the dashboard clock, there were still forty minutes to go until the next broadcast. As long as they got to Stanton Moor before then, the news wouldn't be an issue. By the time it came on, they'd be walking on the moors and

Jen would have no idea about the body that had been found a few miles north of here.

Elly felt as if she were in a bad sitcom, trying to hide the news from someone—with hilarious consequences. Except this was real life and there were no hilarious consequences, only guilt and dishonesty. And how long did she think she could hide something like this from her sister? The story had already hit the national news. Jen was bound to find out.

She took a deep breath and said, "Jen, there's something I need to tell you. But you can't let it worry you, okay? And no matter what you say, I'm staying here and finding out what happened to those girls."

Jen gazed at her steadily for a moment before saying, "Do you mean the body the police found last night?"

"You know about that?"

"It was all over the radio when I was driving up here."

"So why didn't you mention it?"

"I wanted to see if you'd mention it first."

Elly pursed her lips to stop herself from saying something driven by the aggravation she felt, something she'd later regret. She didn't like being tested. *Let it go*, she told herself. *You're going to be nice to Jen even if it kills you.*

"Don't give me the silent treatment now," Jen said.

"No, I'm fine," Elly said, keeping her voice even. She nodded at the map. "You know where we are?"

"Of course. I told you—Girl Scout training."

They arrived at the edge of Stanton Moor fifteen minutes later. An area of packed dirt by the side of the road served as the parking area. Elly guided the Mini onto it and killed the engine. The road was bordered by a high hedge but a gap had been cut to allow access to the moor. A path led through the moor and a signpost bore the legend: NINE LADIES STONE CIRCLE.

Elly peered at the gap in the hedge and wondered if a killer had carried the lifeless body of Lindsey Grofield through that gap eighteen years ago on a cold and dark New Year's Eve. Or had Lindsey still been alive, forced to walk across the moors at knifepoint to the stone circle where she met her fate?

This was all speculation, of course. Just because the passage in the journal contained the capitalised word Ladies didn't necessarily mean it referred to the Nine Ladies. The capital L might even be a mistake. Elly doubted that, though. The writer of the journal seemed to choose his words carefully. She couldn't imagine him capitalising a word by mistake.

"Are we going to do this, then?" Jen asked with a sigh of resignation.

"Yes," Elly said, trying to sound upbeat. The truth was, she didn't know what she was going to do if she found a "grave of daisies" at the stone circle.

Call the police? Tell Mitch to bring shovels? And even if there were daisies growing at the Nine Ladies, it didn't really mean anything. Daisies grew everywhere.

She opened her door and got out, going to the back of the car to get her boots and jacket. Jen did the same. When they were dressed appropriately, Elly slung her camera around her neck and said, "Let's go."

They stepped through the gap in the hedge and began walking along the path that cut through the purple heather. The landscape was rugged and flat, dotted here and there with boulders. Elly could see a village in the distance but there was a feeling of isolation on the moor that was amplified by seeing how far away the closest buildings were. If Lindsey Grofield had screamed out here, no one would have heard her.

Stop being morbid, Elly told herself mentally.

They'd been trudging across the moor for ten minutes when Jen said, "Can we go back now? My feet hurt."

"Jen, we haven't even walked a mile yet. You can't be tired already."

"It's these boots. They're too tight."

"No, they're not. We're both the same size. They fit perfectly. Come on, stop complaining. We can rest when we get to the stone circle."

Jen rolled her eyes. "How much farther is it?"

"You see those birch trees up ahead? I think it's

in there." The closer they got to the trees, the more anticipation Elly felt building up inside her. What if she was right about the journal entry and Lindsey Grofield really was buried there? The fact that she'd discovered one of the girls' graves would be a huge selling point for the book. Glenister would never belittle her again.

But more importantly than that, Lindsey Grofield would finally be found after all these years. Her family would get some closure. She could be given a decent burial and laid to rest in a real grave, not some hole where her killer had dumped her. She deserved a proper headstone, not just a patch of daisies to mark her final resting place.

"I'm hungry," Jen said.

Elly sighed. "It's like hiking with a five-year-old."

"Well, I can't help it. I was on the road all morning and then you dragged me out here without a bite to eat."

Elly stopped walking and took the keys to the Mini out of her jacket pocket. "Here are the car keys. If you want, you can go back and wait in the car. But I have to see the stone circle, okay? Now, are you coming or not?"

Jen hesitated. She glanced at the keys dangling from Elly's fingers, then back along the path to the gap in the hedge. She narrowed her eyes and turned to Elly with a look of suspicion. "Why is the stone circle so important to you? Is it something to do with that serial killer?"

"Maybe," Elly admitted. "I don't know yet."

Jen's eyes widened again. "What is it? What's up there?" She turned to examine at the trees in the distance.

"I think it's possible that he may have buried one of his victims there."

"Really?"

Elly nodded. "It's just a theory."

"Well, come on then, let's find out." Jen went marching along the path towards the trees.

Elly caught up with her. If she'd known getting Jen to the Nine Ladies easily was simply a case of involving her in the investigation, she'd have done it ages ago and saved herself a lot of frustration.

"What are we looking for?" Jen asked as they reached the tall birch trees. "Some kind of grave marker? A symbol etched on a tree trunk?" She sounded genuinely excited and seemed to have forgotten all about her hunger and tight boots.

"A grave of daisies," Elly said.

"A grave of daisies? What does that mean?"

"I think he marked the grave with daisies."

"But there are daisies everywhere," Jen said, pointing out an abundance of daisies flourishing in the woods.

"The ones we're looking for are within sight of

the stone circle," Elly said. "A grave of daisies in a glade watched over by the Ladies."

Jen arched a quizzical eyebrow. "What does that mean?" A worried expression crossed her face. "Elly, has the killer been communicating with you?"

"No," Elly said. "Not directly, anyway." She couldn't tell Jen about the journal because to do so would break the trust Mitch had placed in her. She saw the Nine Ladies ahead, a circle of stones standing in a clearing ringed by trees. Elly walked into the circle and scanned the surrounding area, searching for a grave of daisies. All she could see were trees and undergrowth. There were daisies in the woods, little white star clusters in the undergrowth, but there was nothing to discern one patch from another.

The Nine Ladies themselves were no more than hip-height and the stone circle was built on a low mound. The fact that these stones had been placed here before recorded history amazed Elly, but she wasn't in the right frame of mind to dwell on it now. She had to know if Lindsey Grofield's grave was here somewhere.

"Do you see anything?" Jen asked.

Elly continued scanning the woods. Seeing nothing out of the ordinary, she walked out of the circle along the circular edge of the woods, peering between the trees. Maybe you had to be at a certain vantage point to see the grave and unless she was standing in the right spot, she would miss it.

Or maybe there wasn't a grave here at all.

Jen was exploring the woods as well now, winding her way between the trees and checking the ground in front of her every few steps.

I looked upon a grave of daisies

In a glade watched over by the Ladies

The verse sprang into Elly's mind. She pushed it away, annoyed at its obscurity.

"Wait a minute," she told Jen. "We're looking for a glade. Trying to find the daisies themselves is too difficult but the ones we need to find are in a glade. Surely that will narrow things down a bit." She couldn't see any glades in the area she was exploring so she turned and examined the trees on the far side of the circle.

There was an area within the woods there that seemed to be brightly lit by the sun. Could it be a glade? She strode back over the Bronze Age mound and into the woods. Jen followed silently.

When Elly reached the trees, she could see the brightly lit area more clearly. It could be described as a glade even though it was no more than a circular clearing less than twenty feet in diameter. The sunlight shafted down onto long grass and a patch of daisies.

But this was no ordinary wild patch of daisies. The little flowers had been planted purposefully in an oblong shape that was a couple of feet wide and eight feet long. The exact dimensions of a grave. The shape was rough and would probably appear natural to a casual observer but to Elly, who was looking for it and knew the journal's verse, there was no mistaking that this was the daisy grave.

"Oh, my God," Elly whispered.

"This is it," Jen said. "This has to be it."

Elly's mind began to race. What should she do next? Call the police? Call Mitch? The police would ask too many questions and Mitch wasn't answering his phone. Deciding to try Mitch again anyway, she took her phone out of her pocket. No damned signal. Typical.

"Are you calling the police?" Jen asked.

"I'm not calling anyone. I haven't got a signal."

Jen checked her own phone. "Me either." She stared at the grave of daisies. "Elly, who's buried under there?"

"I think it's a girl named Lindsey Grofield. She went missing on New Year's Eve, 1999."

"She's been under there for eighteen years?"

Elly nodded. "Come on, we need to get back to the car. I'll just get a couple of pictures and then we're out of here." She unslung the camera and took half a dozen shots of the daisies. Then she put the camera back around her neck and began retracing her steps through the woods to the path.

A couple of minutes later, when they were

walking back across the moors, Elly got a signal on her phone. She called Mitch's number but still got no answer. They'd agreed to share any information they discovered with each other but the fact that he wasn't answering his phone was putting her in a difficult position. She knew where Lindsey's grave was and that was knowledge that had to be acted upon. Calling the police meant betraying Mitch's trust but what choice did she have? She couldn't let Lindsey spend another night in that grave, another night lost from the world. She had to do the right thing. For Lindsey's sake.

"What's wrong?" Jen asked.

"I need to call the police," Elly said, reaffirming her decision to herself.

"What's wrong with that?"

"I promised someone I wouldn't do that without speaking to him first. He needs to find his sister and he's afraid that if the police get involved, he'll lose his chance."

"That's ridiculous. The police need to handle this."

"I know," Elly said.

"So call them. Or do you want me to do it?"

"I'll do it." As she found the number for the Buxton police station and dialled it, Elly still couldn't help but feel as if she were betraying Mitch.

When her call was answered, she gave her name and said she thought she knew where the body of a missing girl was buried. She was asked to hold while she was transferred to the correct department.

After a minute's wait, during which Elly wasn't sure if she'd been disconnected, a woman's voice answered. "Hello, Miss Cooper, this is DS Morgan speaking. Apparently, you might know where a missing girl can be found, is that correct?"

"Yes, that's right."

"And what girl is this? Do you know her name?"

"Lindsey Grofield. She went missing on New Year's Eve 1999."

There was a slight pause, then, "And you know her whereabouts?"

"I know where she's buried, yes."

"Just a moment, please."

Elly heard the phone being covered, probably by the police officer's hand. DS Morgan's voice was muffled when she spoke again but Elly could still make out what she was saying. "guv, I've got someone on the line who says she knows where Lindsey Grofield is buried."

A gruff male voice said, "Bloody hell. Get the details. As if we haven't got enough on our plate."

The hand was removed and DS Morgan said to Elly, "Where is she buried, Miss Cooper?"

"The Nine Ladies stone circle. I'm telling you the truth. That man seems to think I'm lying."

"Miss Cooper, you have to understand, Lindsey Grofield has been missing for eighteen years. How do you know the location of her body? Are you involved in her disappearance in any way?"

"What? No! I'm telling you where she is. You need to get people here with digging tools. That girl needs you."

"Are you at the Nine Ladies now?"

"Yes."

"Miss Cooper, please don't go anywhere. We'll be there shortly."

"All right. Fine." Elly ended the call, even though DS Morgan was about to say something else. She understood that the police got crank calls all the time and they were probably under pressure because of the body they'd found on Blackden Edge last night, but she thought they'd jump at the chance to finally find Lindsey.

She jammed the phone back into her pocket.

"What did they say?" Jen asked.

"I don't think they believed me."

"Are they coming?"

"Yes, apparently. We'll wait in the car." She wasn't sure now if she'd done the right thing by calling the police. What if they thought she was crazy and refused to dig up the grave of daisies? What if they didn't even investigate the area and left Lindsey there?

Elly glanced over her shoulder at the woods and made a mental promise to Lindsey Grofield. *I'll dig you up myself if I have to.*

24

DISCOVERY

The first thing Mitch became aware of was a series of beeping sounds. It was a sound he knew well after spending many days and nights beside his mother's hospital bed. She'd been hooked up to various machines and all of them had emitted beeps and alarms of some kind. He'd wondered how nurses could put up with hearing that noise all the time.

He opened his eyes and discovered that he was in a hospital bed. The machines were attached to him. He tried to sit up and felt a burning sensation in his side. Groaning, he sank back against the pillows. The machines beeped more urgently.

A dark-haired nurse came into the room, a look of concern in her eyes. She grabbed a clipboard from the foot of the bed and began writing as she consulted the readouts on the machines. "How are you feeling, Mr. Walker?"

"My head is pounding. Where am I?"

"You're in Manchester Royal. You were brought here by an ambulance. You've been stabbed but the blade didn't penetrate too deeply. The doctor is more concerned with the bump on your head. Do you remember anything about that?"

Mitch recalled the intruder at Edge House. He remembered crawling across the kitchen floor to his phone and calling someone for help. "I remember," he said.

"Well, the police will want to speak with you about that. But there's someone here who's been waiting for you to wake up. If she hadn't called the ambulance, you probably wouldn't be here with us now. I'll just go and get her." She replaced the clipboard and left the room.

Mitch wondered if Jess had somehow heard about what had happened and was here with Leigh. But when the nurse returned, the woman accompanying her wasn't his ex-wife or daughter.

Mitch frowned, confused. "Tilly. How?"

His cousin smiled and came over to the side of the bed. "You rang me, asking for help. You sounded like you were in an awful state so I called an ambulance and drove over to Edge House. Don't you remember? You regained consciousness for a while when you were being put into the ambulance."

"No, I don't remember. The last thing I

remember is talking to a woman while I was lying on the kitchen floor."

She nodded. "That was me."

Mitch couldn't remember putting Tilly's number in his phone. As far as he knew, her number was only written on the card she'd given him at the bank. How had he managed to call her? "I don't understand," he said.

The nurse smiled at him. "You might be feeling a bit groggy because of the drugs. The doctor will be along shortly and he'll explain everything to you." She left the room again.

Mitch looked at Tilly. "Did they catch the person who stabbed me? I think he's involved in Sarah's disappearance."

She shook her head. "No, not yet. I don't think they've got anything to go on. You're the only witness, Mitch, and you haven't been able to give them a description yet."

"I don't know what he looks like. He was wearing a ski mask."

Her face fell slightly. "Oh, well that's a shame. Why do you think he had something to do with Sarah?"

Mitch wasn't going to tell her about the journal or that he thought his father had been murdered. So he just shrugged and said, "I don't know."

She eyed him closely as if trying to decide if he was confused or lying. She seemed to shrug off the answer. "Is there anyone you'd like me to call? What about your daughter?"

"My phone," Mitch said, trying to sit up and again experiencing the burning sensation in his side.

"It's okay, you lie back. Your phone's right here." She picked it up from the bedside table and handed it to him.

Mitch keyed in the passcode and checked his phone calls. The last call he'd made was to "Aunt Tilly." He smiled to himself. Leigh had obviously put Tilly's number into his contact list. He found Jess on the list and rang her. There was no answer. He hung up when his call went to voicemail.

"Is there anything I can get you?" Tilly asked. "I think they're going to keep you in here for a while. If you want me to go to Edge House and get your pyjamas, toiletries, or anything, just ask."

"That would be great, thanks," he said. A thought occurred to him. "Tilly, how did you get into Edge House? Did you go through the garden gate and the back door?"

"No, I've got a key. I've had it for years, since before I had trouble with Mum and Dad. It's been sitting in a drawer at home, gathering dust. When I knew you were in trouble, I grabbed it and drove over to the house." She looked sheepish. "Sorry, I suppose I should have given you the key now that it's your house."

Mitch ignored her comment about the key. He

was more interested in what trouble she'd had with her parents. He still wasn't sure that Silas was innocent, despite the man being confined to a wheelchair. And Alice was a real piece of work. Mitch wouldn't put anything past her. "What trouble with your parents?" he asked.

Tilly shrugged. "Oh, you know, the usual. They didn't approve of me having Faith."

Mitch frowned in confusion. Was she saying Silas and Alice didn't approve of her being religious in some way? "Faith?"

"My daughter, Faith. I was twenty-two when I had her, but Mum and Dad acted as if I was fifteen and had got knocked up at school. They practically disowned me, told me I was bringing disgrace to the family." She shook her head at the memory. "They said it was because I wasn't married but I think really it's because Faith was a girl. Mum and Dad don't like girls." She let out a humourless laugh. "You only have to compare how they treat Jack to how they treat me to realise that."

"I didn't know you were badly treated," Mitch said.

Tilly smiled but it appeared more like a grimace. "It wasn't too bad. I suppose I should think myself lucky. The other young Walker women have had it worse; they've all vanished."

Mitch sat up, ignoring the pain that flared in his side. "Tilly, what was my father like?"

She considered that for a moment. "I think he was a good man. It's a shame you didn't get to know him. He really helped me when I fell out with my parents."

"How did he help you?"

She shrugged. "He was just there, a shoulder to cry on. He listened, which was more than my mum and dad ever did. They treated me like I was stupid. When I was younger, I used to dream of running away and starting a new life in London. I should have done it. Not that they would have cared."

"But Michael was different," Mitch said, bringing the conversation back to his father. He wanted to know more about him, wanted to see if Tilly would let slip that she knew Michael was a killer. Had she known? Had Michael confided in her? Maybe she'd seen something that had made her suspicious.

"Yes, he was different," she said. "He cared about other people. After you and your mother left, Uncle Michael spiralled into a depression for a while. He cut himself off from the rest of the family and became reclusive. He barely left Edge House except on rare occasions when he'd go outdoors to sketch or paint. He became obsessed with finding out what had happened to Sarah. I think he thought that if he could solve the case of her disappearance, you and your mum would come back to Edge House and you'd all be a family again."

"That doesn't sound like he cared about other people," Mitch said. "Only that he cared about getting what he wanted. When my mum took me away, she was terrified. I think she was terrified of him."

Tilly let out a sigh that seemed borne of exasperation. "Mitch, you've got the wrong idea about your dad. Honestly, he was a caring guy. Every time I went to visit him, he asked me about Silas. He wanted to know all about his brother even though he'd cut all ties with him. He was interested in his family."

That caught Mitch's attention. Had his father been asking about Silas because he wanted to know about his brother's welfare, or for some other reason? "What kind of things did he ask you?"

"All kinds of things. Where Silas had been recently. If he'd painted anything new. Whether he'd been out of the house or stayed indoors. I told him my dad's life was mostly regimented but Uncle Michael wanted to know all the details anyway. He liked hearing everything. I suppose it was the only way he knew to connect with his brother since they'd gone their separate ways."

"You said my dad asked if Silas had painted anything new. I didn't realise he was a painter."

"Of course he is. The artistic streak runs in the family. Don't you remember when we were kids and our parents took us on field trips to paint landscapes?"

"No," Mitch admitted.

She grinned. "They used to take us up to Dark Peak and we'd all have our easels and watercolours. You, me, Sarah, and Jack. I'm sure my dad kept those paintings. They're probably still at Blackmoor House, in the attic most likely. That's probably for the best, I'm sure they're quite horrendous." She laughed lightly.

Mitch tried to take in this new information. If Silas was an artist, could the journal have been written and illustrated by him? But it still didn't make sense that he could be the Blackden Edge Murderer. He'd been wheelchair-bound since the quarry accident in 1977. He couldn't have abducted and murdered Sarah or Lindsey Grofield. Not without help, anyway. He hadn't been in his wheelchair when Olivia went missing but he had a rock-solid alibi for that night; he'd been drinking in the Mermaid pub with his wife and father.

Silas and Michael could have been working together, Mitch supposed, but it sounded as if they'd had nothing to do with each other for years.

He took a deep breath and let it out slowly. He wondered if he'd ever unravel the mystery of Sarah's disappearance. The journal had given him hope but now that hope had been snatched away.

"Tilly, do you know anything about a journal? I

think it was my dad's. He might have kept it in the safe at Edge House." He watched her closely for some sort of reaction but she was either good at hiding her emotions or the journal didn't mean anything to her at all.

"Journal?" she said. "No, I don't think so. I don't remember seeing your dad with a journal. That's more *my* dad's thing."

"Your dad keeps a journal?"

She nodded. "Always has. Mum and Jack too. It was a big thing in our house when I was growing up. I only stopped a few years ago and that was only because I couldn't find the time to keep filling it in."

"But your dad still keeps a journal?"

"As far as I know," Tilly said.

Mitch's mind began sorting through the information, trying to arrange it into a logical pattern. If Silas kept a journal out of habit, didn't it make sense that he'd journal everything he did, including visiting the graves of dead girls? But if the journal belonged to Silas, how had Mitch's father gained possession of it and locked it in his safe deposit box?

Mitch reassessed everything he knew from a different angle. He'd been working on the assumption that his father was guilty of murder. But what if his father had been innocent? Tilly said he'd tried to find out what had happened to Sarah. Had he come upon some clue that led him to suspect Silas? Had he somehow managed to get his hands on the journal by nefarious means? Had he been trying to decode it just as Mitch had been?

But how would he even know of its existence? Michael had no way of knowing that Silas had written a journal that contained clues to the locations of the missing girls' graves.

"Mitch, are you okay?" Tilly asked.

He realised he'd been staring into space while his mind worked overtime. And his mental gymnastics were all for nothing. He had no way of knowing how his father had come across the journal, assuming he hadn't written it himself. Mitch felt like he was trying to solve a complicated mathematical equation but that half the equation was missing, rendering the entire thing meaningless.

"I'm fine," he said. "If I give you a list of things, could you get them for me from the house? I'd really appreciate it."

"Of course, I said I would. Just let me know what you need."

Five minutes later, after Tilly had left the room, Mitch tried Jess's number. There was still no answer. *Probably in a meeting at work*, he told himself. He hung up and dialled Elly's number. He should probably tell her what had happened to him since he'd agreed to share information with her. At least he could tell her that her assumption was correct, the killer—or at least his accomplice—was still at large. He had the stab wound to prove it.

She answered immediately. "Mitch, where are you?"

"I'm in the hospital in Manchester."

"What? What happened?"

"Somebody broke into Edge House last night and attacked me." He lowered his voice. "They took the journal."

"Oh, shit," she said. "Are you all right?"

"I've been better but I'll survive."

"Have you heard the news?"

"What news?"

"I found Lindsey Grofield's grave. The police are digging it up right now. They haven't told me much but I've seen them load a body bag into their van."

"Where are you?"

"A place called Stanton Moor. There's a stone circle here called the Nine Ladies. I figured out a piece of the journal. I found the grave of daisies."

"'I looked upon a grave of daisies in a glade watched over by the Ladies,'" Mitch recited.

"Yes, that one. Mitch, I found her. I found Lindsey." She sounded both upset and elated at the same time.

Mitch felt his heart sink. He had always known that there was no way Sarah was still alive, but now that Lindsey had been found in a grave of daisies, just as the journal had described, it brought home the fact that somewhere out there was a grave of forget-me-nots in which Sarah was lying.

Would the police soon be exhuming her remains, putting them into a body bag, and loading them into a van? It would mean the end of a thirty-years' search but it wasn't an end Mitch looked forward to facing.

He knew that facing it would be for the best, though. A worse ending would be to never find the grave of forget-me-nots and never know for certain what had happened to his sister.

"Listen," he said, "I've been thinking. What if Michael was innocent? I think the journal might belong to Silas and my dad somehow got his hands on it."

"Speaking of the journal," Elly said, "I'm going to have to tell the police about it, Mitch."

He sighed in resignation. He'd hoped to keep the journal a secret from the police, at least until he'd used it to find Sarah, but that was impossible now. He supposed that since the journal was back in the hands of the killer, it didn't really matter anyway. "It's okay. It's either that or tell them you're psychic."

"Yeah, there's a DCI here who wants to know how the hell I pinpointed the location of Lindsey's body. Of course, he isn't saying it's Lindsey but I think we all know it is."

"Is it Battle?"

"That's right," she said. "DCI Battle. He's a grumpy old sod."

Mitch grinned. "His day probably just got a lot busier."

Elly gasped as if suddenly realising something. "Of course, you don't know about the body they found last night, do you?"

"What body?"

"They just released her name an hour ago. It's a girl named Rhonda Knowles. They found her body at Blackden Edge. She'd been strangled and slashed with a knife."

"Just like Josie Wagner," he said.

"Yeah, just like Josie."

Mitch's hand instinctively went to the bandage that covered the wound in his side. He wondered if the knife that had sliced into his flesh was the same knife that had been used to kill a woman at Blackden Edge hours earlier.

25

FROM THE GRAVE

"I don't know if I should take you to the station and interview you under caution or just take a statement from you now," DCI Battle said to Elly. He was standing next to her Mini, his manner gruff. Elly and Jen were leaning against the car, watching police personnel teeming over the moors.

"There's no need to take me to the station," Elly said. "I have an alibi for New Year's Eve, 1999. I was at a night club in Birmingham celebrating the arrival of the new millennium. In fact, my sister was with me. Do you remember that night, Jen? You were off your face by midnight." She was beginning to regret letting the police in on this. But she couldn't think like that. Lindsey had been found. That was all that mattered.

Battle grimaced. "All right, there's no need to be smart-arsed about it. I know who you are. Working on a new book, aren't you? That's what Gordon Farley told me, anyway. So how did your research lead you here?" He indicated the moor with a wave of his hand.

Elly decided the best way to deal with Battle was just to tell him the truth. He looked like the type of man who valued honesty and wouldn't stand for anything less. "I deciphered a clue in a journal," she told him.

Battle appeared lost for words. His forehead furrowed and he stared at Elly for a moment before asking his next question very slowly, as if he were trying to control his emotions. "What bloody journal?"

"Mitch found it in his dad's safe deposit box. At first, it seemed like nothing more than a journal of walks in the countryside with drawings but it actually describes the graves the girls are buried in. The poem that was sent to the police after Lindsey disappeared contained lines from the journal."

"Why am I only hearing about this now?" Battle asked no one in particular. He gazed up at the grey sky and let out a long breath. When he looked at Elly again, his eyes were steely. "Right, where's this journal? I want it."

"It's gone," she said. "The intruder that broke into Edge House last night stole it."

"Of course he did," Battle said, throwing up his hands in frustration. "Why should I have expected anything else? The only piece of concrete evidence we might have had to put the bastard away has been stolen, probably by the murderer himself."

Elly shrugged. She could understand Battle's frustration but there was nothing she could do or say to alleviate it. The journal was gone and there was nothing she could do about it.

The understanding she felt for Battle paled in comparison to the sympathy she felt for Mitch. The detective had lost a piece of evidence but the journal had been Mitch's only chance to find his sister. There was no question who had lost the most when it had been stolen.

A female detective with long dark hair, who had been leaning on a green Range Rover talking into a phone, shouted to Battle, "The preliminary lab reports on Miss Knowles are ready, guv."

Battle nodded to her. "Right," he said to Elly and Jen. "You two go back to your cottage and stay there. I'll send an officer around to get your statement. I don't want either of you to leave the area for a while. At least not until I've gotten to the bottom of this journal business."

"But I'm supposed to go home tomorrow," Jen protested. "I have a husband and kids."

"Jen had nothing to do with this," Elly said. "I just brought her along for the ride. She didn't know anything about the grave and she's never seen the journal."

Battle inspected each sister in turn, his eyes narrowed. Then he said to Jen, "When I've reviewed your statement, I'll decide if you can go home yet or not. All right?"

Jen nodded meekly.

"Until then, stay put," Battle said, turning to the Range Rover. He walked a few steps and then turned back to Elly and Jen. "And be careful. There's a murderer out there somewhere." He resumed his walk to the Range Rover and got into the driver's side, saying something to the dark-haired detective, who was already in the passenger seat, before starting the engine and tearing off up the road.

"He has to let me go home," Jen said, a note of concern in her voice. "He can't keep me here."

"That was all bluster," Elly assured her as she got into the Mini. "Don't worry, you'll see Trevor and the kids tomorrow."

Jen climbed in next to her and said, "You really shouldn't have gotten me involved in all this, Elly."

Elly started the engine. "I had no idea we were going to find that grave. It was a long shot."

"But now we have found it and I'm mixed up in all of this." Jen turned her face away from Elly and stared out of her window silently.

Elly put the Mini into gear and guided it past the police cars and vans parked on both sides of the road. The police had closed the road to the public and, after driving for a couple of minutes, Elly saw a group of uniformed officers keeping members of the public and press on the other side of a length of police tape that had been stretched across the road.

Elly slowed the car, surprised that the gathered crowd was so large. She could see vans bearing the logos of several news channels and there were reporters talking to various cameras, positioning themselves so that the police cordon was visible in the background of their shot.

The uniformed officers waved Elly through and removed the tape to let her pass. As soon as she was on the other side of the cordon, reporters flocked to the Mini, shoving their microphones at the windows and gesturing for Elly to roll the windows down. Some of them stood in front of the car, slowing Elly's progress. She kept moving forward slowly enough not to kill anyone but fast enough to make it clear she wasn't going to stop.

One of the reporters shouted, "Aren't you the writer Elly Cooper? Is this something to do with the Eastbourne Ripper?" She indicated to her camerawoman to point the lens at Elly. Then she asked, "Miss Cooper, what can you tell us about what the police found on the moors? Is it one of the Ripper's victims?" and pointed her microphone at Elly's window.

Elly recognised the blonde reporter as Jillian Street, a freelancer who, when Elly had been interviewing Leonard Sims, had knocked on Elly's front door and pointed a camera in her face, trying to get a scoop on what the Eastbourne Ripper was telling the only person he'd let inside his mind.

Elly had told her to get the hell off her property before she called the police and had only seen Jillian Street one more time since then, when the reporter had turned up at a book signing in Manchester and asked Elly what information the Ripper had divulged that hadn't made it into the book. Did Elly know where some of his undiscovered victims' remains were buried?

Despite wanting to get past the throng of reporters as quickly as possible and despite her reluctance to give Jillian Street a story, Elly had to let Street know that there was more to who she was and what she did than just the Eastbourne Ripper. Her life and career wasn't defined by a single case.

So she put her window down and said, "No, this has nothing to do with the Eastbourne Ripper. Some of us have moved on since then, Miss Street." She pressed the button that slid the window back up and stared dead ahead, gunning the engine slightly to warn the vultures in front of the car that they'd better get of the way or else.

They reluctantly stepped aside and she accelerated away.

When the reporters and their vehicles were nothing more than an indistinguishable dot of colour against the bleak landscape in the rear-view mirror,

Jen turned to Elly and said, "Why did you have to do that? Why did you have to speak to them?" She'd shrunk back into her seat and appeared more shaken by the experience of facing the cameras than that of finding a dead girl's grave.

"Ever since *Heart of a Killer* came out, everyone associates me with the Eastbourne Ripper. I don't want my name to be synonymous with Leonard Sims. I have to show the world that there's more to me than that. I refuse to be defined by that evil bastard. I want to put him behind me but I can't do that until everyone else lets me."

"Well, they'll let you do that now," Jen said. "You found that poor girl's grave."

"Yes," Elly said, feeling a sudden flood of emotion. Because of her, one of the lost ones was no longer lost. "Yes, I did." Her eyes blurred with tears and she pulled over to the side of the road. Killing the engine, she put her hands to her face and wept. She wasn't sure if she was crying with elation at finding Lindsey Grofield or with pity after seeing the place where the girl had lain, lost to the world, for eighteen years.

All she knew was that the emotions that had been building up inside her ever since she found out about the lost girls needed to be released.

Jen reached across and drew Elly into a hug. Saying nothing, she simply held her sister while Elly's raw emotions spilled out.

I CAN'T BELIEVE what I'm seeing on television. It makes my blood boil and my skin prickle with rage. According to the news, the police have found a body at Blackden Edge. They say the girl, named Rhonda Knowles, was found there last night. She's been strangled and slashed with a knife.

This can't be. Is someone playing with me? Taunting me?

I was nowhere near Blackden Edge last night and I've never heard of Rhonda Knowles. She isn't one of my girls. So why has she been left at the Edge in the same sorry state in which I left Josie Wagner all those years ago?

If I was at home right now, I might put a fist through the television, so angry has the newscast made me. But I'm not at home, I'm in the cafe in Matlock and the television is bolted high on the wall behind the serving counter. I'm not the only customer watching the screen; the discovery of a body so close to here has everyone enthralled.

An old woman sitting in the booth opposite catches my eye. "It's a travesty," she says. "No one deserves that."

"She certainly didn't," I say. I realise I'm holding the handle of my teacup so tightly that it might break. I loosen my grip and force myself to breathe deeply. The air smells of cooking oil and coffee. I try to focus on that and not on the scenes playing out on the screen, but the broadcast catches my attention as surely as a trap springing shut on a mouse.

The newsreader puts a finger to her ear for a moment and then says to the camera, "*We're getting reports that police in Derbyshire have now found a second body. Apparently this second body was found on the moors twenty-five miles South of Blackden Edge where Rhonda Knowles' body was discovered. We have this report from Jillian Street.*"

The screen changes to a view of the road near Stanton Moor. I know the road well but I've never seen it like this, with police vehicles and news vans parked everywhere. Half a dozen officers stand behind a police line, keeping reporters and local busybodies away.

A blonde woman is standing on the grass by the side of the road, a microphone in her hand as she talks to the camera. "*We're not exactly sure yet whose body the police have found on the moor situated behind me but we do know that a number of scenes of crime officers, or* SOCOs, *drove down this road an hour ago and have yet to emerge. A local helicopter pilot flew over the area half an hour ago and apparently he saw a number of officers digging in an area near a stone circle called the Nine Ladies.*"

I put the teacup down and grab the edge of the table, holding on tightly, feeling as if the cafe is tipping and rolling like a boat on a stormy sea. They've found Lindsey Grofield's grave. How can this be? And on the same day that they find a body at Blackden Edge, a murder victim who is nothing to do with me?

Mitch must have led the police to the grave. He has the journal, and the location of Lindsey's grave isn't too hard to figure out from my poetic little passage in there. I should have been more obtuse in my word choices but when I wrote about Lindsey, I was getting sloppy. The journal hadn't been seen by another living soul for over twenty-five years and I was overconfident. How was I to know Michael Walker would steal it from me eighteen years later? He's ruined everything.

Now his son has the journal and now Lindsey is no longer in her grave of flowers, a grave I have tended lovingly since burying her there.

On the television screen, a blue Mini can be seen driving out from behind the police cordon. The reporter rushes over to it and pushes her microphone at the driver's window. There's a redhead behind the wheel and a blonde in the passenger seat. Who are they? Did they stumble upon the grave by accident?

No, that's not possible.

The reporter seems to know who the driver is. She says, "*Aren't you the writer Elly Cooper? Is this something to do with the Eastbourne Ripper?*" The camera zooms in on the redhead and the reporter says, "*Miss Cooper, what can you tell us about what the police found on the moors? Is it one of the Ripper's victims?*" Again, she shoves her microphone at the car window.

I realise I've seen this woman before. She was at Edge House with Mitch, standing in the window as I watched her from the woods. I knew she was familiar. Elly Cooper, the writer. Has she seen my own writings in the journal? Did Mitch show it to her and she figured out my reference to the Ladies?

The car window opens and Elly Cooper looks directly at the camera, saying, "*No, this has nothing to do with the Eastbourne Ripper. Some of us have moved on since then, Miss Street.*" The window buzzes back up and she stares straight ahead, forcing her way through the other reporters.

As the Mini drives away, the camera again focuses on the reporter. "*Well, this is interesting. Elly Cooper, the author of* Heart of a Killer, *seems to have been at the site where the police discovered the body. Despite Miss Cooper's claims otherwise, this could mean that the body on the moors is a victim of Leonard Sims, the Eastbourne Ripper. It doesn't fit what we know of Sims because he buried his victims in the Eastbourne area but the presence of Elly Cooper is strong evidence that Sims wandered farther afield and buried one of his victims here in Derbyshire.*"

No. No, no, no, no. This won't do at all. Lindsey

Grofield was not the victim of a serial killer from Eastbourne. I gave her eternal rest from her cruel life and honoured her memory by giving her a grave of flowers. No one else is going to take the credit for that. The police have obviously allowed Elly Cooper onto their investigation. Is she some sort of psychologist? What does she know about me?

I get up from the table and walk unsteadily to the door. The air outside is cool and damp and for a moment it invigorates me. Then I remember that Lindsey is no longer where I put her and a wave of nausea creeps over me. I lean against the wall with one hand, causing a passer-by to ask me if I'm all right. I nod and stagger forward, making my way to the car.

By the time I get behind the wheel, I don't feel any better about the situation but I'm thinking more clearly. I have no idea how the body of a girl named Rhonda Knowles came to be at Blackden Edge but I do know that I didn't put it there. I can't worry about that now; it has nothing to do with my girls.

I feel rage and sadness that Lindsey has been taken from her grave but also a renewed sense of purpose.

Tonight, I'll drive to Manchester. There are plenty of girls there only too willing to get into my car, girls who are already lost to the world and won't be missed by anyone when they're gone.

The girl who gets into my car tonight will be

given a gift, something she won't be able to thank me for but something she longs for deep down inside without even realising it.

Her miserable life will end and she will know no more suffering.

26

THE VISIT

"You seem to be in quite good condition considering what you've been through," the doctor said, switching off the pen light he'd been shining into Mitch's eyes. "The wound in your side isn't deep at all. It's a good thing you were falling backwards at the time you were stabbed or we might be looking at something much more serious. You've suffered a concussion but there's no sign of brain injury."

"When can I get out of here?" Mitch asked. There was too much happening for him to be stuck in hospital. He wanted to talk to Elly about her conversation with the police. He wanted to talk to Battle about his investigation into the Blackden Edge Murderer. That investigation must surely be further along now that the police presumably had clues from Lindsey Grofield's body and the body of Rhonda Knowles.

He felt helpless lying here in a hospital bed in Manchester while everything was happening in Derbyshire. Apart from a headache and a slight burning pain in his side, he felt fine.

"I'd like to keep you in for at least another night," the doctor said. "I want to make sure you're fit and well before I send you home."

Mitch pursed his lips, considering his options. He wasn't sure he could stand being here all night. "What if I discharge myself?"

The doctor's face fell. "I would highly recommend you don't do that, Mr. Walker. Look, it's late afternoon already. All I'm asking is that you stay here tonight under observation. If you feel okay in the morning, you can leave then. How does that sound?"

Mitch thought about it. He supposed he could call Elly, and Battle was probably on his way here anyway. Hadn't the nurse said the police wanted to talk to him about what happened last night? He nodded slowly. "All right, I'll stay here tonight."

"Good. You won't regret it. It's better to be safe than sorry. I'll see you in the morning," the doctor said as he left the room.

Mitch turned his attention to the TV on the wall but there was no further news regarding the bodies yet, so he settled on a programme about cars and watched it half-heartedly while his thoughts revolved around the events of the night before.

He barely heard the knock at the door. Turning his attention from the TV, expecting to see Battle entering the room, he was surprised to see Silas wheeling through the door.

"Silas," he said, "what are you doing here?"

"I had an appointment with my consultant this afternoon," Silas said. "I ran into Tilly downstairs. She told me you were here. It sounds like you've had a bad time of it."

"It's not too bad," Mitch said. "Just a concussion, really."

Silas brought the wheelchair to a stop beside the bed. "Have they got any idea who did it?"

"I haven't spoken to the police yet. I'm sure they'll be coming to see me later."

"Well, hopefully they catch the bastard." He paused and then said, "Look, Mitch, I'm here because we started out on the wrong foot. I shouldn't have lost my temper the other day and for that, I apologise."

"It's fine," Mitch said. He wasn't sure if Silas was really here to apologise or if he was going to offer to buy Edge House again, but he realised he could use this opportunity to get a measure of his uncle. "Tilly was telling me that she doesn't have much contact with you and Alice anymore."

Silas shrugged. "That's true. You know how families are. Sometimes people just lose touch with each other." He looked closely at Mitch and said, "It's probably for the best, anyway."

"What do you mean by that?"

Silas looked towards the door, then back at Mitch. "All I'm saying is that Tilly is better off where she is, apart from the rest of the family."

"Why should she be better off?"

Silas looked at the open door again and Mitch followed his gaze. Alice and Jack were walking along the corridor towards the room.

"Listen," Silas said quickly. "Olivia and Sarah, our sisters, are in a better place. Don't go digging up things that are best left alone. Everyone is better off where they are right now."

"What do you mean by that?" Mitch asked, but Silas was already wheeling his way towards the door.

"Silas," Mitch said.

"Don't ask any more questions," Silas said.

Alice and Jack reached the door. They looked at Mitch in the bed but neither of them said anything.

"What are you doing here?" Alice asked Silas.

"I came to see the lad," Silas said, nodding towards Mitch.

"Well, come on now, we need to get going. I've got a meeting at the centre tonight."

"All right, all right," Silas said.

Jack took hold of the wheelchair's handles and pushed his father out into the corridor. Alice followed after giving Mitch a look of disdain.

Mitch watched them walk away down the corridor and then a realisation struck him.

Jack was limping.

27

CONNECTIONS

Battle didn't arrive at the hospital until the following morning. Mitch had spent a restless night unable to sleep, constantly checking the news on his phone to see if there was any more information about the bodies the police had found.

When Battle arrived at nine, Mitch was certain the detective had also had a sleepless night. His eyes were bloodshot and there was an air of weariness that seemed to follow him into the room.

"Mr. Walker," Battle said, "Good to see you're up and about."

Mitch had made an effort to get up earlier and sit on the chair next to the bed, believing his chances of being discharged were greater if he appeared fitter than he actually felt.

"It takes more than a stab wound and knock on the head to keep me down," he told Battle.

"Yes," the detective said, leaning against the wall. "So it seems. It also seems that you've been telling me lies. I had a chat with your friend Elly Cooper yesterday. She told me about a journal you found in your father's safe deposit box. Funny, but I don't recall you mentioning that to me, even when I specifically asked you if you had any information that would help my investigation."

"I didn't tell you because the journal seemed like nothing at first, just aimless ramblings set down on paper."

"But they weren't aimless ramblings, were they, sir? Those so-called ramblings led Miss Cooper to the grave of Lindsey Grofield. So I want to know everything about that journal. Everything that was written in it, every picture that was drawn on its pages, every comma and full stop."

Mitch sighed. "I'll tell you what I can remember but it isn't much."

Battle took a notepad from his coat pocket and flipped it open. "It's a shame you didn't tell me about the journal before, isn't it? We might still have it in our possession."

Mitch recounted what he could remember from the journal. Some of the lines came to him easily, but Battle already knew those bits and pieces because they'd been in the poem that had been sent to the police. When Mitch recalled something Battle wasn't already aware of, such as the descriptions of walks to visit flowers that were out of season, the detective scribbled notes on the pad.

Mitch could only describe the drawings in the simplest terms because he had no idea where the places that had been sketched were. He realised Battle would probably have identified every location instantly had he seen the sketches.

Of course if he'd told the detective about the journal, it would have been taken from him and locked up in an evidence room, but the journal was gone now, anyway. Any clues it held to Sarah's whereabouts were lost to him now.

When he'd told Battle everything he remembered about the journal, the detective questioned him about the intruder at Edge House, making Mitch go over every detail numerous times.

Finally, Battle seemed satisfied with Mitch's account of the attack "Is it all right with you if I send some officers over to search the garden? The knife may still be in the weeds somewhere. The intruder might not have been able to locate it in the dark. That's probably why he ran away and didn't stick around to finish you off. That and the fact that you'd called for help. For all he knew it was the police you were talking to and not just your cousin."

"There's something else," Mitch said. "It may be nothing but I think it's worth checking out."

"Go on," Battle said, pen poised over his notebook.

"I told you I hit the intruder in the leg with the vase. Last night, Silas came to see me here. He told me to stop digging into things that were best left alone. Anyway, Jack and Alice came to the room to collect him and I noticed that Jack was limping."

Battle raised an eyebrow. "Are you telling me that you believe the man who assaulted you at Edge House was your cousin, Jack Walker?"

"I don't know. It's possible, isn't it? I know he doesn't like me."

"Mr. Walker, there's one thing I know for sure. Unless Jack Walker has a time machine, he can't be responsible for what happened to the Hatton sisters, Olivia Walker, or Josie Wagner. He wasn't even a twinkle in his father's eye when those girls met their end. And although he was around when your sister was abducted, he's innocent of that as well, unless he was a criminal mastermind at the age of five."

"I know that," Mitch said, "but I've been thinking about something Silas said to me a few days ago. He said that Jack did everything Silas couldn't do for himself anymore. What if that includes murder? What if Silas is responsible for the older crimes and then Jack took over when his father was unable to carry on?"

"You think murder runs in the family, do you, sir?" Battle let out a tired sigh. "It's not impossible, I suppose. Silas could have groomed the lad to become a murderer from an early age but it's a lot of supposition. There's no proof for any of it and, besides, Silas has an alibi for his sister's abduction, remember? He was drinking in The Mermaid with his wife and father. None of them left the pub until closing time and by then, Olivia had vanished."

Mitch threw his hands up in frustration. "I don't know the answers to any of this, I'm just thinking out loud." None of this was leading him any closer to Sarah.

"All right, Mr Walker, there's no need to stress yourself out. You've probably struggled into that chair this morning so the doctor will discharge you but it looks to me like you need more rest. If you are discharged today, perhaps you should consider returning home to Leamington Spa instead of Edge House. I'll contact you if we find anything regarding your sister. There's nothing more you can do here."

Mitch wondered if the detective was right. He'd exhausted his resources where finding Sarah was concerned. The journal had been his single strand of hope and now it was gone. "What about Jack Walker's limp?" he asked.

Battle shrugged. "I'll speak to him but he'll probably say he was injured at the quarry or playing football, or even gardening. If he got that injury because you smashed him with a vase, he's not going to admit it." He put the notebook back into his coat pocket. "So do you want me to ask him about it?"

"No," Mitch said. "What's the point?"

"If we find that knife, we'll have something concrete to go on," Battle said, walking to the door. "In the meantime, think about what I said. There's nothing more you can do here. You've gone thirty years without looking for your sister's remains, so a bit longer shouldn't make that much of a difference."

Mitch watched the detective walk away down the corridor. He knew Battle was probably right; there was probably no point in going back to Edge House. For one thing, it seemed like everyone either had a key or was willing to break in. The house wasn't safe.

There was no way he could take Leigh there for the weekend, so he was going to have to return to Leamington Spa before Friday anyway.

And he had to be realistic about his chances of finding Sarah's grave. Without the journal, he had no clues, not even obscure ones.

As for Jack's limp, Battle was right; it could have come from anywhere.

The doctor came into the room, smiling. "How are we today, Mr. Walker?"

"I feel fine," Mitch lied, forcing a smile onto his own face.

The doctor looked at him closely. "Are you sure? It doesn't look like you slept very well. Are you in any pain?"

"Nothing a good night's sleep in my own bed won't cure," Mitch said. And the bed he had in mind was the one in his flat in Leamington Spa, not the bed in the sparse bedroom at Edge House.

"Well, I'll just give you a final examination and we'll see about getting you out of here."

AN HOUR LATER, Mitch was packing his things into a sports bag Tilly had used to bring them from Edge House. The TV was on, the volume turned down low. A morning show was being broadcast live. As he continued packing and half-listening to the TV, Mitch realized they were talking about the bodies recently discovered in Derbyshire. He found the remote and turned up the volume.

Sitting on the sofa with the presenters was a woman Mitch had seen before. She was some kind of psychologist and Mitch was sure he'd seen her on a programme about the Moors Murderers.

She was telling the presenters that the body of Rhonda Knowles wasn't the first to be found on Blackden Edge and that the body of a nurse named Josie Wagner had been found in the same location in 1977. A picture of Josie's smiling face appeared in the upper right corner of the screen.

"That's the picture they have on the wall in the orthopaedic ward," a voice said from the doorway.

Mitch turned to see the nurse who had been looking after him standing there. "Sorry?"

"That picture," she said, nodding at the TV. "It's on the wall in the orthopaedic ward downstairs. Josie was a nurse there in the seventies. She and some other nurses raised a lot of money for the hydrotherapy pool. There's a photograph of them and some of their patients by the pool after it was built." She pointed at the TV. "That's a close-up of Josie from that photo. I don't know how the TV people got hold of it, though."

"She worked here?"

The nurse nodded. "It's a shame how she ended up. They never caught her killer. I don't think it's anything to do with this new body they found, though. Too much time has passed."

"I'd like to see that photo," Mitch said. "Do you think I'd be able to?"

She looked at him with undisguised suspicion. "Well, you can't just walk onto the ward. What do you want to see it for? You're not with the TV station, are you?"

"No, I just have an interest in history," Mitch said. He told himself that he wasn't really lying because for the last few days he'd been obsessed by the brief period of history during which Josie Wagner had been alive.

The suspicious look on her face lessened but remained in place. "I could take you there, I suppose. You'll be going downstairs on your way out anyway. If I take you, we'll just have a quick look at the photo and then you'll be on your way, all right?"

"Of course," Mitch said. He felt a strong need to see the picture. Josie Wagner had been in his thoughts many times over the past few days and every time he'd thought of her, the images in his mind had been of her naked and bloody, exposed on Blackden Edge. Seeing a photo of her alive during a happy part of her life might realign his mental image.

"Come on, then," the nurse said.

He finished packing his things and slung the bag over his shoulder, trying not to wince when pain exploded in his side.

Five minutes later, they were standing outside the door to the orthopaedic ward. The nurse pressed the buzzer and spoke through the intercom to a nurse called Sandra, whom she seemed to know. They were buzzed in and Mitch was led to a group of framed photos hanging on the wall of the main corridor.

"There it is," the nurse said. "Just like I told you. See, there's Josie and it's exactly the same as the photo on the TV."

Mitch studied the picture. Six nurses stood in their uniforms at the edge of a small pool, smiling at the camera. Josie Wagner was among them, her eyes vibrant and alive. Mitch resolved to see this version of Josie whenever he thought of her and not the version his mind had cobbled together from police statements and newspaper articles.

Also in the picture were four patients in wheelchairs. Mitch scanned their faces and then felt a chill run up his spine as he recognized one of them.

In the photograph, sitting in his wheelchair and smiling at the camera, was Silas.

28

FREEDOM

When he got outside the hospital, Mitch called Elly. During the walk from the orthopaedic ward to the main exit, he'd considered telling Battle of his discovery but, remembering the detective's parting words, decided against it.

The police obviously weren't going to look into anything without concrete evidence. The photo in the orthopaedic ward proved that Silas had known Josie Wagner before she was murdered, but little else. Because Silas wasn't even on their radar as a possible suspect, the police would pass the photograph off as inconsequential.

For Mitch, though, the coincidences that connected Silas to all the girls who had gone missing or been murdered were impossible to ignore.

Elly answered after a couple of rings. "Hey, Mitch."

"How's it going? I saw you on the news."

"Ugh, not my finest moment. You still in hospital?"

"No, they let me out. I just walked out the door and I'm taking my first breath of fresh air."

"Well, that's good news. How are you getting home?"

He realized he hadn't thought about that. He'd been brought here by ambulance. His Jeep was parked at Edge House.

He supposed he could ring Tilly but she'd be at work and he didn't want to impose on her any more than he already had done. It was only by chance that he'd called her from Edge House but she'd gone above and beyond the call of duty. "I don't know," he told Elly. "I'll probably get a taxi."

"Want me to pick you up? My sister's just about to leave and then I'm free. I can be there in a couple of hours."

"You sure? That'd be great, thanks. We can talk about where we are in our investigation during the ride."

"Our investigation, huh? Didn't Battle warn you off? He came around here last night and told Jen and me to stop sticking our noses into police business. Said we should go home and forget about it."

"Funny, he told me the same thing," Mitch said.

"Did you listen?"

"No, did you?"

"Nope."

"That's settled, then." His earlier doubts were dispelled. It felt good to be back on the case, especially with Elly. She had a confidence that made him believe anything was possible, even finding Sarah.

He looked over towards the car park and was surprised to see Tilly walking over to him. She was waving.

"Elly, my cousin's here. I'll get a lift back with her."

"Okay, no problem. Then come to the cottage and we'll discuss where we are and what to do next."

"See you later," he said and ended the call.

Tilly reached him and said, "They let you out, that's great. I was coming to see how you were before I go to work. I can't believe they discharged you so quickly."

Mitch shrugged it off and gave her the same line he'd given the doctor. "I feel fine."

She gestured to the car park. "Let's go, then. Once you get back to Edge House, you can relax. I'll do some shopping for you after work. I noticed the other day that your kitchen cupboards are empty."

"There's no need to do that," he said, following her to the car park.

"Of course there is. You need to rest. Here, give me that bag." She reached out for the sports bag.

Mitch shook his head. "It's okay, I've got it."

Tilly's level of care was escalating from endearing to stifling.

Her car was a black Hyundai. She opened the rear door and Mitch slid the sports bag off his shoulder and onto the back seat.

Then he gingerly got in the front passenger side, trying to hide the pain he felt as he settled into the seat. If Tilly saw him wince, she'd probably bundle him into a wheelchair and wheel him back to the ward.

She got in behind the wheel and started the engine. Then she paused, seemed to come to some sort of decision, and said, "Mitch, I'm sorry. I'm only trying to help but sometimes I go too far. I know I'm doing it but I can't seem to help it. I apologise."

"No problem," he said. "I'm just not used to someone running around after me."

"No, it isn't that. It's me. I'm always the same if anyone is sick or injured. I go too far trying to help them and I end up pushing them away. That's why Faith's father and I aren't together anymore, you know. He got pneumonia the first Christmas after Faith was born and I tried so hard to care for him but I just stifled him. It was so bad that when he was well enough, he moved out."

She put the car in gear and headed for the exit. "I think I inherited it from my mother. When we were young, if we got a cold or even a sniffle, she'd put us to bed immediately and make chicken soup from scratch. I remember when I had scarlet fever, she didn't leave my bedside for a whole week."

Tilly looked wistful for a moment. "Those were the days when she still cared for me at all." She stopped at the exit barrier and inserted her ticket into the machine. The barrier lifted and Tilly drove out of the car park.

"You said your mum and dad weren't too keen on girls," Mitch said.

"Yeah, that's right," she said. "At least that's what I told myself when they started ignoring me. But that doesn't really make sense considering the volunteer work my mum does at the Women's Centre."

"Women's Centre?" Mitch asked.

"Oh, that's right, you don't know about 'Saint Alice.' For a woman who mostly ignores her own daughter, my mum more than makes up for it working with victims of domestic violence. There's a shelter in Matlock she visits two or three days a week. She's on the board of directors."

She shrugged. "She can do what she wants, of course, and it's a good thing for her to be involved in, but she certainly never heard the saying that charity begins at home. At least not when it comes to me. After I got to nine or ten years old, she never spent any time with me, was never interested in my schoolwork, friends, or anything like that."

"I'm sorry to hear that," Mitch said.

"It is what it is," Tilly said. "Jack would tell you a

totally different story, of course. He's the apple of her eye." She pulled out of the hospital grounds and onto the main road, joining the heavy traffic heading southeast out of Manchester.

"I saw them yesterday, you know," she said. "In the hospital. Dad spoke to me but Mum and Jack barely said two words."

"Your dad came to see me," Mitch said.

Her face brightened slightly. "Oh, that's nice."

Remembering Silas' warning to stop digging into the past and deciding not to mention it, Mitch simply said, "Yeah, real nice." Then he added, "I noticed Jack was limping."

"I noticed that too. He's always injuring himself doing some crazy stunt or other. He's a thrill-seeker, an adrenaline junkie. He broke his leg hang-gliding once. Dad went ballistic, told him he could have ended up in a wheelchair like him, or worse."

"I don't suppose Jack listened to him," Mitch said.

"Yes, he did. Jack does everything Dad tells him to. He dotes on our father. He never went hang-gliding again after that. It'd be easy to think he gave it up because he broke his leg doing it, but that isn't the case. He stopped because Dad told him to."

Mitch's interest was piqued. This was adding fuel to his theory that Jack was responsible for the more recent killings. "So he'd do anything Silas told him to do?"

She thought about it for a few seconds and then said, "It wasn't always like that. Up until eighteen years ago, Jack seemed to be ashamed of our father. I don't think he liked that he was in a wheelchair and couldn't do any of the stuff Jack liked doing.

"But then Jack's attitude to Dad totally changed. Just like that. I'd like to say he grew up but the words 'grown-up' and 'Jack Walker' don't really belong in the same sentence. But, he's Dad's primary caregiver now and does everything for him."

Everything? Mitch wondered. *Even murder?*

29

DRIVE

Jen sat in the dining room of Windrider Cottage, looking through the window at her black Nissan X-Trail parked next to Elly's Mini.

She wasn't looking forward to getting into her car and driving home. She wished someone could just invent teleportation already so she didn't have to face the prospect of a couple of hours on the busy motorway.

She wanted to be at home, of course, and was looking forward to seeing Wendy and William, and even Trevor, but the journey itself worried her.

For one thing, she would be alone in the car and she hated being alone, it made her nervous. The drive here had been a nail-biting, nerve-wracking test of endurance. She liked to surround herself with other people because she wasn't really fond of her own company. She didn't know how anyone could live on their own and not go crazy from the lack of human interaction.

Elly came into the room, putting her phone into her jeans pocket. "That was my friend Mitch," she said. "He's going to come round later."

"Is he feeling better?"

"Well, they discharged him so he must be all right." Elly turned to Jen's weekend case, which was sitting by the front door. "Right, are you ready? If you go now, you can beat the lunchtime rush."

Jen nodded and got up. "It was good to see you, Elly. When you get back to Birmingham, you must come and visit. Trevor and the kids would love to see you. I could invite Mum and Dad as well. We'll have a party."

"In celebration of what?" Elly asked.

Jen resisted the urge to roll her eyes at her sister. Did they need an excuse to have a party? That was just like Elly, always questioning everything. "In celebration of your new book," she said. "It's sure to be a bestseller now. You discovered one of the victims yourself. Not many authors can say that."

Elly offered her a smile that seemed to hold no joy. Jen wasn't surprised at her sister's dour outlook. Paul had left her and she faced a life alone until she found someone else. It couldn't be easy to have that prospect looming in front of you.

And finding the grave at the stone circle had upset Elly a lot. Since crying in the car, she'd become distant. Jen had gotten out of bed last night to get a drink of water and had heard Elly crying in her bedroom. Jen wasn't sure if it was because of the grave or because of the Paul situation. A bit of both, she supposed.

She knew that, as a sister, she was supposed to offer support in some way but she didn't know what to do. She and Elly weren't close, so Jen wasn't sure if an attempt to console her sister would be rejected and push her and Elly even further apart.

"Will you be okay?" Jen asked. The question was vague enough that Elly could confide in her if she wanted but wouldn't see it as prying if she didn't.

"Fine," Elly said.

"All right, I'll be going then." Jen leaned in to give her sister a hug. "You take care and don't get yourself into any trouble."

"I won't." Elly returned the hug.

"I don't know what I'm going to tell Mum and Dad," Elly said, breaking the hug and going to the hallway to get her case. "Now that you've been on the news—at a murder scene, no less—they'll be worse than ever."

Elly smiled and this time Jen detected genuine humour in it. "Don't forget that you were on the news too. At a murder scene, no less."

Jen pursed her lips. That was true, of course. She wasn't sure how she was going to explain that to her parents. The last thing her mum had said before Jen left for Derbyshire was, "Make sure you keep Elly out of trouble while you're there."

She'd just have to find a way to smooth it over when she talked to Mum later, put a spin on it somehow. She had plenty of time to think of something to say during the drive home.

She picked up her case and opened the front door. It was a grey day and there was a sense of impending rain in the air. Jen supposed this was what most days were like here. Maybe the weather would improve when she got closer to home.

She went out to the car with Elly following close behind. Jen opened the boot and slid the case inside, then remembered something. "Oh, my umbrella. It's by the back door."

"I'll get it," Elly said, going back inside the cottage.

Standing alone by the cars, Jen wondered if the sense of impending rain she'd felt a minute ago had actually been a sense of impending doom. It was so quiet out here in the middle of nowhere and Elly was vulnerable in the isolated cottage on her own.

Elly came back out and handed the Hello Kitty umbrella to her.

"Thanks," Jen said, putting it into the boot next

to her weekend case. "Wendy would have killed me if I'd left that here. It's her pride and joy."

"Good job you remembered it, then." Elly gave her another brief hug. "Be careful driving home. Text me when you get there safely."

"I will," Jen said, climbing into the car. "And you be careful too. You're in the middle of nowhere here. I'd prefer it if you were staying in a town, close to other people."

"I'm fine," Elly said.

Jen closed the door, gave Elly a brief wave through the window, and started the engine. The X-Trail's GPS was telling her she'd arrived at her destination. She pressed the button that told it she wanted to go home and while it was calculating the route, she reversed onto the main road. The GPS told her to go straight on and, after waving to Elly again, Jen followed its instruction.

The road took her south, although—like most of the roads around here—it did so via an indirect route, snaking through the countryside with sharp bends and very few straight stretches.

This meant Jen had to watch her speed because she didn't want to go flying around a bend and crash into the back of a tractor that might be dawdling along the road unseen in front of her.

The only other vehicle she could see was a blue Land Rover that appeared every now and then in her rear-view mirror. It was far enough behind her that she only saw it when she was on one of the few straight stretches of road. Every time she hit a bend, the Land Rover disappeared again, hidden from view by the bushes and trees that bordered the road.

She felt the same sense of impending doom she'd felt at the cottage and realized how isolated she was on this road. What if her car broke down? What if she hit one of the bends too fast and went careening off the road and into the trees?

She reduced her speed slightly and put the radio on. She kept the radio tuned to BBC 4 because it was a spoken-word station and hearing other's people's voices while she drove comforted her. *Woman's Hour* was on and a discussion about eating disorders was well under way.

Jen half-listened to the presenters and their guests while she concentrated on navigating the tight bends the road threw at her. She wasn't really bothered about what was being discussed, she just liked to hear other people's voices in the car. It eased her fear of being alone. Eased it, but didn't dispel it.

Because she'd slowed her speed, the Land Rover gradually got closer. Jen could see the driver, a dark-haired man, in the rear-view mirror. She wondered if she should pull over and let him get past her. He was probably a local who knew this road like the back of his hand and was probably annoyed at sitting behind

Jen's SUV as she slowed to a snail's pace at each bend.

He flashed his headlights at her twice. Jen groaned. So he was annoyed after all and wanted to overtake her. She checked the side of the road ahead. There was nowhere to pull over. This part of the road was narrow and was bordered with thick bushes. If she pulled over and scratched the side of the car, Trevor would be furious.

He flashed again.

Jen looked at him in the rear-view mirror and shrugged, a gesture that was supposed to let him know that she wanted to let him past but couldn't at the moment.

The Land Rover's headlights flashed again, three times in quick succession.

Jen increased her speed slightly. Maybe that would make him happy. She realized she was taking a chance each time she came to a bend but she couldn't bear to have this man tailgating her and flashing at her. Why couldn't he hang back like he'd been doing before? Why was he now desperate to get past?

The Land Rover's horn sounded, making Jen jump.

"All right, all right," she muttered, spotting an open farm gate at the side of the road ahead. She could go through the gate and wait on the dirt track while the dickhead in the Land Rover drove on.

Then she could reverse back onto the road and continue on her way at her own pace.

She slowed as she approached the gate and steered the SUV onto the track that led to a farmhouse in the distance.

She was surprised when the Land Rover didn't speed past her as she had expected but instead slowed down as well. It stopped at the gate.

"Oh, great," she said. It seemed the man in the Land Rover lived on this farm and now she was blocking his way. There was a ditch at each side of the dirt track so she couldn't very well turn around unless she drove on to the farmhouse and turned around there.

The driver got out of the Land Rover and began walking towards the SUV.

"Bloody hell," Jen whispered. The farmer was going to give her a piece of his mind and probably throw in a comment or two about women drivers. Trevor was always complaining about her driving, always belittling her, telling her the X-Trail was too big of a car for her to handle. And now she was going to get the same treatment from a total stranger.

She pressed the button to lower her window all the way down and prepared to apologise. There was no need to enrage the guy any further. Jen just wanted to apologise and get out of there.

As the man came alongside the car, she said, "I'm

sorry, I didn't realise you lived here. If I can just turn around at your house, I'll be out of your hair."

He got to her door and shoved his arm through the open window.

When Jen saw the knife in his hand, she realised she should never have stopped at all.

30

THE BLADE

When Mitch arrived at Edge House, there was a police car sitting on the gravel near the side of the house.

"Perhaps they've come to tell you they've caught the man who broke in," Tilly suggested as she parked behind the police car.

"No, I think they're here to look for the knife in the garden," Mitch said. "Battle thinks the intruder might not have been able to see it in the dark."

"Well, that's good," she said. "Finding the knife will bring the police one step closer to finding the guy."

"If it's still there," Mitch said, getting out of the car and trying to ignore the pain in his side. He went around to the boot and grabbed the sports bag.

Tilly's window buzzed down and she shouted back to him, "I've got to get to work now but if you want to go out for a meal sometime in the week, let me know."

"Okay, I will," he said, shutting the boot and walking around to her window with the sports bag over his shoulder. "And it's my treat. I have to thank you for saving my life."

She smiled and said, "That's what family is for," before giving him a quick wave and accelerating away.

Two police officers appeared from around the side of the house. Mitch recognized them as the two officers who had been here before. He searched his memory for their names. The blonde woman was Sergeant Preston, he was sure of that. The dark-haired man was Constable White or Waite, or something like that.

"Morning, sir," Preston said. "Good news. We found the knife in your garden." She turned to the constable, who held up a clear plastic evidence bag containing a short knife with a black handle. It was like no knife Mitch had ever seen. It couldn't have been more than four inches long from pommel to tip and the blade was double-edged but one edge was straight while the other was serrated.

"Diver's knife, sir," Preston said, seeing the confusion on Mitch's face. "It's not a common item so we'll probably be able to track down where it was purchased."

"That's great," Mitch said. "I'm glad you finally have a lead to follow."

"Thanks to you, sir. That was quick thinking, kicking the knife away into those weeds."

"It was purely reflex," Mitch said. But he felt a glimmer of pride. If this knife led the police to arrest Sarah's killer, then he'd helped her in some way after all.

Preston smiled. "We'll get this to the lab and have it processed. Have a good day, Mr. Walker." She and the constable got into their car and left.

Mitch didn't bother going into Edge House. He had no taste for the place anymore. He'd even consider selling it to Silas now, if the man turned out not to be a killer.

He went to the Jeep and put the sports bag into the boot. He'd stay at a hotel tonight. He climbed into the Jeep and felt a stab of hunger as well as pain. He wondered if Elly had eaten lunch yet. Maybe he should pick up something on the way to her cottage and they could eat while they went over the case. He set the GPS to the postcode Elly had given him and put the vehicle into gear.

As he set off, it began to rain. *Typical*, Mitch thought. *Just when my mood is lifting, the weather tries to dampen it.*

He turned on the wipers and turned up the radio. It was tuned to an eighties station and Duran

Duran were singing "Hungry Like the Wolf." Mitch took that as an omen; he needed to get food.

When he arrived at Windrider Cottage, he was ravenous. He'd stopped at a supermarket on the way and picked up baguettes, cooked ham, cheddar, cherry tomatoes, strawberries, cream, and a bottle of red wine.

If Elly had already eaten, then he could use her kitchen to make himself a ham-and-cheese baguette. If she hadn't, he had enough food for both of them. Even if Elly wasn't hungry, he was sure she wouldn't say no to a dish of strawberries and cream and a glass of wine.

He wasn't exactly sure why he'd bought fresh ingredients and wine rather than just grab some pre-packaged sandwiches and a couple of cans of Coke, but he thought it was something to do with the fact that he was going to see Elly.

The truth was, he liked her. She was a strong woman who exuded confidence, and Mitch found that attractive. And they worked well together. He didn't have any designs on her but he also didn't want her to think he was a pre-packaged-sandwiches type of guy.

Yet one of the things he found attractive about her was that he knew she wouldn't mind even if she thought he was that type of guy. Elly didn't have any airs and graces at all.

Yet you're still trying to impress her.

No, I'm not. I just want us to have a nice lunch. With wine. You never have wine at lunchtime.

Mentally switching off his internal monologue, he parked the Jeep next to Elly's Mini and got out into the light rain. The cottage stood alone overlooking the moors. It was quaint but looked like it had been built to withstand the harsh weather up here on the hillside.

Pretty and tough, just like Elly.

"Shut up," he muttered at his own thoughts.

The front door opened and Elly came out. She was wearing jeans and a red long-sleeved top with the Nike swoosh on the left breast. She gave Mitch a wave and came over to him, smiling. "Hey, good to see you're still among the living."

"Yeah, it feels good," he said. "Have you eaten? I've got some food."

"Not yet. I'm starving."

Mitch congratulated himself for his quick thinking. He unloaded the shopping bags from the boot and followed Elly into the cottage. She led him to the kitchen, where the windows offered a view of the moors and the distant peaks.

"Wow," he said, putting the bags down on the table. "That's a view."

She grinned. "At last, someone who appreciates it."

"What do you mean? Who didn't?"

"My sister. She said she'd rather look out her window and see shops."

He laughed and indicated the bags. "I've got some baguettes and ham here, that kind of thing."

"Sounds good. We can have a working lunch." She opened the cupboards and took out a couple of plates. She took a packet of butter from the fridge, and from a drawer near the sink, she produced a selection of knives and put them on the table next to the plates.

"That reminds me," Mitch said. "The police found the knife I was stabbed with. It was still in the garden at Edge House. Apparently, it's a diver's knife."

She raised a quizzical eyebrow. "An odd choice of weapon. I don't think any of our suspects are divers."

"Jack might be. Tilly told me that he's into that kind of thing. She didn't mention diving specifically but apparently he broke his leg once while hang-gliding."

Elly nodded slowly. "Okay, so it could be him. It's a bit circumstantial, though."

"I guess we just have to hope the police might connect the knife to him. Or if it's not him, then to whoever used it to stab me and probably kill Rhonda Knowles."

Elly began cutting into the baguettes with the bread

knife. "Let's say it was Jack who killed Rhonda and stabbed you while he was retrieving the journal from your house. Are we saying he was Michael's accomplice and that Michael carried out the earlier crimes?"

"No, I don't think that's the case," Mitch said, opening the cherry tomatoes and placing some on each plate. "I think Michael was innocent and Jack is doing the dirty work for Silas."

She thought about that for a minute and then nodded slowly. "It's possible but are you sure you're not being biased, though? Michael is your dad, after all."

Mitch told her about the photograph he'd seen hanging on the wall of the orthopaedic ward. He told her about Silas coming to the hospital room and telling him to stop digging. And he repeated what Tilly had said about Jack doting on his father and doing everything Silas told him to do.

By the time he was done, the baguettes were ready and the strawberries and cream were in the fridge.

"I brought wine," Mitch said, pulling the bottle out of the bag.

"I'll pass on the wine," Elly said. She reached into the fridge and took out a bottle of Coke.

Mitch put the wine on the table. "Coke sounds good to me too."

They took their food and drinks into the dining room, where Mitch was surprised to see the whiteboard Elly had filled with bits and pieces of the case.

"This is impressive," he said. Then he noticed the photo of him and Sarah and added, "Where did you get this?"

"It doesn't matter." She went to the board and grabbed a red marker. "Based on what you've told me, we can now draw a line connecting Silas to Josie Wagner." She drew the line. "He's already connected to Olivia and Sarah, of course. That leaves the Hatton sisters and Lindsey Grofield." She frowned at the board. "There must be a connection, we just don't know what it is yet."

Her phone, which was sitting on the dining room table, began to ring. Elly picked it up and rolled her eyes when she looked at the screen. "My mother," she said. "I'd best take this." She walked into the hallway and Mitch heard her say, "Hi, Mum."

He studied the board. Elly had done a good job of listing everything relevant to the case and drawing connections where they existed. The board didn't give Mitch a flash of inspiration or show him anything he didn't already know but it sorted the information into a neat, visual form.

Elly returned to the room, a look of concern on her face.

"Something wrong?" Mitch asked.

"I don't know. My mum said Jen hasn't arrived home yet. She was ringing to see if she left later than planned this morning. She didn't. She should be home by now." She sighed. "Maybe the traffic's just bad."

"The motorway can get really busy," Mitch offered. "Especially if there are roadworks."

Elly smiled but it was thin. "Yeah, Mum's probably worrying about nothing as usual."

Mitch pointed at her phone. "Have you tried ringing your sister?"

She shook her head. "No, but Mum's rung her about a dozen times, I think. No answer." She began pressing the phone's screen and then held it up to her ear. After a couple of minutes, she said, "No, nothing," and ended the call.

"I'm sure she's fine," Mitch said. "What's her car like? Is it possible she broke down?"

"It's a brand new Nissan. She could have gotten a flat, I suppose, but then she'd call the AA and she'd be answering her phone." She went to the window and looked out, as if expecting to see her sister standing there in the rain.

"I'll check the traffic report, see if there's any hold up on the motorway," Mitch said, fishing his phone out of his pocket. "There could be an accident or an overturned lorry or something." He brought up the news and a headline caught his eye.

"They've arrested someone," he told Elly.

She turned to him with a questioning look. "What?"

"Put the telly on. They've arrested someone for Rhonda Knowles' murder."

She went into the living room and Mitch followed. Elly used the remote to turn the TV on. The headline that Mitch had just read on his phone was written across the bottom of the screen: MAN ARRESTED IN RHONDA KNOWLES MURDER CASE.

The screen was showing video footage taken from a helicopter. Mitch could see a country road and four police cars surrounding a blue Land Rover. It looked like the police cars had forced the Land Rover to stop because its front end was partly embedded in the bushes at the side of the road.

The voice of the female newsreader was saying, "*This is the footage we're getting at the moment. Apparently, the police were involved in a high-speed chase, which resulted in the suspect crashing his car. He was then arrested and taken to Buxton police station where he is currently being held in custody. I can confirm that the suspect is a man in his thirties who lives close to Blackden Edge, the place where Rhonda Knowles' body was found in the early hours of yesterday morning.*"

On the screen, a police van arrived and three white-suited SOCOs got out and went over to the Land Rover. They began inspecting it inside and out.

"*We can confirm that the police will give a state-*

ment later today with more details but what we know at the moment is that a man in his thirties, who is local to the area, has been arrested in connection with the murder of Rhonda Knowles."

"It's got to be Jack," Mitch said. "He's the right age and he's a local."

"So are a thousand other people," Elly said. "We have no way of knowing if it's him or not."

There was a knock at the door that made them both jump. Mitch looked out of the window and saw Battle's dark green Range Rover parked on the road.

Elly went to answer the door and Mitch followed.

DS Morgan stood on the step, her face grim. "Can I come in?" she asked Elly.

"Yes, of course," Elly said, ushering her inside. "Have you come to tell us about the man who's been arrested?"

"That isn't why I'm here, no, although I've come about something that's connected to the arrest. I think you should sit down, Miss Cooper."

Elly frowned, confused. "What? Why?"

"Please," DS Morgan said, indicating the living room.

Elly complied, her face suddenly worried. She sat on the sofa and Mitch noticed that her hands were clasped tightly together in her lap. "What is it?" she asked Morgan.

"The man we arrested earlier today was Jack

Walker. His fingerprints were found on the diver's knife we discovered at Edge House."

"But he was wearing gloves," Mitch said. "When he attacked me, he was wearing gloves."

DS Morgan nodded. "He wore gloves when he broke into your house, sir, but he'd touched the knife before then and not bothered to wipe it down. As you can imagine, DCI Battle is having a field day with that one."

She turned back to Elly. "We arrested Mr. Walker on a road twenty minutes south of here. He made a run for it but we caught him. When he was arrested, he was in possession of another knife, similar to the one we found at Edge House. The blade was bloody. When asked about it, Mr. Walker refused to comment."

She cleared her throat. "We made another discovery on the same road, an abandoned Nissan X-Trail that belongs to your sister, Jennifer Townsend."

"Oh, my God," Elly said. A stricken look crossed her face. "You said abandoned. You mean Jen wasn't in it?"

"No, she wasn't. We have reason to believe that before he was arrested, Jack Walker had some sort of contact with your sister."

Elly looked at her with fury in her eyes. "Some sort of contact? You mean he killed her?" Tears spilled from her eyes. "Jen," she said weakly.

Mitch sat next to her on the sofa and put his arm

around her shoulder. Elly collapsed against his chest and sobbed.

"No, I don't mean that at all," DS Morgan said. "We found blood on the Nissan's driver's seat and door but we don't know what's happened to your sister. We have the entire force out looking for her."

"But Jack Walker knows," Elly said, pushing away from Mitch and getting up. "I want to speak with him."

"I'm afraid that isn't possible, miss. DCI Battle is interviewing Mr. Walker at the moment and he'll get all the information we need regarding your sister." She checked her watch. "Now, I have to get back to the station but I promise we'll call you the moment we know anything."

Turning to Mitch, she said, "Will you be able to stay with her, sir?"

Mitch nodded. "Yes, of course."

"I'll see myself out." She left and Mitch heard the front door close.

"Oh God, I don't believe it," Elly said. "Not Jen. She wasn't involved in any of this until I dragged her into it. It's all my fault. She's dead and it's all my fault."

"It isn't your fault and we don't know what's happened to her," Mitch said.

"Jack knows," she said, "but they won't let me speak with him."

"Whatever he knows, Battle will get it out of

him," Mitch assured her. "I'm sure Battle is like a dog with a bone in the interview room."

She looked at him and wiped at her tears with the sleeve of her top. "Silas," she said.

"What do you mean?"

"If you're right about Jack doing this for his father, then Silas knows what happened to Jen. I'm going to go and see him." She strode into the dining room and snatched her keys from the table.

"Let me drive," Mitch said.

She nodded. "Okay."

They went out to the Jeep. The rain was falling softly now, gently whispering over the cars and the road.

"I guess he'll be at Blackmoor House," Mitch said.

"I know the way."

Mitch started the engine and reversed onto the road.

"That way," Elly said, pointing north.

Mitch followed her instructions and headed north. He had no idea what they were going to say to Silas when they got to Blackmoor House or if he was going to have to restrain Elly from assaulting the man.

They were probably going to have to confront Alice too. Did she know about her husband's and son's crimes? Mitch thought she must know. A secret like that was too big to hide from someone you lived with. But he'd heard of murderer's spouses being unaware of their partner's misdeeds. Could Alice be unaware that she was living with not one but two murderers?

"You need to go faster," Elly told him. "If Jack confesses to Battle and incriminates Silas, the police will be on their way to Blackmoor House. I have to talk to Silas before they arrest him."

"You think Jack will snitch on his dad?" Mitch asked her.

"Probably."

Mitch put his foot down and the Jeep sped north towards Dark Peak.

31

INTERVIEW

Battle was tired. The events of the last couple of days had taxed his mind and given him sleepless nights during which he had lain in bed with a million thoughts tumbling through his head.

Now, at last, they had Jack Walker in custody. Jack couldn't be responsible for the earlier crimes but he was certainly responsible for the murder of Rhonda Knowles. His fingerprints were on the diver's knife and the pathologist had matched that knife to the wounds on Rhonda's torso.

Battle looked across the interview room table at Jack and his lawyer. So far, Jack hadn't said much, but it was coming, Battle could sense it. The lad desperately wanted to say something. What it was, Battle had no idea, but he knew that his patience would be rewarded if he just sat it out.

"Come on, Jack," he said, "tell me why you did it. Tell me about Rhonda Knowles."

"She was nobody," Jack said.

"So you did know her, then?"

Jack shrugged. His eyes were fixed on the table between them. "No, not really. I've seen her around, that's all. What happened to her wasn't right."

"You mean her being killed?"

Jack shook his head. "No, I mean the way it was done. It was all wrong. A pale imitation." He looked up at Battle. "I don't understand, you see. I want to make him proud of me but I don't understand the meaning behind what he did. I thought it would all become clear when I killed Rhonda, but it didn't."

"Jack," the lawyer said quickly, "I advise you not to say anything else."

"Shut up," Jack said. "It doesn't matter now. It's going to all come out anyway. And it's about time it did."

Not too much patience required after all, Battle thought. *He's going to give me everything gift-wrapped and tied up with a neat little bow.*

Jack pointed at Battle. "You are going to be so humiliated when you find out what he did, how many years he evaded you." He laughed. "He'll go down in history as the greatest killer of all time."

"Who will?" Battle asked.

Jack paused, seemed to be thinking, and then

said, "My father. Silas Walker. He's had you lot baffled for decades."

Battle raised an eyebrow. "Your father? I'd be interested to know how he's managed that. It can't be easy killing fit young girls when you're in a wheelchair."

"He's got drugs. Strong drugs for his back. He puts them in a syringe and sedates the girls. Then he kills them while they're lying there helpless."

Battle's mind began poring over his recollection of the toxicology reports from Josie Wagner's autopsy. There were drugs found in her system. And the pathologist had determined that Lindsey Grofield had been sedated and then buried alive. That nugget of information had been leaked to the press and mentioned on the radio and TV, so Jack could simply be regurgitating information he'd head in the news. "Does he indeed?" he asked. "You've seen him do it, have you? You've witnessed him murdering someone?"

The question wiped away the smug look from Jack's face. "I haven't seen it with my own eyes, no, but I've seen the syringes." A slight grin returned to his mouth. "And the journal."

Battle nodded. "Ah, the journal. Do you mean this journal, Mr. Walker?" He picked up the clear plastic bag containing the black leather journal that had been found in Walker's Land Rover.

"Yes, my father's journal."

Battle nodded slowly, deciding to goad the young man. "I've had a look through this journal and it seems to me to be a load of nonsense. Nothing more than descriptions of flowers and a few sketches. Not exactly the diary of Jack the Ripper, is it?"

"It's about the girls. The girls are the flowers."

"Oh, is that right?" Battle asked, feigning ignorance. "You figured that out all by yourself, did you?"

"Not at first. But the newspaper articles of the disappearances of those girls were with the journal in the attic and they helped me understand what it was all about. I still don't fully understand everything but I understand the most important thing: my father is a clever, powerful man. All this time, people thought he was poor old Silas, stuck in that wheelchair but he's outfoxed all of you."

"Mr. Walker, I think you don't understand anything at all. You find a journal and some press clippings in an attic and you use that as a motive to go out and kill Rhonda Knowles?"

Jack looked closely at him. "All of my life, my father has been in a wheelchair and do you know what? When I was young, I was ashamed of him. He wasn't like the other dads who played football with their sons or went walking with them along the fells. My dad couldn't do that and because he couldn't do that, everyone thought he was weak."

He pointed at his own chest. "I thought he was weak. But all the time, he was living a secret life. He wasn't weak at all, he was strong, holding the power over life and death in his hands. I pitied him because I was getting my kicks from hang-gliding, rock-climbing, and diving, and I thought he could never have that, never know that rush of adrenaline. But little did I know, he was doing something far more exhilarating."

"Killing girls," Battle said.

"Yes, killing girls."

"So when you found the journal, you thought you'd have a go yourself, experience the ultimate thrill. Is that why you did it? For the adrenaline rush?"

Jack nodded. "Not right away. At first, I didn't have the guts to do it. I thought about it, though. It played on my mind for years."

Battle interrupted him. "Years? When exactly did you find the journal?"

"Eighteen years ago. I was seventeen. I went into the attic to find some rock-climbing gear I thought was up there. While I was up there, I noticed an old cardboard shoe box. When I opened it, I found the journal and the clippings inside."

"And the syringes?" Battle asked.

Jack nodded. "And the syringes and some of my dad's meds. That was the day I realized my father wasn't the weak man everyone made him out to be. Even my mum is always putting him down and telling him he's a disappointment to her. If only she knew the truth." He grinned. "Well, she will soon, won't she? Soon, everyone will know what kind of man my father is. He certainly fooled you and your cronies."

"Wait a minute," Battle said, performing a mental calculation. Jack must have found the journal shortly after the murder of Lindsey Grofield. "You sent the letter to the police, didn't you?"

"Yes, that was me," Jack said. "I wanted to bring some attention to the killings. I sent the same letter to the papers as well but nobody published it. It could have been huge, like the Zodiac case in America but nobody paid any attention."

Battle tried to form a timeline in his mind. "So why did you kill Rhonda Knowles now, eighteen years later? It doesn't make much sense to me, lad."

Jack stared down at the table. "I couldn't work up the courage to do it. I came close a few times but never actually went through with it. I wanted to, wanted to be like my father, but I couldn't."

"And then suddenly, you could," Battle said, "And Rhonda Knowles paid the price."

"My dad was growing weak," Jack said. "My cousin Mitch arrived and took Edge House from us. My dad wanted to buy it but Mitch said no and brought up Olivia and Sarah. My dad broke down. I realised that he'd grown a lot weaker over the past few years. He was upset because he can't do what he used to. I told myself that I had to finally find the courage to continue his work. And I did."

Battle said, "Excuse me a moment, sir." He left the interview room and went upstairs to the incident room that had been set up for the Rhonda Knowles case. "Where's DS Morgan?" he asked as he entered.

"She's giving Elly Cooper the bad news, guv," DS Johnson said.

"Right, get on to dispatch. I want a unit over at Blackmoor House. We're going to bring Silas Walker in on suspicion of murder. His son has fingered him as the Blackden Edge Murderer but something about it doesn't sit right with me." He turned to leave the room.

"Aren't you going out there as well, guv?" Johnson asked.

"No, I'm not bloody going out there. I need to find out what Walker's done with Jennifer Townsend, don't I?"

"Yes, guv."

"Yes, guv," Battle mimicked, closing the door behind him and going back downstairs to the interview room.

DS Morgan was driving north after leaving Windrider Cottage wishing she hadn't had to be the one to deliver the bad news to Elly Cooper. She knew it was part of the job but some parts of the job were terrible. She just hoped they'd find Elly's sister soon and that she'd be alive when they did.

She'd intended to return to the station to get an update about the interview with Jack Walker but as she drove towards Blackmoor House, she saw a white Honda CR-V with Alice Walker at the wheel come speeding out from between the eagle pillars and onto the main road. The vehicle turned north.

Morgan followed. When she'd first joined the CID, she'd been told that she'd been told that she'd develop a gut instinct about some things and right now, her gut was telling her to follow Alice Walker. She was the mother of the accused, after all, and it looked like she was running away from something.

Keeping her distance but making sure she had the white Honda in view at all times, Morgan followed the vehicle off the main road and onto side roads that snaked through the woods.

32

BLACKMOOR HOUSE

WHEN MITCH TURNED off the main road and guided the Jeep between the eagle-topped pillars that marked the entrance to Blackmoor House, he felt a jolt of déjà vu.

The track that led from the road to the house was straight, unlike the track at Edge House, and the house could be seen from the road.

The dream-memory Mitch had dismissed came back to him with frightening clarity. This was the track he'd run along in his pyjamas as a child. This was where he'd looked over his shoulder and seen that single light burning in the upstairs room.

What had he seen that had made him flee the house? Fragments of memory returned to him. He and Sarah had been staying overnight here while their parents went out somewhere. He couldn't remember where and it didn't matter. What mattered was that he and Sarah had been staying here with Tilly and Jack. Silas and Alice were looking after all four children.

Mitch remembered waking up during the night. He'd been playing army all evening with Tilly, pretending to be a soldier and stalking her around the house with a plastic machine gun. She had a gun too and was also stalking him.

The house was so large that the game sometimes went on for a while without them finding each other. But then, when they finally met, the toy machine guns rattled off imaginary bullets and he and Tilly pretended to die in agonizing ways. It was a good game but all that running around had made him thirsty later. He'd remembered there were some cans of Pepsi in the fridge downstairs.

He had slid out of bed and opened the bedroom door quietly so as not to wake Jack, who was asleep in the next room. The girls were sleeping at the other end of the long hallway that ran along the second floor so Mitch didn't have to worry about waking them.

Moonlight shone in through the windows, so he didn't have to turn any lights on. He padded along the hallway to the top of the stairs and began to go down to the kitchen, his hand sliding along the smoothly-polished wooden bannister.

When he was halfway down, a noise reached him from the floor he'd just descended from. It sounded like someone crying. Curious, Mitch went back up and listened, trying to pinpoint where the sound was coming from.

He crept along the hallway until he reached a closed door. The sound was definitely coming from the room behind that door. There was a girl crying in there. Was it Sarah or was it Tilly? Mitch couldn't be sure.

The only way to find out was to open the door. The trouble was, this room was one that the children had been warned not to enter. Tilly had told Mitch that it was her mother's private room and there were fragile things in there that might get broken if they went inside. She didn't know what those fragile things were because she'd never been inside herself. She said that to disobey her parents meant you'd get a slap or hit across the back of your legs with a wooden spoon.

Mitch had heeded the warning and hadn't gone into the room, not even during the game of army. But now there was someone in there crying. Whoever it was, he'd tell them to cheer up and then he'd get them a Pepsi.

He grabbed the handle and opened the door as quietly as he could so he didn't wake anyone else in the house.

What he saw sent a shiver of shock through him and made him step back and gasp.

Sitting on the bed was Alice. She was dressed in

a white nightgown and she was rocking back and forth, tears streaming down her cheeks. Clutched in her arms were the bodies of two dead girls. They wore long blue dresses and lay limply in Alice's arms, their faces covered by long, blonde hair.

Alice heard Mitch gasp and turned to face him. The sorrow in her eyes turned to fury. "How dare you!" she spat. "How dare you come in here!" She threw the girls down on the bed and then Mitch realized they weren't real at all—they were dolls. But they weren't little dolls like Sarah's Tiny Tears or Barbie, they were life-size.

They were also life-like. Most dolls, like Sarah's, didn't look real because their eyes always looked fake. The eyes were made of glass or plastic, Mitch knew. But Alice's dolls had their eyes closed, which made them look more real.

He backed away from his advancing aunt. "I'm sorry," he pleaded. He didn't want to get a wooden spoon across the back of his legs.

"Get out!" Alice shouted.

Mitch fled down the stairs and to the front door. He had no desire for a drink now, he just needed to get out of the house. He was in trouble and he needed to escape whatever punishment was coming his way. The key was in the door. He turned it and ran out into the night.

When he was halfway along the track the led to the road, he looked over his shoulder and saw the light burning in the room where Alice had been sitting on the bed with the dolls. He should never have gone in there. Why hadn't he stayed out?

He reached the road, panting for breath. He heard a shout coming from the house but it wasn't Alice shouting at him, it was Silas calling his name. His uncle had come out of the house and was sitting in his wheelchair by the front door, peering into the darkness and calling for Mitch.

Mitch stood where he was for a moment, wondering if he should keep running. But where would he go and what would he tell his parents tomorrow? That he'd been frightened by a pair of dolls? Maybe it was better to go back to the house now and take whatever punishment he deserved for breaking the rules. If he was lucky, Silas and Alice might not even tell his parents.

Reluctantly, he turned towards the house and walked back along the track.

Silas waited for him and, when Mitch got closer, asked, "Are you all right, lad?"

Mitch nodded slowly. "I'm sorry, Uncle Silas."

"Come on, let's go inside." Silas turned the chair around to face the doorway. "Aunt Alice was just surprised to see you looking into her room, that's all."

"Am I in trouble?" Mitch asked, following Silas back into the house.

Silas stopped in the foyer and put a hand on Mitch's shoulder. "I'll tell you what; let's not mention this to anyone. You keep quiet about the room and I won't have to tell your parents you were in there. How does that sound?"

Mitch nodded. He didn't want to be in trouble.

As he parked the Jeep outside Blackmoor House, Mitch recalled that he never told anyone about what he had seen in Alice's secret room. At the time, he'd thought that a grown woman crying over dolls was strange but nothing that concerned him.

Now, he wasn't so sure. He got out of the Jeep and went to the front door. Elly beat him to it. She was pounding on the door with her fist before he reached it.

"Silas," she shouted, "I want to talk to you." She stepped back from the door and glanced at the windows, probably looking for an open one she could climb through, so desperate was she to get into the house.

"Get down here," she shouted at an upper-floor window.

Mitch followed her gaze and saw Silas looking out at them. Because he was in his chair, only the top part of his face showed through the window. His eyes were unreadable.

"Silas!" Elly shouted again.

The face disappeared and Mitch wondered if Silas wasn't going to open the door at all. Then he realised that Silas' only means of getting from the upper floor must be a stair-lift or an elevator, both of which took time.

At last, the door opened. Silas said nothing to either of them. He merely wheeled himself back into the centre of the foyer.

Elly strode up to him. "Where's my sister, you bastard? What has Jack done with her? Where is she?"

"I don't know for sure," he said simply.

"Don't lie to me," she said, grabbing his shoulders and shaking him. "Where is she? Where is Jen?"

"Please, Miss Cooper," he said. "I'm not lying to you. Not at all."

"You tell me where she is or so help me, I'll—"

"Elly," Mitch said. "I think he's telling the truth." There was something different about Silas. He seemed deflated somehow, as if his life-force had leaked out of him. It could be nothing more than the fear of being caught, but Mitch detected something else in Silas' bearing as well: a great sorrow.

Elly stepped back and looked at Silas, really looked at him, for the first time. "It isn't you," she said. "You're not the Blackden Edge Murderer."

Silas shook his head slowly and said, "No, Miss Cooper, I'm not."

"Not even the early abductions, the ones before your accident." She said it as a statement, not a question.

He shook his head again and then looked down at the floor as if ashamed.

"If not you," she said, "then who?" Her brows furrowed as she thought about it. Then she said, "You knew Josie Wagner and she ended up dead. You knew Olivia and Sarah and the same happened to them. If you didn't do that, then it had to be someone who had the same connections." Understanding flashed in her eyes. "Your wife. She had exactly the same connections. But why kill Josie?"

Silas sighed. "You have to understand, Miss Cooper, Alice and I have had a strained relationship from the moment we met. That didn't stop us from marrying at eighteen.

"We knew nothing about the world. We were both so young and innocent. Well, one of us was innocent, I suppose. The year before we were married, Evie and Mary Hatton disappeared from their home in Leath, the same village Alice was from. So, of course, it came up in conversation every now and then, especially since the police were still scouring the countryside looking for the two girls. But every time I mentioned it to Alice, she acted strangely. A faraway look came into her eyes and she said the girls were in a better place, away from their father."

"So you suspected her," Mitch said. "But you didn't go to the police?"

Silas scoffed. "With what? I had no evidence, nothing but a nagging suspicion.

"Then Olivia disappeared," he said. "And I saw the similarity between her and those poor Hatton girls."

"You mean she was abused," Elly said. "I've seen photos of her with you and Michael when you were children. It was easy to see she was an unhappy child."

"Yes, that's what I mean. Our father, Frank Walker, was a mean old bastard. And he was as misogynistic as they come. As far as he was concerned, women were good for cooking and breeding. He said so, too." Silas let out a long breath. "Olivia had a terrible time of it. But it wasn't Frank abusing her, it was Michael."

"What?" Mitch said. He felt as if he'd been punched in the stomach. He'd convinced himself that his father was innocent.

"Oh, yes, your father was no saint," Silas said. "I knew what was going on, and so did Alice."

"Yet you did nothing," Elly said.

"What could I do? My father—and Michael, for that matter—were untouchable. The police would never investigate my claims. Alice kept saying that Olivia would be better off if the same thing happened to her as happened to the Hatton girls. At least she'd be free of her abusers. I kept trying to convince her that wasn't the case, but she wouldn't listen. Alice has very strong opinions regarding abuse. I think, from some things she's told me, that she was abused herself during her childhood. Her mother had a temper and often took it out on her."

"So she killed Olivia," Elly said. "To save her?"

"Olivia disappeared," Silas said. "Then everything went quiet for a while. It was a couple of years later that my suspicions were aroused again. Alice came home with two dolls that she'd asked a seamstress friend to make for her. They had their eyes closed, as if they were sleeping, and they wore long blue dresses. These weren't ordinary dolls, they were life-size." He looked at Mitch. "You've seen them, lad."

"I remember," Mitch said.

"She kept them locked away in their own room but, every now and then, she visited them and held them in her arms while she cried. I realised that one of the dates she always did that without fail was the anniversary of the disappearance of the Hatton sisters. And those dolls looked like those poor girls. It was bloody creepy."

He shrugged. "It didn't prove anything of course but it got me thinking again. I started wondering where she'd dumped the bodies of those two girls. Eventually, I thought about the quarry. Alice had access to it and there are tunnels there that go deep into the ground. So, one night I decided to investigate. I drove out there and began searching the tunnels by torchlight."

Silas gazed at the floor, as if he were seeing the past being played out there. "What happened next changed my entire life. Alice had followed me. She wasn't stupid; she knew why I was there. Before I knew what had happened, she swung a steel scaffolding pole at my back. And then, when I went down to the ground, she continued hitting me with it."

"It said in the papers that you wouldn't tell anyone why you were at the quarry," Elly said. "Why didn't you go to the police? You had evidence now. You'd been attacked."

"Do you know what state I was in? I could barely move my body at all, not just my legs. I was sure in my mind that Alice was a murderer but there was no way I was going to report her. She could have killed me easily. I didn't want to die, Miss Cooper."

"So you stayed quiet," she said, "and another girl died."

He sighed. "What happened to Josie was my fault. She and I built up a relationship while I was in hospital. I tried to hide it from Alice but she figured it out. And then I heard on the news about Josie's body being found at Blackden Edge. Alice wasn't just taking revenge on the woman she thought had slighted her, she was also sending me a message, telling me that if I stepped out of line, the result was going to be my death or the death of someone I cared for."

"Tell me what happened to Sarah," Mitch said.

"I don't know," Silas said. "Ten years had passed since Josie's murder and life had quieted down. Then Sarah went. It ripped your family apart, of course. You and your mother left and your father took it very badly."

"Was he abusing Sarah?" Mitch asked, dreading the answer.

"I think so."

"So you're saying that Alice is some kind of 'angel of mercy' killer," Elly said. "She sees girls who are being abused and takes their lives to end their suffering."

Silas nodded. "She isn't sane."

"But you've lived with her for all these years and never even hinted of your suspicions to the police," Mitch said.

Silas hung his head. "Ever since I've been in this chair, she's controlled me. I know what she's capable of and there's nothing I can do to stop her."

"And now Jack is killing women," Elly said. "If he's hurt my sister in any way, I won't just hold him responsible, but you and your wife as well. You think Alice is scary? You can't even imagine what I'll do to you if...if Jen..."

Mitch put a comforting arm around her shoulder. "Where's Alice now?" he asked Silas.

"I don't know. When she heard that Jack had been arrested, she left. I have no idea where she's gone."

"This isn't helping us find Jen," Elly said. Realisation suddenly dawned on her face. "Jack knows who Jen is because he saw her on the news with me, after we'd found Lindsey. Because of us, Lindsey was removed from the flower grave. I bet he's put Jen in there to make up for the loss." She turned to Mitch and a panicked look crossed her face. "Come on, we have to go. We'll call the police on the way. Maybe they can get there before us."

She ran to the Jeep and Mitch followed.

33

FINAL GRAVE

As I DRIVE NORTH from Blackmoor House, I resist the urge to put my foot down to arrive at my destination quicker. I can't risk attracting the attention of the police.

Jack has ruined everything by meddling with things he knows nothing about. What game is he playing? He knows nothing about my girls or their flower graves. What does he know of suffering? Nothing, the boy has been spoiled his entire life.

But whatever he knows or doesn't know, his arrest is going to cause an investigation into the family. I can't trust Silas not to talk and I can't trust Jack at all. The boy is a fool and the police will have no trouble getting everything he knows out of him and into a statement.

I have to face facts; it's all over. My work will end now. That saddens me because it means many girls will be left to struggle and never know the release I could have given them.

I know I should be proud of what I've achieved--I have liberated many girls from suffering over the years--but I feel like a failure because I could have done more. But isn't that the lament of every person who has worked for the good of humanity, that they could have done more?

I turn off the main road and onto a narrow secondary road that winds through the woods. Not much farther now.

Ten minutes later, I arrive at a place I've visited before. The last time I came here, I marked it by tying a red ribbon to the branch of a tree. It flutters in the breeze. The last time I came here, I also brought a shovel but there's no need for that now. No more digging.

I grab the three syringes from the passenger seat and open the door. Leaving the car by the side of the road, I make my way into the shadowy woods. The car will be found sooner or later but by then, it will be too late for the police to act against me.

I refuse to be punished for helping those poor girls.

I reach the clearing where the grave waits. This is a nice spot. Pink foxgloves grow in the shade of the trees and daisies carpet the ground like a constellation of white stars.

The grave sits in the centre of this abundance of

bright flora. This will be a good place to rest. My work is done.

I remove the lid of the packing crate in the hole and lower myself down into the crate itself. Lying back, I can see the twisted patterns of the branches above the grave and the infinite sky beyond. I can't see the wildflowers now but I know they're there and that's enough.

I position the needle of the first syringe over my forearm and then quickly press it through the skin. There's a sharp sensation for a second but hen I press the plunger and feel a slight sting as the drugs enter my veins.

Even though I have three syringes, I can't trust that their contents will kill me. So, before I use the second and third syringes, I will make sure the job is done properly. The razor blade brought from home seems to shine bright silver as I unwrap it. This will get the job done. The razor will ensure that I experience the same relief from suffering as I gave my girls. I gave it to them as a gift and now I must accept that gift myself.

Morgan spotted the white Honda abandoned by the side of the road and parked the Range Rover behind it. She'd seen Alice Walker get out of the vehicle and enter the woods but she had no idea what was going on.

She radioed in her location and told Control that she was pursuing a suspect into the woods north of Blackmoor House but didn't require backup. Then she entered the woods, stepping beneath a piece of red ribbon that fluttered in the breeze.

The first thing she did when the stepped into the shadows was stop and listen. Alice couldn't be too far ahead and there was no way she could move silently through the undergrowth that covered the ground.

But the woods were deathly silent.

Morgan moved forward, trying to be as quiet as she could. Low ferns swished against her trousers and their wide leaves hid twigs that snapped as she stepped on them.

She could see that Alice had passed this way. Some of the ferns ahead were broken, their branches dangling down like dead arms.

When Morgan stepped into a clearing, the first thing she was an oblong hole in the ground. When she moved closer, she saw Alice inside it, lying inside a wooden crate. The wood near her wrist was stained red and three syringes were lying in the growing pool if blood.

"Shit!" Morgan jumped down into the hole and slid her belt out of her trousers. Luckily, Alice had only slit one wrist and not both of them. Maybe whatever drug had been in the syringes had stopped her completing her task.

Morgan removed her jacket and wadded it into makeshift bandage, which she wrapped around Alice's wrist before looping the belt around it to apply pressure.

She fumbled her radio out of her pocket and called Control. "This is DS Morgan. I'm in the woods north of Blackmoor House and I need an ambulance now!"

34

EXHUMATION

WHEN THE JEEP screeched to a halt at the gap in the hedge that led to the Nine Ladies stone circle, Elly was alarmed that there were no police vehicles already there. She'd called them as soon as she and Mitch had left Blackmoor House. So where the hell were they?

She jumped out of the Jeep and scrambled through the hedge. As soon as her trainers hit the trail that led through the moor to the trees, she ran. She had no reason to believe that Jen was still alive but she had every reason to hope. Because without hope, she might as well go and curl up in a corner and sob her heart out.

She had to believe that Jack had been in a hurry when he brought Jen here. He still had to go back and move her SUV off the road. So maybe he'd simply tied Jen to a tree or drugged her and left her in the woods. Then he'd been arrested and was unable to come back here and finish his plans regarding Jen.

Until she knew otherwise, that was the hope she was going to cling to.

She looked over her shoulder and saw Mitch running after her, a shovel in his hand.

"No," she told herself, "we won't need the shovel. We won't need the shovel because Jen isn't buried in Lindsey's old grave. She's alive and well and above ground."

She heard sirens in the distance. *About bloody time.*

When she reached the trees, she began to shout Jen's name. There was no answer other than the sound of rainwater dripping from the branches onto the ground.

Elly got to the stone circle and spun around, calling her sister's name, her eyes scanning the undergrowth. Still no answer. Maybe she was wrong and Jen wasn't here at all.

She arrived breathlessly in the glade and her heart sank when she saw that the grave had been filled in again and the dead daisies had been scattered over it.

"No," she cried out. "No!"

Her fingers sank into the wet earth and she began

clawing at it, scooping handfuls of mud away and throwing them aside. "Jen," she said hopelessly. "Please."

Mitch arrived and dug the blade of the shovel into the wet earth. He began tossing clumps of soil away, then thrusting the shovel back into the ground.

Elly refused to believe that her sister was here, dead and buried in the ground beneath her clawing hands. The thought was too much to bear. What would she do without her sister? What would Jen's kids do without their mum?

"She's not here," she told herself over and over. "Jen isn't here."

Mitch was bathed in sweat, working like a machine to move the earth out of the grave as quickly as possible.

"Why are we hurrying?" Elly asked. "If Jen is buried here, she's already dead. This is hopeless."

"Didn't you hear the news today?" Mitch said. "Lindsey Grofield was drugged and then buried alive. She suffocated in the grave. Jack would have heard that too. Wouldn't he do the same thing?"

"Oh, my God, Jen," she said, clawing at the earth with every ounce of strength she had left in her body.

Mitch's shovel hit something solid. He used the blade to clear away the dirt, revealing a flat wooden surface. "Looks like a packing crate," he said. "Stand back."

Elly moved a few feet away while Mitch brought the shovel down on the crate. The wood splintered. Mitch struck it again and there was a cracking sound. "She's in there," he said. "I can see her."

"Jen," Elly said, crawling forwards to the grave, "can you hear me?" Through the hole in the crate, she could see Jen's jeans but nothing else.

Mitch removed more earth, exposing the crate's lid. Elly heard people approaching them through the woods and looked over to see half a dozen police officers making their way through the trees.

"Help us," she shouted to them.

The officers rushed over.

Mitch dug the edge of the shovel into the top of the crate and used leverage to pop the lid. The officers lifted it out of the way. Elly heard one of them radioing for an ambulance.

Jen lay in the crate, her eyes closed, hands folded on her chest. Elly was sure her sister was dead. Mitch leaned into the crate and grabbed Jen's wrist. After a moment, he said, "There's a pulse."

Elly felt as if her heart would burst. She reached down and took hold of Jen's legs while Mitch and a police officer lifted her by her shoulders. They laid her on the grass and someone shouted, "Get a stretcher and a blanket!"

Jen's eyes fluttered open for a moment.

"Jen, it's me," she said. "It's your sister, Elly."

Jen's eyes closed again.

"It's going to be okay," Elly said. She wasn't sure if she was talking to herself or to her sister. Probably both. "Everything's going to be okay."

35

FACE EVERYTHING AND RECOVER

ELLY SAT STARING at the early evening sky through the window of the hospital room. The rain had stopped and the clouds were painted bright orange by the low sun.

"Sorry if I'm boring you," Jen said from the bed.

Elly looked back at her sister and smiled. "You're not boring me. I was just thinking how easy it would have been for this to have all turned out differently."

"Well, it didn't," Jen said. "Thank goodness for your man's prowess with a shovel."

"He isn't my man," Elly said. "After Paul, I don't think I'll ever have another man again. They're too much trouble. Maybe I'll become a nun and go live in a convent on an isolated island."

"And leave all this excitement behind? That isn't the Elly I know."

"The Elly you know is beat. She's got wet feet

and has broken all of her fingernails trying to dig her sister out of a grave."

"It could be worse. You could be stuck in this bed."

"True." Elly looked around the room. "I hate hospitals. As soon as Trevor and the kids arrive, I'm out of here. Sorry, sis, but there's a hot bath and an early night with my name on it. Ah, speak of the devil."

The door opened and Trevor entered the room, his arms laden with bags of clothes and toiletries that Jen had asked him to bring. Wendy and William ran into the room and threw themselves on the bed, both of them shouting, "Mummy!" at the top of their lungs.

"Hi, Trevor," Elly said. "I was just leaving."

He nodded at her and dumped the bags on the chair next to the bed.

"Don't forget to come visit when you get home," Jen reminded her. "Bring your man, if you like."

"I told you, he isn't my man." Elly left the room and took the elevator down to the ground floor. Mitch was waiting outside the cafeteria.

"How is she?" he asked.

"She's doing well. I reckon she'll be out of here by tomorrow morning."

"That's great. Battle called. "They have Alice in custody. Apparently, she tried to kill herself. DS Morgan saved her life."

"Alice will probably be declared insane and end up in a secure mental hospital," Elly said.

"Maybe. Battle said the girls we know about aren't the only victims. Alice has been picking up runaways and homeless girls too. She used the women's centre where she worked to find her victims and also picked them up off the street." Sorrow tinged his voice as he said, "She refuses to give the locations of the graves."

"Oh, Mitch, I'm sorry."

He shrugged, trying to put on a brave face. "I might not know where Sarah is but at least now I know what happened to her."

"Is that enough?"

"What choice do I have? It's going to have to be."

"Did Battle say what's going to happen to Silas?"

"He'll probably end up in jail for a while. They've arrested him for perverting the course of justice."

They reached the exit. "Fancy a drink?" she asked.

"Sure. There's a pub just down the road."

Elly shook her head. "I mean in Derbyshire. I've still got a book to write and I still need to do some research for the early chapters. Let's have a pint at The Mermaid."

"Okay," Mitch said, nodding. "Let's do that."

36

CONFESSION

One week later
HM Prison Sudbury

MITCH ENTERED THE VISITORS' room and looked for Silas among the prisoners seated at the tables. When he spotted his uncle, he walked over and sat down opposite him. He wasn't sure why Silas had requested that Mitch visit him. He'd have thought he'd be the last person Silas would have wanted to see.

"Hello, Mitch," Silas said.

"Silas. How are you?"

"I'm fine, under the circumstances. Although I have to tell you, it doesn't feel good to know that my son is disappointed in me because I'm *not* a serial killer."

"Yeah, I heard about that," Mitch said.

Silas sighed. "I suppose you're wondering why I asked you to come here."

Mitch nodded but said nothing.

"I've had some time to think," Silas said. "I'm going to tell you something but I want your word that you won't tell anyone else. Not the police, not my lawyer, not anyone. Understand?"

"I don't know," Mitch said. "Are you going to confess to a crime or something?"

"No, it's about Sarah."

Mitch sat up. "Sarah?"

"Do I have your word?"

"Yes, of course."

Silas leaned in closer and lowered his voice. "I haven't been honest with you. The version of events I told you at my house wasn't the entire truth. It's the version I've told the police and everyone else but I'm going to tell you what really happened. If you want to hear it."

"Of course I do."

Silas looked around to make sure no one was eavesdropping. Mitch looked too. The other prisoners were too focused on their own visitors to listen to anyone else's conversation.

"You remember I told you that Olivia was being abused?"

"Yes," Mitch said. "Are you saying that isn't true?"

"No, that's true. Let me tell this in my own way, lad."

"Sorry, go on."

"She was being abused," Silas said, "and Alice was aware of it and she kept saying that Olivia would be better off if she met the same end as the Hatton sisters. I told you all that. What I didn't tell you was that Olivia came to me one day and told me she was going to run away."

"Okay," Mitch said.

"I knew how bad she was getting it and I also suspected that Alice was planning to be Olivia's angel of mercy, so I helped my sister plan her escape route. She wasn't abducted, Mitch. She ran. That's why I made sure I was in The Mermaid that night with my dad and Alice. I didn't want the police sniffing around in my family's business so I made sure we had a cast-iron alibi."

"Are you saying she's alive?" Mitch asked.

"Sshh, keep it down." Silas looked over his shoulder again. Satisfied, he said in a low voice, "Yes, she's still alive. She's in Scotland. She left her jacket at Blackden Edge so it would look like the killer everyone was talking about had taken her. It was also her way of sticking a middle finger up at Alice, I assume. Alice would know the killer hadn't taken Olivia at all, since she was the killer. "

A verse from the journal came unbidden into Mitch's head, the verse referring to Olivia.

Don't look in the woods or in the glade

The pimpernel's not there

"Well, I'm glad she's not dead," he said. He wasn't sure what else to say.

"There's more," Silas said. "Olivia and I kept in touch via letters. I kept a PO box in Matlock that no one else knew about. We contacted each other very rarely but in 1987, I wrote her and told her that her niece needed her."

"Her niece," Mitch said. "Sarah."

Silas nodded. "Sarah was in the same situation Olivia had been in twelve years before. I told her that if Sarah didn't escape the family soon, she was going to end up like those Hatton girls."

Mitch felt his throat tightening. He knew where this was leading and he could hardly fathom that he'd believed something for thirty years that was untrue.

"Olivia didn't want to come back to Derbyshire," Silas said. "But she knew she was Sarah's only hope. So she came back and watched Edge House, waiting for an opportunity. She planned to break in through the back gate but, apparently, you and Sarah went wandering over the moors. Olivia saw her chance and saved Sarah's life."

"She abducted her," Mitch said. "She's the one who hit me on the back of the head and took Sarah."

The import of this information hit him like a blow to his gut. "Is Sarah still alive?"

Silas nodded slowly. "She and Olivia live together."

"In Scotland."

"Yes, in Scotland."

"Where exactly?"

"If I tell you, you're going to go there."

"Of course I am."

"Then I want you to take a message for me. Tell Olivia what has happened, tell her Alice is locked away and won't be getting out. With Frank and Michael gone and Alice out of the picture, Olivia and Sarah will finally be free of their past."

"Give me the address," Mitch said. He was still trying to process the information he'd just been given. His sister was still alive. Leigh had an aunt she'd never met. He had to see Sarah as soon as possible.

"Fell Cottage," Silas said. "On the shore of Loch Rannoch."

Mitch pushed his chair back and stood up. "Take care," he told Silas.

"You too, lad. You too."

37

LOST AND FOUND

It was a bright afternoon and the sun shimmered off the surface of Loch Rannoch. Mitch drove the Jeep onto the short road that led to Fell Cottage. The place wasn't known to his GPS so he'd had to get directions at the local garage.

"Are we there yet?" Leigh asked from the passenger seat.

Mitch spotted a cottage on the right-hand side of the road, a small, quaint white building with a thatched roof and a front garden full of flowers. A wooden sign next to the front door said FELL COTTAGE.

"This is the place," Mitch said. He parked the Jeep and turned to Leigh. "I want you to wait here while I knock on the door, okay? Olivia and Sarah haven't seen anyone from the family for a long time and they might turn me away. So you wait here until I know they're friendly."

"Okay," Leigh said, pouting a little and sliding down in her seat.

Mitch knew how she felt but he didn't want her involved in any ugliness. "No matter how this turns out, we'll go and get ice cream later, how does that sound? And the hotel we're staying at is really nice and has a pool."

That seemed to cheer her up a little. She smiled and nodded. "I know, you already told me that."

"Well, I'm telling you again in case you forgot."

She raised an eyebrow and looked at him incredulously. "As if I'd forget that, Dad."

He grinned. "I'll be back in a minute." Taking a deep breath, he got out of the Jeep, went through the gate, and walked along the stone path that led to the door. Before he had a chance to knock, a woman opened the door. She was in her sixties and had grey hair cut in a simple bob style and eyes that reminded Mitch of Silas, her brother.

"Yes?" she asked.

"Olivia," he said.

She inspected his face closely. Her own face became grim. "I think you'd better leave," she said and began to close the door.

"Olivia, I have a message from Silas," he said. The door halted. When she didn't say anything else,

Mitch continued. "Alice has been arrested. You don't have anything to worry about anymore."

"You came all the way here to tell me that? Why can't Silas write me?"

"He's in prison at the moment. I don't think he wants anyone to know about you, including the prison guards who read his mail."

"Yet he told you where I am."

"I'm not my father," he said. "I'm—"

"I know who you are. The last time I saw you, you were lying in the snow. I apologise for that. Now, you can turn that car of yours around and go back to where you came from." The door resumed its journey towards being closed.

Mitch put his foot in the way. "I came to see Sarah, my sister."

"Oh, did you? And what makes you think she'd want to see you?"

He frowned. "I've never done her any harm."

"Then don't do her any now."

"I'm not sure what you mean."

"Sarah has a life here, free from the troubles of the past. She has nightmares every now and then, of course, but on the whole, she's doing well. She's got her own family. Do you think seeing you would do her good or do her harm?"

"But I'm her brother. I love her."

"And Michael was her father, but that didn't mean he had the girl's best interests at heart. It took

Sarah years before she trusted anyone when she came here. She's taken some positive steps forward. Not leaps, steps. And now you arrive on my doorstep thinking you have the right to push her back down a road she doesn't want to travel just because you're her brother and you *love* her."

Mitch didn't know what to say.

"Just because you've gotten over the events of thirty years ago doesn't mean everyone has," Olivia said. "Some of us had to deal with a lot more than you did. You lost your sister, but think about what she lost every time...well, every time she was forced to do something she didn't want to do."

"I told you, I'm not Michael."

"No, but you're his son and Frank's grandson. And in my experience, the apple doesn't fall far from the tree."

"My dad is a nice man," Leigh said from behind Mitch.

He turned around. "Leigh, I told you to wait in the car."

Olivia bent forward slightly so her face was level with Leigh's. "Hello, who might you be?"

"I'm Leigh. Leigh Walker. This is my dad." She pointed at Mitch.

"I see," Olivia said. "And you like living with your dad, do you?"

"Well, I don't live with him anymore but that isn't his fault. That's because my mum had an affair."

She said it so matter-of-factly, that Mitch wondered exactly how much she knew about her parent's breakup. He and Jess had simply told her at the time that they couldn't live together anymore.

"I live with him at the weekends, though," Leigh continued. "And he lets me do stuff my mum doesn't, like stay up late sometimes and watch TV. And he makes my favourite food, which is spaghetti. He's really nice and I'm sure you'd like him if you got to know him."

Olivia smiled. "Oh, would I? And I suppose you came all the way here to meet your aunt, is that right?"

"If she wants to meet me," Leigh said, nodding.

Olivia straightened her back again and looked from Leigh to Mitch. "Sarah doesn't live here anymore, she's got a house with her husband and their son. She's moved on as best she can. I suppose I can ring her and ask her if she wants to see you."

Mitch nodded. "That would be great, thank you."

Olivia pointed at the Jeep. "You go and wait in your car there and I'll see if Sarah wants to see you or not. Whatever she says, whether yes or no, I will abide with her wishes."

"Okay," Mitch said, giving Leigh a nudge back towards the Jeep. When they got to it and climbed in, he asked her, "What did you mean back there when you said your mum had had an affair? I never told you that."

She gave him the incredulous look again. "I know what's going on, Dad, I'm twelve. I'm not a child anymore."

"Right," he said, nodding with a straight face.

The door of Fell Cottage opened again and Olivia came out. She beckoned them over. When they got to the front door, she said, "Sarah will see you. I don't know if it's a good or bad thing but I told you I'd abide by her wishes and I stick to my word."

"So where do we find her?" Mitch asked. "You said she doesn't live her anymore."

"I told you she lives with her husband and son and that's true. But they've gone fishing today so Sarah is here at the moment, visiting me."

"She's here," Mitch said.

"I just said that, didn't I?"

"Hello, Mitch." The voice came from the side of the house. Mitch looked over to see a woman with long chestnut hair standing by a tree of white dog rose flowers. She wore a yellow summer dress and sandals. Her face was thirty years older than when he'd last seen it but she was unmistakably Sarah.

"Sarah," he said, going to her and wrapping his arms around her. Her hair smelled of honeysuckle.

"It's good to see you," she said. She broke the hug and turned her attention to Leigh. "And who's this?"

"I'm Leigh. You're my aunt."

"Yes," Sarah, said, nodding. "Yes, I am. Would you like to see the loch?"

Leigh nodded.

Sarah took her hand and led her around the side of the house to the back garden, which sloped down to the water.

Mitch took a deep breath of flower-sweet air and looked at the distant high hills and the sun glittering on the water. It seemed that Sarah had found a good life here.

He'd believed her to be dead for thirty years but the journal of a killer, locked in a vault by the very man who was responsible for Sarah's flight from her old life, had opened the doors that had eventually led Mitch back to her.

He walked down to the loch where Sarah and Leigh were talking by the water's edge.

It was time for the shattered pieces of their family to be reunited and form something good.

PLACES TO VISIT

Join The Suspense List to get an email when Adam J. Wright releases a new book:

http://eepurl.com/cWw36Y

Adam J. Wright's Facebook page:

https://www.facebook.com/authoradamjwright/

Contact the author:

adamjwright.author@gmail.com

Thank you for reading DARK PEAK. I hope you will consider leaving a review. Reviews help authors write more and better books for your enjoyment!

35185125R00246

Printed in Great Britain
by Amazon